MURDER
IN A
MAYONNAISE
JAR

For Barry & Jody,
May you enjoy this book.
        Best wishes,
            Molly

Molly McPatterson

MURDER
IN A
MAYONNAISE
JAR

MOLLY MCKITTERICK

ST.
MARTIN'S
PRESS

New York

MURDER IN A MAYONNAISE JAR. Copyright © 1993 by Molly
McKitterick. All rights reserved. Printed in the United States of
America. No part of this book may be used or reproduced in
any manner whatsoever without written permission except in
the case of brief quotations embodied in critical articles or
reviews. For information, address St. Martin's Press, 175 Fifth
Avenue, New York, N.Y. 10010.

Design by Sara Stemen

Library of Congress Cataloging-in-Publication Data

McKitterick, Molly
    Murder in a mayonnaise jar / Molly McKitterick.
      p.   cm.
    ISBN 0-312-09346-2
    1. Television stations—Missouri—Saint Louis—Fiction.
  2. Women journalists—Missouri—Saint Louis—Fiction.
  3. Saint Louis (Mo.)—Fiction.   I. Title.
PS3563.C38324M8   1993
813'.54—dc20   93-10335
                                       CIP

First Edition: September 1993

10 9 8 7 6 5 4 3 2 1

To J.G.B.

Special thanks to my unnamed source, who put me on to the method of murder and helped me with the details.

I also want to extend thanks to Linda Cashdan for once again going the distance with me (back and forth, back and forth), to Ann Belenky, and to Zuzanna, Lady Shonfield, for her titular suggestion.

MURDER
IN A
MAYONNAISE
JAR

1

BENTON PARK, AFTER the last rays of the late summer sun had faded and deepened into serious shadow, was crawling with curious nightlife. Insects freed from a covered jar; park people flew blind in the glow of the streetlights.

They came from the houses on the park's periphery, tall brick houses that gawked through curtainless windows and cried out with a jarring melange of radio, television, sobbing children, and shouting grown-ups. In those houses anger grew and spread like mold.

But there was refuge in the park and balm in the act of hurting someone, even if that person were no more than oneself. Warmed with cheap whiskey and still sucking on the empty bottle, a gaunt, baggy man lay in the curve of a hillside. Blue tattoos reached out of the dark for the soggy joint two brewery workers were sharing along with a six-pack. And in the shadow under the park pavilion a drugged girl in a fringed leather vest flirted with three men as if she were being presented with a choice.

In the children's play area a blond boy leaned his cheek against the metal links of the swing chain and pushed gently with his toe. His skin was quartz white in the darkness, and dirty designs showed up on it like veining.

At an hour when most ten-year-olds were safely ensconced in the family circle, this boy was isolated in the halo of a streetlight. The cheek resting against the cool of the swing chain had a bruise on it, and the boy's eye sockets formed soft, brown hollows in the fairness of his skin. But he seemed content to sit and revolve on his toe.

Abruptly the boy planted both feet on the ground and pulled a plastic bag out of the pocket of his shorts. He held the bag over his nose and mouth and inhaled deeply. Inside was a dirty, wet rag and nothing else.

A few miles away at a local motor lodge, KYYY-TV anchorman William Hecklepeck brought his fist crashing down on the wooden podium with malicious intent. The South St. Louis chapter of the Rotary Club had insisted on listening to detailed reports from its president, secretary, and treasurer and then presenting several awards before allowing him, the evening's guest of honor, to speak. And the guest of honor was peeved.

But in the instant that Hecklepeck felt the smack of contact with the wood surface, he also felt the panic rise up through his torso to meet it. There it was again, the now familiar, whole-body sensation that his life was closing in on him, choking, immobilizing, eventually exterminating him or at least the vibrant parts of him. Hecklepeck was no stranger to the panic. It had been coming over him intermittently for months now, but it caught him by surprise every time.

Fist on podium, Hecklepeck looked back at the Rotarians with an expression as startled as their own. "When we talk about the electronic media today," he boomed suddenly in tones loud enough to overpower his feelings, "we cannot avoid talking about the people who watch it. To put it simply, the problem with television news is . . . you." The 'you' was accompanied by a glare that touched each drowsy Rotarian personally.

The Rotary Club chapter had asked Hecklepeck to speak because he anchored the number one newscast in St. Louis. He was the most recognized television personality in town and had been for years. St. Louisans didn't get tired of him. They had continued to find Hecklepeck highly entertaining because he gave them the option of watching the news at face value or, alternatively, for the editorial value added by his face.

The Rotarians should have derived a warning from that. They should have known that a man who read a poorly written news story as if a horrible smell were emanating from the teleprompter and who had been known to publicly castigate a reporter for "missing the story" was not the sort of guy to come and make a few funny, innocuous after-dinner remarks, particularly not after being left to cool his heels while the Rotarians conducted their interminable club business.

"This is the age of technology. Information is being thrown at you from all directions—from car radios, from telephone receivers, from omnipresent squawking television sets. It is critically important to play a role in separating the matter from the chatter." *Why?* The question blinked like a semaphore in Hecklepeck's mind. There was so much babble. It was filling every nook and crevice like sickly scented lather from a shaving cream can. Was there any point in diving into it for one true, clear thought? Any point at all?

"You"—Some of the Rotarians jumped. Midlevel managers and small businessmen, Hecklepeck thought, avid Reagan supporters but not rich enough to have gotten richer under Reaganomics. They could benefit from what he had to say about taking the critical view.—"are the consumers of the stuff we put on the air. Take a good, hard look at it. Start listening for a change. If you don't like it, you should say so, loud and clear. Better yet, you should write. I"—Hecklepeck threw back his shoulders and puffed out his chest. His panic was once again going into remission.—"read my mail. In these days of declining viewership, the news director and station manager even read theirs. And they pass it along with memos attached to the people responsible."

The now-wakeful South St. Louis Rotary Club was an earnest group, and the meeting room was silent except for a few clinks of cutlery against stoneware. Some Rotarians were thoughtfully finishing the last of their chocolate pudding.

"What I'm speaking to is values, and I don't mean emotional values like home and m-m-mother. I'm talking about intel-l-l-lectual values." As he said this Hecklepeck swept the room with his eyes, willing the audience to have standards in spite of all appearances. "Yesterday the president announced the almost immediate phaseout of chlorofluorocarbon production in this country. The deterioration of the ozone level has become so alarming that we can no longer wait, as previous timetables would have it, until the end of the century to stop producing CFCs. Now you know as businessmen this regulation is going to affect all of you. Chlorofluorocarbons are widely used as refrigerants. They're critical to your air-conditioning systems, and they have a host of other industrial uses."

Hecklepeck tucked his thumbs and forefingers into his vest pockets and rocked back on his heels. Without facial expression he was a handsome, dark-haired man, although not particularly distinctive. It was only when Hecklepeck's brown eyes flashed (his face talked) that he commanded attention. His eyes were flashing now, and his face was shouting righteous indignation.

"Now, did any hint of this appear on our newscast last night? No! It was on the front page of the *New York Times* this morning, but the producers at KYYY didn't think it worth mentioning. One of them told me it was national news and didn't belong on a local newscast." The Rotarians laughed tentatively. Club members were suddenly uncertain about the direction in which things were moving.

"I know it's easy to be complacent about what you see—and don't see—on television." Hecklepeck's baleful eye made the rounds again. "There's so much that's truly terrible. But it's not going to change if you don't work to change it.

Here's another example: our commentary. Or, the chalky substance that passes for commentary these days. Whatever happened to the good old-fashioned editorial? In the past few weeks my station has come out against hot weather, deplored the skirt lengths this fall, and, in a particularly tough stance, decried litter in the streets." Hecklepeck wasn't exaggerating. KYYY commentator Ivan (pronounced Ee-vahn) Sandler favored subjects that went down easily and did not upset the stomach when they got there.

"What if you were what you watched?" Hecklepeck's expression indicated that his audience was indeed what it watched and that that was reruns of "Gilligan's Island." "Is that how you wish to be thought of? Well, when the history books are written, that is how our society is going to be characterized. Unless you and others act to do something about it, this will go down as the era of 'Dynasty,' of 'Geraldo' and of the watered-down, crowd-pleasing newscast." Members of the Rotary Club looked down into their empty dessert plates and tried to feel bad.

The boy in Benton Park swayed drunkenly on his swing and almost pitched into the dust. He rescued himself and giggled.

He was no longer alone on the swing set. Someone was sitting on the swing two swings down from him. The boy was not surprised; it did not occur to him to question the appearance of a grown-up in a playground.

Without speaking, the newcomer held out a quart-sized jar.

4

The child saw that it contained a clear liquid. He smiled at the grown-up on the swing, understanding now that they had something in common.

Reaching, the boy took the jar, unscrewed the top, and held it over his nose and mouth.

Hecklepeck was winding up. "Think of this as your chance to talk back to your TV set, and for once your set, embodied by me, will answer back. I am here to hear any well-founded complaints and criticisms, and I will see that they get addressed by my station." Hecklepeck's gaze swept the room. He had spoken well, inspiringly, and there was reason to hope he might have stimulated discussion.

The Rotarians were not quick to respond. After a long pause, a man in a salt-and-pepper double-knit jacket got up. "How come . . ." The jacket was big for him, and he seemed hesitant about asking his question.

"Yes?" encouraged Hecklepeck.

"How come . . . you make all those faces when you're reading the news? I thought newsmen were supposed to be impartial, but sometimes it looks like you're making some kind of commentary as if to say you don't like what you're reading about." The man in the double-knit had been exhorted to speak his piece, and now he was going to do it. "My wife . . . thinks some of that facial massage, or even a face-lift, if it were to become necessary, would have the effect of giving you some relaxation, smoothing it out. I mean to say, they fire you when you don't look good."

Just then Hecklepeck looked like an incipient clap of thunder. But his words came out short and very quiet. "Thank you. Thank you for your observation."

"The massage would probably do it, but even if you had to go in the direction of the face-lift, it's not too bad. My wife—"

Hecklepeck whirled in the direction of someone else with a hand in the air. "Your question?"

"I find that there's a real liberal bias among the various news media." The questioner was wearing a three-piece suit but had loosened his tie for the evening.

"I hear that a lot," Hecklepeck replied with relief. "And I've given it some thought. I think there's something inherent in the journalistic process that passes as liberalism. Reporters tend to focus on society's ills—the poor, the sick, the corrupt. So it often looks like they're taking up the liberal torch even though they're not. I personally believe the news media has a responsibility to bring the ills of our society to public attention because that is how things get better. Now I bet you're going to say we cover too much bad news, not enough good news."

The man in the three-piece suit shrugged. No, he hadn't thought of that.

But Hecklepeck was glad to have the discussion launched at last, even if the other participant was himself. "Well, good news often is not news. It takes something out of the ordinary, and usually that's something negative, to constitute news."

A little man standing at the back of the meeting room waved his arms wildly. Hoping that the momentum was building at last, Hecklepeck recognized him. "It seems like you guys miss a lot of good stories." The man's chest was covered with matted hair. It showed up even on the other side of the room like a fur dickey in the vee of his open shirt. "F'r instance, yesterday the president announced the immediate phaseout of all chlorofluorocarbons. In my business, which is electroplating, we have been using that stuff . . ."

Hecklepeck glared at the beast. Where had he been? Hadn't he just heard him talk about the president's decision? The guy must have taken a powder in the middle of his talk! Or, his mind had wandered off somewhere alone. It was one thing to listen, as most of the Rotarians clearly had, and come up with some off-the-wall interpretation. It was another to prevail upon a guest speaker and not even have the common courtesy to hear him.

"We saw this thing coming and started phasing out the fluorocarbon we use this spring. Now I see that as a local angle for a news story . . ."

It was a good point; the guy was right. But Hecklepeck wasn't going to give him the satisfaction of acknowledging it. He nodded curtly and pointed to a man in a short-sleeved knit shirt.

"I like 'Geraldo' the man said in an aggrieved tone. "He's very informative."

The boy was convulsing. His arms and legs had taken on frenetic little lives of their own and appeared to be dancing but all of them to different tunes, each raising a small cloud of dust under the swing.

Unable to lift his head, the boy brought in the powdery air in

6

short little gasps that somehow could not fill his lungs or get from there to his bloodstream. His chest muscles pumped wildly, but they were no more effective than a bellows with a hole in it. Finally they stopped.

Shortly afterwards the dancing ended and the dust began to resettle.

William Hecklepeck stabbed at the lock in the silver side of his car with the key.

Inside he yanked at the rearview mirror. His face looked back at him, the same face it always was, always had been. He hadn't begun to show signs of aging yet. There was, incredibly, no gray in his dark hair, and the lines on his face, while deepening, had not yet begun to change him into somebody older. He looked angry, of course, but that was because he was angry. he had a right to look angry if he felt that way. And after what he had been through he had a right to *be* angry.

But suddenly Hecklepeck grinned and readjusted the mirror for driving. Was he really considering a face-lift?

The car started with a hum that foretold real power. Hecklepeck fastened his seat belt, pushed back into the leather seat, and let out a long breath. The evening at least was behind him. And, he smiled ironically at the windshield, he had been a big hit. The Rotary Club Chapter of South St. Louis had had the kind of evening it wanted, even if he hadn't.

Hecklepeck eased off the parking brake and let the car drift toward the parking lot exit. They had crowded around him at the end. One man in a baby blue windbreaker had babbled about how Hecklepeck had made television accessible, humanized it. He for one would never see it as mere electronic gadgetry again but as his new friend . . . Bill Hecklepeck.

Another, an older Rotarian, who moved like a praying mantis, slapped Hecklepeck on the back and declared himself ecstatic to discover that his favorite newscaster was a conservative at heart. Where that came from, Hecklepeck could only guess. He shook his head over it.

Then the guy with the furry chest, who hadn't bothered to hear his speech, appeared. In contrast the hair on his head was sparse and wispy. He shook hands firmly, a little too firmly, and looked Hecklepeck right in the eyes as if to impress himself on the anchorman's memory. Clearly he had taken some Carnegie course on how to sell himself to potential customers. All that trouble and he couldn't make the effort to do something as elementary as listen. It was particularly galling because the guy wanted Hecklepeck to come out to his plant and shoot a news story. After only a brief glance Hecklepeck put the man's card in his pocket and vowed never to go anywhere near Metalcote Inc.—Electroplating.

He stopped the car to wait for a gap in the traffic. That guy was the most blatant, but all those Rotarians had just been using him in one way or another, if only as a sounding board for their own strange opinions. Hecklepeck marveled again at how many interpretations could be derived from a simple statement on his part. In the early days of his career he had forced himself to adopt a benign view of this phenomenon because not to was to give up on the communication business altogether.

But lately it seemed that nothing he said ever shot true to anybody. Nor did other people appear to do any better. Talking, yes. Speaking the same language, no. What if the world were at the brink of total fragmentation? Worse, what if this fragmented, dark world was a result of (yes!) the electronic media. Hecklepeck felt a sharp stab of guilt cut through his incipient panic. Could it be that civilization was drowning in the babble of a thousand talking heads from which not one clear word was heard by anybody? If so, the only thing to do would be to take a vow of silence and join a monastery. That way he could simultaneously atone for his role in it all and aid in the preservation of ideas through the coming dark ages.

Hecklepeck applied his foot hard to the accelerator of his car, and the machine whooshed out into the street in a smooth, effortless arc. Relief washed over him; he was still in control. He eased into the left lane and passed four or five cars before pulling back in front of them and stopping at the light. And what he controlled was raw, brute power. This (he massaged the steering wheel), this miracle of crafting, this magnificent mean machine, his new Porsche Carerra 911. They wouldn't let him drive this in a monastery.

The Porsche was a refuge from his panic attacks. He hadn't had one, not one choking, paralyzing sensation, when actively engaged in driving his new car.

The Porsche had also eased the malaise that came over Hecklepeck during the past year, the thirteenth year of his anchoring the news in St. Louis. In that time life had somehow, suddenly and completely, lost its poignancy and left him with an emptiness inside, except recently for the overstuffed and airless feeling of panic.

But when he first saw the Porsche, Hecklepeck had felt excitement. And in the month and a half since he'd bought the car for his forty-sixth birthday, he had rediscovered something like the wide-flung euphoria of his youth.

It was welling up in him now. "Old Man River," he sang loudly, while the fingers of his right hand fiddled with the buttons of his radio, playing radio roulette, hoping to come up with a song he liked. There had been fewer and fewer of them as time went by. Incredibly, however, the country music station was playing a Hank Williams, Jr., song, and Hecklepeck subsided in order to listen.

He felt as if he were floating down Jefferson Street, taking in the sights from a position of luxury and power. On either side were big brick turn-of-the-century houses built for working-class St. Louis. South St. Louis was an area that fascinated Hecklepeck because it was so foreign to his own eastern background. It had been settled largely by German Catholics, who whitewashed their front steps, scrubbed their walkways, and kept their grass so well-groomed, their yards appeared to be covered with lawn toupees.

South St. Louis, it seemed to Hecklepeck, had never really come into the sixties, much less the seventies, eighties or nineties. There were lots of bridal shops and German bakeries. The church had a presence there. Hecklepeck felt the weight of old-fashioned values when he drove through South St. Louis. It was all very strange and interesting. He loved to look at the solid midwestern architecture that was nevertheless varied, to picture streets full of horse-drawn vehicles and, most of all, to sense the presence of the Mississippi River just a few blocks away.

The song ended. Punching at the radio buttons, Hecklepeck brought the Porsche to a graceful stop at the intersection of Jefferson and Wyoming. In the shadows beyond the streetlights he recognized Benton Park. He had left South St. Louis and come into a very different neighborhood. Hecklepeck switched the radio off and wondered how ordered South St. Louis could just shatter into Benton Park. Architecturally, the buildings around the park were just as sound. The difference lay in their inhabitants, many of them poor white people whose existences were isolated, purposeless, and largely unredeemable.

He gazed into the depths of the park until the light changed and the Porsche sailed on down Jefferson Street to the highway.

2

GLUE-SNIFFING!" HECKLEPECK was wary. It was four o'clock the next afternoon, and he was sitting in the news director's office at KYYY-TV. "Glue-sniffing was something you heard about in the sixties, and then they took whatever it was out of airplane glue and that was the end of it."

"Evidently not," said James Turnbull drily. "It's in the newspaper this morning: evidence of solvent abuse. That's glue."

Hecklepeck shrugged. "It's also aerosols and other household chemicals. Big deal."

"Whatever. It makes me curious. Why would a kid do that? There are plenty of other drugs around." Something slight and indefinable in Turnbull's tone of voice suggested that Hecklepeck ought to be curious too.

Hecklepeck merely shrugged again. "Cheap," he said. "So what? No big deal."

"The boy died," said Turnbull in his deceptively mild tone of voice.

Hecklepeck did not reply. He was not going to betray himself with even the slightest show of interest.

"The story was in the late edition . . . buried . . . inside." Turnbull seemed to imply that Hecklepeck hadn't read it and should have.

He hadn't. But he wasn't responsible for knowing about every person who died anywhere in the metropolitan area. Nor was it anywhere written that he had to care. He was tired of caring.

The news director looked out of the glass window that encased his office at the newsroom beyond. It was busy. Everybody out there had something to do for the five o'clock news show and appeared to be doing it. Turnbull approved of that.

What he didn't approve of was an anchorman who thought his job consisted solely of sitting on the news set for the hour and a half duration of the station's evening newscasts and reading into a camera. In Turnbull's view anchormen should be part of the news team. They should write and report and be visible to the community as working newsmen.

William Hecklepeck had not covered one story during the last year. Turnbull knew he was more than capable of it. Before he turned to anchoring, Hecklepeck had been a well-known investigative reporter. Even as an anchor he had done a fair amount of it, good stuff; Turnbull had been impressed. But then a year ago the trickle had stopped and Turnbull had no idea why.

He couldn't out and out order Hecklepeck to cover a story. There was nothing in the anchorman's contract that required him to report and little to be gained from enraging him. Hecklepeck was, after all, vital to the number one standing of KYYY's news. Turnbull didn't want to take the slightest risk of losing him. If he were going to get Hecklepeck to cover a story, he had to maneuver him into it.

"I was thinking it would make a good series: some stats on substance abuse, a profile of a glue-sniffer, perhaps a look at the ghetto where the kid lived."

Hecklepeck raised his eyebrows and nodded, as if he didn't know what Turnbull was trying to get him to do and simply approved of the idea. "Yep," he said. "Maybe an interview with some kind of drug counselor, if there is one for that kind of thing."

It was Turnbull's turn to nod. "I wonder"—he swiveled his chair toward the newsroom window and looked out at his employees— "who I could assign it to."

"Handy," said Hecklepeck automatically. He was referring to KYYY reporter Joe Handy. There is a Joe Handy at every local television station and more than a few at each of the networks. They have the kind of white male presence that white male television management deems to be credible to viewers. And they are never a threat to management. Joe covered all the major stories at KYYY.

Turnbull shook his head. "I've got Handy looking into something down at city hall for the November book," he said, referring to the

November ratings period, when Channel Three always made every effort to beat the competition by as many points as possible.

"Ah. Who does that leave?"

Given the opening, Turnbull listed each of the rest of his reporters and the projects they were currently working on. "And so," he wound up, "that leaves only Jennifer, who is doing the early morning cut-ins, and, in any case, is still getting adjusted." Jennifer Burgess had only been at KYYY for three months. What Turnbull was saying by intimation was that Jennifer was young and inexperienced. She brought a fresh, and, hopefully, eye-opening presence to the local portions of the network morning show. But Turnbull wasn't giving her any credit for reporting ability.

"Jennifer's through with the cut-ins by 8:30," Hecklepeck pointed out. "That leaves her free for the rest of the day."

"Until 3:00," qualified Turnbull. "She's off at 3:00. And I'm not sure she'd bring the kind of tough approach to this story that I'm looking for."

Hecklepeck knotted his forehead and looked thoughtful as if he were reviewing all the candidates in his mind. "Well, I don't see who else you have to do it," he said finally. "And," he sighed deeply as if he were being forced to volunteer for an onerous task, "I'd be willing to help her out a little, advise her."

Turnbull barely blinked, although his blue eyes looked hard enough to cut glass. "Help out?" The tone of his voice was just slightly incredulous. Did it reflect the generousness of Hecklepeck's offer? Hecklepeck didn't think so. He didn't care either. He wasn't going to investigate glue-sniffing.

"Help out?" Tipping back in his chair, Turnbull tried it again. "Well, I suppose you can." It was something anyway "I'll tell her you're going to be helping her."

Hecklepeck nodded. "Fine. Now, there's a series I want to do."

Turnbull lost his balance and came down hard in his chair. But his voice, when he spoke, was as mild as ever. "Oh," he said. "A series?"

"Yes."

"About?"

"Steamboats. Did you know that at one time St. Louis was the most important riverboat capital in the United States, more important even than New Orleans? Because of the three rivers that come together here—the Illinois, the Missouri, and the Mississippi."

Before Turnbull could comment, Hecklepeck pulled a small notebook out of the chest pocket of his khaki suit jacket. "But it was a risky business. The average life of a steamboat was only five years. In 1852 alone there were sixty-seven steamboat accidents on the inland waterways and they killed 466 people. In the six years between 1819 and 1825 more than 400 steamboats were sunk or damaged trying to navigate the Missouri River alone. Of course, the Missouri was the most challenging waterway in the Mississippi River system. It was sandy down here by the mouth and rocky on the upper reaches. They used to call it 'harlot'," Hecklepeck added in an aside.

"Ah," said Turnbull, who had never seen Hecklepeck this enthusiastic before and wasn't sure when it got right down to it that it was what he really wanted.

Hecklepeck was chronicling great Missouri steamboat wrecks. ". . . The Malta. The Seabird. The Saluda. The Edna. And of course, the White Cloud, which caught fire right on the St. Louis levee and burned fifteen business blocks. The fire was followed by an outbreak of cholera. Thousands of people died."

"Interesting," said Turnbull expressionlessly. New Englander that he was, he had so far been impervious to the romance of the river, which struck him as merely dull and muddy.

After a pause, he added, "But don't you think it lacks a certain immediate impact? You wouldn't call it today's news . . ."

"I wouldn't call it news at all," Hecklepeck replied, huffy. "I call it history."

"Well."

"Missouri's history. Our history. Our heritage. Anyway, I intend to give it a newsy twist."

"A newsy twist," murmured Turnbull.

"What if . . . ," Hecklepeck paused dramatically before delivering the punchline, "I rode an authentic steamboat from here to New Orleans and did a series of stories on it."

"Oh, that is news," said Turnbull ambiguously. "But I can't afford to pay for you and a photographer to take a steamboat cruise on the *Delta Queen* or whatever."

"What does the *Delta Queen* use for fuel?" Hecklepeck's tone was deeply scornful.

Turnbull shrugged.

"Fuel oil." There was a pause during which Turnbull tried to

14

figure out what was so terrible about fuel oil. "The original steamboats burned wood. About three cords a day. Eventually the switch was made to coal. Fuel oil never came into it."

"Ah."

"I'm talking about making a real steamboat trip down to New Orleans. I'd rather go up the Missouri like Pierre Chouteau and his fur traders did. But the engineers have messed around with it so much, it's too shallow."

"Too bad."

"Anyway, Gus wants to do the Mississippi."

"Gus?" But Turnbull had a sinking feeling he already knew.

"Gus Bussard."

Turnbull closed his eyes. Gustavius Bussard VI. Nicknamed by the media Gus Bus. There were three venerable families associated with St. Louis: the Danforths of Ralston Purina, the Busches of Anheuser-Busch, and the Bussards of Bussard-Dusay. Pet food, beer, and soap.

The Bussards had been among the earliest settlers in St. Louis. They had been fur traders. But well before the fur trade diminished they had adeptly switched to soap and perfume, a low-overhead choice since both products were made with what the fur traders rejected. Gus Bus's ancestors had dogged the footsteps of the trappers collecting discarded animal parts. Right up until after the famous world's fair, Bussard-Dusay perfumes and soaps outsold French perfumes in the midwestern United States. But when St. Louis went into decline, so did the Bussard products. By the mid-twentieth century "perfume made in St. Louis" had developed a very different ring from "perfume made in Paris." But by then Bussard-Dussay had diversified into more mundane products, like detergent, which could originate in St. Louis and still sell.

At forty Gus Bus was the titular head of the company. His father had died after flying a plane into the Lake of the Ozarks while trying to buzz the lakeside estate of one of his cronies. Gus ran the company by hiring a competent management team and staying away. He had found his calling in public service, and Gus had his own ideas about public service. Establishing foundations, buying baseball teams, and building stadiums weren't for him. He had come up with various other schemes to benefit his city and its inhabitants, including the commissioning of a work of earth art that involved erecting a huge dome of parachute silk across the Mississippi River.

The dome had been tied to the feet of the arch on the St. Louis side of the river and anchored with a pair of grain silos on the Illinois side. It was true the scheme gave St. Louis worldwide publicity. But when the dome collapsed on a fleet of barges and created a massive traffic tie-up on the river, there was some question as to whether the city had benefited from its fame.

"Gus has built a coal-burning boat, or had it built at a boatyard in Indiana, across the river from Louisville. He's bringing it up here next week. His idea is to use it to entertain dignitaries, foreign businessmen, that sort of thing. Take them on short cruises. Get them to invest their money here.

"But first he wants to run it down to New Orleans. I want to take a photographer and go with him."

If Hecklepeck would just follow along and report what he saw, it wasn't an entirely bad idea. Gus Bus was nothing if not news, and it sounded like a comparatively reasonable scheme, certainly after the dome idea Turnbull had heard about. But he couldn't help wondering how Hecklepeck had gotten hooked up with Gus Bus.

He dug a little deeper. "You and Bussard and who else will be making this trip?"

"Gus has hired a captain and an engineer and some firemen to keep the boilers running. Of course, there's a cook . . ."

No other media. That made the story an exclusive. It was sounding better. "And this captain is somebody with a lot of experience?"

"Yes. He was once captain of the *Julia Belle Swain*. Gus says he was also a narc; he worked for the Drug Enforcement Agency in the Florida Keys."

"Ah, well that qualifies him."

"Frankly I'm hoping it doesn't."—Like a sudden gas pain Turnbull's misgivings returned.—"because I would like to try to pilot that boat." The anchorman looked into the distance over Turnbull's shoulder. In his eyes was a fierce and unassailable light. "I don't have a license, but there's no law you have to have one, and I know the river. I've been studying it for years, and I've been down and back several times on the *Delta Queen*. Like Mark Twain I have learned the river to where I can see it in my head."

Turnbull was saddened but not surprised. He had seen this happen many times before to television people. They fell in love with themselves. News became an extension of their own egos, and news reports, minimovies in which they were entitled to star. At various

16

times in his career Turnbull had had a skydiving anchorman, an anchorwoman who made a news series out of her hysterectomy, and a small army of news personalities who had each undergone basic training for the small screen. The research showed these schemes went down well with audiences. But Turnbull deplored them. They were self-promotion rather than public service.

He suppressed a sigh and made one last effort to steer Hecklepeck away from steamboats. "What if you aren't quite as familiar with the river as you think you are?"

"Then we hit a snag and go down."

Turnbull could have put a stop to it then. But the news director believed in meting out rope to his employees until they succeeded in getting their necks into nooses. It took great restraint on his part, but he never interfered unless it was absolutely necessary.

Yet he remained disappointed. He'd always viewed Bill Hecklepeck as being too self-confident to need general approbation and, in any case, too lazy to wave his ego around publicly. It was his profound and last hope that the boat would sink before it arrived in St. Louis.

"Sha-eeke, rattle, and roll." In the middle of the newsroom the producer of the ten o'clock news show was organizing his desk. The room itself resembled a rectangular recycling center where various types of trash had been isolated into large piles for trips to various reclamation facilities. In the center of each pile was a writer or a reporter or a producer, who, while presumably writing, reporting, or producing, could actually be seen manipulating trash. One writer yanked a sheet of paper out of a battered typewriter, balled it up, and tossed it at a metal trash can that had long passed overflowing. Phone at his ear, a reporter aimed a ballpoint pen at a ceiling panel on which he had drawn a target. The pens sometimes stuck but more often dropped to the ground. The floor around the reporter's chair was a sea of broken, leaky ballpoint pens appropriated from the station storeroom.

The ten o'clock producer's desk, presuming he had one, was totally obscured by stacks of videotapes, newspapers, and old news show scripts. The producer, thirty-six-year-old Richard Markowitz, was taking items off a mountain in the center of his desk and distributing them to various piles. "Sha-eeke," sang Richard as he tossed some papers at a pile of papers. "Rat-tle." A videotape clattered as it found a home on a stack of videotapes. "And roll." Feigning a hook shot, Richard slipped a script onto the script pile.

He came to the central pile and rocked back and forth on his Nikes while he tried to decide what to do with the next item.

"Live a little. Throw it away." Hecklepeck grinned at Richard from behind a pile.

Richard scowled back, an expression that with his black hair and beard made him look foreboding and unpleasant. "Yeah, and if I do, who's going to help you out with the facts next time you come looking for them?" Hecklepeck didn't contradict him. Richard produced an excellent news show, but more than that he had a good memory for facts and faces as they had appeared in old news stories, and he was KYYY's living and only substitute for a newspaper morgue.

"So, what was Jim Tourniquet squeezing you for?" The newsroom was Richard's sun, moon, and stars, his entire universe. He had to know everything that was going on there so he could assess and pass judgment on it.

"Blood, he wanted blood."

"Doesn't he always."

"Actually, he wanted sweat and tears: somebody to cover the death of a glue-sniffer."

"Humph. Could be a good story." Richard looked keenly at Hecklepeck to see if Hecklepeck had found it interesting.

"Yeah," said Hecklepeck absently. "I got him to assign it to Jennifer Burgess."

"Jennifer? She has no experience. The story'll end up like a Disney movie. Little mice singing, 'Just a whiff of glue makes the medicine go down . . .' "

Ignoring the heavy sarcasm (Richard was almost always sarcastic), Hecklepeck intoned mildly, "She's young. She's eager. And I promised to help her."

"My ass, you'll help her." Richard knew bullshit when he heard it.

But his words failed to needle Hecklepeck. "I'll try but I may not have time. I am going to be very busy with my own series."

Richard sat down, folded his arms, and leaned back in his chair in a demonstration of shocked surprise that was every bit as contrived as it looked. "Well," he said, "what prizewinning material are you going to thrill and delight us with?"

18

"I am going to help pilot a steamboat down to New Orleans."

Richard snorted. "What steamboat?"

Hecklepeck explained about Gus Bussard, his steamboat, and their plans to take it down to New Orleans.

Richard was unimpressed. "Well, I guess there's not much to it nowadays with all the engineering work that's been done on the Mississippi."

"Not much to it? Not much to it?" Hecklepeck launched into a lengthy description of the hazards of steamboating on Missouri waterways and his own ability to handle them.

Richard knew better than to interrupt Hecklepeck midenthusiasm. And the flow of talk gave him a moment to pursue a thought of his own, something that had occurred to him when Hecklepeck mentioned the series on glue-sniffing. Richard began sifting through one of his stacks of newspapers.

". . . a sawyer was a tree stuck into the riverbed, waiting to pierce the unwary hull . . ."

Richard let out a little cry. He had found it, a little paragraph buried on page six in the August 21st morning newspaper. "What?" snapped Hecklepeck, irritated at the interruption.

"That series on glue-sniffing might be better than you think." Richard leaned back in his chair, his forefinger on the little article.

"Yeah, yeah?"

"It's the second one. The second glue OD in . . . ," Richard looked at the date of the newspaper he had his finger on, "in a month." He looked at the article again, excited. "Roughly a month. August 21st. No, it says he died the day before. August 20th. September 17th."

At first Richard thought that he'd hooked the anchorman. Hecklepeck stared at him for one long, keen moment. But then, "Coincidence, Little Richard?" The use of "Little Richard" was intended to remind the producer of Hecklepeck's seniority and the ten-year difference in their ages. "Could we be talking about coincidence here? Must we look for the conspiracy in everything?"

"I'm not talking about conspiracy, but what if glue-sniffing has become a fad again? Since I've been here whole years have gone by without reports of death by solvent abuse, and now suddenly there are two."

"Mere coincidence. How many drug overdoses in general do you think there are in this city every year, many of them unreported in the news media?" Richard rolled his eyes 180 degrees and fixed them on a pitted ceiling panel. "What is so remarkable about the fact that two of them involved inhalants? And what possible significance could it have that those two died roughly a month apart?" Richard brought his eyes back to earth and looked at Hecklepeck to see if the tirade were over.

"Another problem on the Missouri was its shallowness."

It wasn't. The diatribe had just reverted back to the waterways.

"One riverboatman said that navigating it at low water stage . . ."

"Porsche 911 46 58 622 XYZ," muttered Richard under his breath. "Steamboats. Piloting. Gus Sawyer and Heck Finn. Hmphf."

". . . 'was like putting a steamer on dry land and sending a boy ahead with a sprinkling pot.' "

"What you have here, Heck, is male menopause." This Richard delivered in clear, audible tones.

And Hecklepeck heard it, Richard was sure of that. He just chose to ignore it. "But the basic problem was that steamboats were built cheaply," he was saying pompously, "often with inferior materials . . ."

3

JENNIFER BURGESS LED her photographer across the patchy grass of Benton Park to the swing set. She looked at the dusty hollow under one of the swings and took several steps backward. "This is where they found him," she said to the photographer.

"Which one, do you know?" asked the invariably cheerful Art Macke. He meant the ground under which swing.

Jennifer shook her head. "I don't know."

"Well," said Art, undeterred in his quest for media accuracy. "I'll just shoot them all. When you find out which one it is, you can use those pictures."

"Yes," said Jennifer, insinuating her finger into one of the curls at the end of her long, silky pony tail. She didn't see any difference between the dust under one swing and another. Whichever one it was, a ten-year-old boy had laid in it and died.

Reassuringly, Art was whistling as he set up his camera on a tripod. The expression on his face was as willing and pleasant as ever. He pulled various cords and other pieces of equipment from the pockets sewn to the legs of his army pants. Art was just as unaffected by the corpse he couldn't see as he would have been by one he could see. He had seen so many.

Tall, big-boned Jennifer tugged the sides of her suit jacket together and held herself around the middle in a comforting way. Looking around, she found Benton Park a little worn, not particularly nice, but definitely not terrible either.

The park was quiescent and almost empty of people in the September morning sunlight. There was barely a ripple on the surface of the small lake. In one corner a city crew was cutting grass, a sight

so normal, so disassociated with death by glue-sniffing or by anything else for that matter that Jennifer could almost believe she was
there to cover some recreational program or a new effort to keep the
parks clean, the kind of story she usually covered. The truth was
that, unlike other reporters, who always yearned to cover what they
did not, she had been content. She had discovered satisfaction in the
crafting of her stories. That they usually appeared midway through
the newscast, after all the important news, did not bother her.
Jennifer's expectations of herself were not that high. She did not see
herself lashed to the catapult of stardom.

Yet here she had been propelled onto the trail of this big story.
Everybody said it was a great opportunity, by which they meant a
great opportunity for Jennifer to shine. What they seemed to forget
or ignore was the simple fact that a ten-year-old boy had died to give
her a break. She felt more like crying than taking advantage of the
situation.

"Tulio!" Psychologist Ben Howell leaned back in his chair. His
cheeks, which looked like big scoops of strawberry ice cream,
moved when he talked. "Tulio, toluene, that's what we're talking
about when we talk about glue-sniffing. There are other solvents . . .
benzene, xylene, hexane, hydrocarbons . . . and they're used in a
vast range of products including fingernail polish remover, paint
thinner, aerosols, glue, gasoline. So, it's not always toluene. But
from what I see around here, tulio is the solvent of choice, as it
were." In his mid-thirties, Howell was slightly ridiculous in appearance. But he sounded competent to Jennifer.

"Tulio." She rolled the word around in her mouth as she wrote
it carefully in her notebook. The word was deceptively pretty and
gave her a thrill that awakened her baby instinct for news.

From Benton Park Jennifer and Art had driven to Malcolm Bliss,
one of St. Louis' two public mental health hospitals, and were in the
office of one of the institution's drug counselors. Art was fussing
with his equipment while Jennifer sounded out Howell. She had
resolved to be as thorough and careful as possible; it was the least
she could do for the boy who had lain in the park dust.

"Why?" asked Jennifer, her whole soul in the question. "Why
would anybody want to sniff tulio?"

"Why do you drink a glass of wine? It makes you feel good."
Howell had on a short-sleeved beige shirt that bunched up under

his arms and a knitted maroon tie. His head ballooned out from the neckline. "It's the same with tulio. In fact, the effect of tulio is much like that of alcohol except it doesn't last as long. That's why the glue-sniffer carries around a plastic bag so he's got it to sniff periodically."

"But sniffing is bad for you, isn't it?"

"Oh, yes," said Howell. "It's bad, bad stuff. But that's not a question that comes into it—any more than side effects come into it when a person takes a drink."

"But glue-sniffing is much worse than alcohol and . . . is it addictive?" Jennifer sat poised on the tips of her toes, her reporter's notebook proffered.

"Sometimes. Not usually. Most solvent abusers move on to alcohol, marijuana, other drugs, as soon as they get older. You might call this group chemically dependent, that is, they're hooked on the act of getting high but not necessarily on tulio. However, there is a certain core group that seems to continue to prefer tulio to other drugs and sticks with it into the late teens and twenties. That's the group I see in here. I would consider that group addicted."

"But then why?" As rapt as she was, Jennifer might have been receiving the gospel. "Why would anybody even risk getting hooked on something like that?"

Howell shook his head. "You can't judge this by middle-class standards. The risks don't even come into it. We're talking about kids who are malnourished, who are no strangers to violence, who face lives of deprivation. With tulio they escape the realities of all that. At the same time they get an identity—not a very exalted one, but in a society built around various forms of abuse, that's something."

Jennifer persisted, her big gray eyes never leaving the glossy, pink face that made her think of baby oil. "But he died. This ten-year-old boy, Hoyt Jenkins, died."

"I didn't know Hoyt . . ." Howell seemed to be searching his memory. "But I don't usually get them until later, when they've developed a real problem." He leaned forward. "They do die. Once in a blue moon. There have been reports of sudden sniffing deaths, usually in cases where there is reduced oxygen content in the blood, which probably has something to do with the plastic bag."

"But this is the second one in a month."

Howell nodded, his blue eyes still sparkling in spite of the seriousness of the conversation. "I did know Mike. His older brother, Pete, is a client of mine. He may be a good one for you to interview."

"That would be great." Jennifer was impressed with Howell's dedication. He seemed to care about his clients. "But don't you think it's a coincidence that two of them died within a month of each other?"

"Yes . . ." Howell hesitated and then clearly decided to level with her, "it's too much of a coincidence if you consider the statistics. Sudden sniffing deaths are rare. With two boys dying close together like this I can't help thinking they were sniffing something other than tulio, something more lethal. I wonder if they didn't get some other chemical by mistake."

"They found a plastic bag for glue-sniffing right beside the body."

"Yeah," Howell conceded with a shrug.

"Couldn't it just be that more people are sniffing glue, and therefore the incidences of sudden sniffing deaths are going up?"

"I doubt that. It's a minuscule problem in the great scheme of things. There was a time when junior high school students experimented with glue-sniffing on a widespread basis, but now you find it mostly in pockets, in populations with certain characteristics. It doesn't spread. It doesn't get worse. It doesn't go away either."

"Populations?"

"Well, poor. Very poor. But it's more than that. Glue-sniffing occurs in neighborhoods that are . . . disoriented. Where there's a question of identity. Where the sense of community is missing."

Howell explained further. "For instance, glue-sniffing has been extensively reported among Indians in the Southwest and Mexican-Americans in California. But you don't see it in poor, black neighborhoods. I think the difference is some degree of self-respect.

"Here in this city, glue-sniffing is confined to roughly a ten-block area just south of here. The area around Benton Park, where that boy was found. Now who lives in that area? The people they call Hoosiers."

Art Macke had just finished setting up his camera. He nodded forcefully and tugged on his dirty blond beard. "Yeah," he said, "yeah."

Jennifer looked at him and back to Howell for an explanation. "I thought Hoosiers came from Indiana," she said.

"Not these Hoosiers. I don't know why they're called Hoosiers,

24

but they moved up here from the country, from the Ozarks mostly," said Howell. "They came during the depression because they couldn't make it down there. Two generations later they haven't done very well here either. They have no job skills suitable for an urban environment, city life is totally foreign to them, and they have no idea how to use what resources are available to them. And what I think is most devastating of all is that these people are now isolated. The old ways, values, such as they were, no longer apply. And there's nothing to replace them.

"As a result the young ones are growing up in total deprivation, not only financial, but also moral, spiritual, and emotional, all those things on which self-respect is based."

The dirty beige office was quiet as Jennifer finished writing in her notebook. In spite of her rising excitement about the story, her fascination with the subject matter, and her growing respect for Howell, Jennifer's note-taking was unhurried and neat. She stared at what she had written. "So these Hoosiers are . . . ," she groped for a way to say it, "are on the, uh, lowest rung of society?"

Howell smiled, pushing his ice-cream-scoop cheeks up into his eyes. "The use of toluene would say they are. There have been no cases of glue-sniffing on the north side." Howell was referring to the poor, black section of segregated St. Louis. "There, they're into crack of course and, more uniquely, abuse of T's and Blues, a combination of Talwin and amphetamines. Talwin is the brand name of the painkiller pentazocaine."

"Yeah?" asked Art. "Why?"

Howell shrugged. "Availability? Fashion? In any case the thing about T's and Blues is you gotta pay for them. Or break into a clinic and steal them, which takes some skill. So they've got a street value and a cachet.

"Now, how do you get toluene? You go to a hardware store and buy some paint thinner. If you haven't got a dollar eighty-nine or whatever, you go down to one of those factories on the river, climb the fence, and fill up your jar from a big storage tank. See the difference in cool? If there can be said to be a hierarchy of drugs, toluene is at the very bottom. It earns you no respect on the street. People who use other kinds of drugs avoid the glue-sniffers. Tulio is cheap and it's also messy. It makes your nose run, your eyes red and watery. It marks you for what you are, a sniffer of glue."

25

"Then why . . . ," aghast, Jennifer repeated the question she had already asked several times, "why do they do it?"

"It's free and available. All you need to ingest tulio is on the street. Pieces of rag, maybe some mattress stuffing soaked with toluene and placed in a plastic bag. The sniffers seem to especially like those Wonder Bread bags. You know, the plastic bags that Wonder Bread comes in." Bent over her notebook, Jennifer nodded. "You see them discarded all over the neighborhood." Howell paused to give Jennifer a chance to catch up on paper.

"Tulio abusers are mostly male for some reason, and they start young, as you've no doubt gathered. Eight or nine years old is not unusual."

"But how? Don't their parents stop them?" To Jennifer this was the most incomprehensible part of the whole saga.

"The parents may try to stop it. Or they may not. What you have to remember is that these kids come from very disorganized backgrounds. A lot of their parents have little or no control over their own lives, much less their kids'."

"But can't they see what it does to their kids?"

Howell shrugged. "Probably not any more than they see the effects of bad diets or abuse. It's no different than they themselves had it as kids."

"What's it do to them?" The question came from Art.

"Chronic use of toluene can damage a whole range of body systems. It's been implicated in kidney, nervous system, and bone marrow disorders. But I think the side effect that is most widespread is brain impairment. There was a study"—Howell whirled around in his chair and pulled a book from the rack behind him. He leafed through it until he found what he wanted.—"in the late seventies that showed 40 to 60 percent of chronic users were brain impaired." Howell snapped the book shut. "I would venture to say it's higher than that. More like 80 or 90 percent."

Jennifer felt her feet go cold. "What . . . what happens to them?" she asked as the chill rose up her legs.

"Almost all of them, without exception, speak like they're coming from far away, and their words are disjointed. They're just having to work very hard to put it together upstairs. But," Howell raised a hand encircled with a gold spandex watch that had worn to silver in patches, "tulio doesn't make them violent. My clients are gentle people. They commit thefts but usually only when it's easy, when the shopkeeper has his back turned and they can slip out with a piece of merchandise. Some of them support themselves by shoplifting. They're not capable of anything more elaborate."

"It must be hard to make a living by shoplifting," commented Art.

"Yes. But there's not much else they can do."

A sense of helplessness pervaded the room and there was a pause. "How do you treat them," Jennifer recollected herself with an effort, "the glue-sniffers?"

"Without a great deal of success." Howell smiled ruefully and climbed another notch in Jennifer's esteem. "To treat someone with a problem of solvent abuse, you really have to treat the underlying problems at home. And, as I already described to you, the problems these people have at home are immense. Then, the problem of treatment is compounded by the inability of the sniffer to see just what he's doing to himself. I use some behavior modification techniques to get them to stop, and for a while they do, but they almost always go back to it." Howell chuckled. "It's discouraging. I try not to dwell on it, to place a lot of emphasis on my life outside the office."

"What happens to them?"

"Eventually something gives, a kidney or something, and they die. But not so suddenly and so soon as Hoyt Jenkins and Mike Cobb. As I said, that's *not* characteristic of tulio use. Pete Cobb, for instance, is nineteen, and he's been sniffing since he was eight or nine. He's much more typical."

"He's the one we can interview?"

"Yes. He's off the tulio right now because of his brother's death. He comes here on Tuesdays. I'll sound him out on it at our next session."

"That would be great. Now, I guess," Jennifer looked down at her notes and up again, "we ought to put some of this on tape." She picked up the microphone.

4

F ROM THE LEVEE in front of the St. Louis arch William Hecklepeck threw a pebble as far as he could into the mud-colored Mississippi. Overhead the sky was a color that Hecklepeck had learned to call midwestern blue, which was to say of the same deep richness as a field of golden brown grain. Across the river in East St. Louis a cloud of smoke from a forever burning pile of tires sat on the horizon. Sedate today, the tire smoke changed with the weather. On windy days it was often mistaken for a major news story. Novice reporters raced across the river to an apparent fire, only to find the same huge pile of smoldering tires, a little post-industrial joke that could not be denied an equal place on the landscape with the fabulous arch.

Hecklepeck watched the ripple from his stone. It was the only apparent disturbance in the continuous flow of water: life itself, literally in the sustenance of plant and animal life, but also metaphorically because of that never-ending roll to the sea.

Yet Hecklepeck knew the Mississippi when it passed St. Louis was not nearly as placid as it looked. It was full of hidden chop and tide rips, various currents fighting it out with one another. They were skirmishes in the battle of rivers that started above St. Louis, where the Missouri and the Mississippi crashed headlong into each other and refused to mingle. They flowed for a short way side by side, the gray water and the brown, until suddenly they engaged and fought a violent ten-mile battle along a reach called the Chain of Rocks. They were still fighting it out on a smaller scale in front of St. Louis. And wasn't that like life too? Hecklepeck asked himself sentimentally.

The muddy tint of the water indicated the Mississippi was winning and would prevail down past Cape Girardeau and Cairo, where it would link up with the much larger Ohio in a wide-ranging ramble to New Orleans. How Hecklepeck longed to make that trip, to ride the willful old river, testing its smooth patches and making close calls around the rough.

The first time he traveled downriver on the *Delta Queen* he had itched to be more than a passenger. On the second and third trips, he had taken Army Corps of Engineers map books and studied the waterway, memorizing everything he could because by then he had conceived the hope of navigating it himself.

Hecklepeck came down with river fever the first time he visited St. Louis, interviewing for the anchor job at KYYY. It breathed adventure to him, and he heard it in the place where his own breath originated and where, if he had stopped to look, the boy in him lived. At one stage he had collected steamboat relics, including a much-prized wheel, which he installed in the hotel suite where he lived. He had spent long periods visiting with the lock master at Alton and the barge hands waiting to lock through. He had endlessly driven the river roads.

Now, just at the point when none of those things any longer soothed him, he had the chance to help pilot a real honest-to-goodness steamboat on the Mississippi. True, it was only the lower river. Hecklepeck would have liked to start in Minneapolis-St. Paul, close to Lake Itasca, the river's source, and navigate the entire length of the waterway, but he was happy with what he could get.

It was all thanks to Gus Bussard. Hecklepeck swung around and took in a yellowish art deco building just inside the right leg of the arch. Across the brow of the structure, peeling white letters spelled "Bussard Building."

Hecklepeck had just come from there, from lunch with Gus. They had eaten in the corporate dining room, a gilded, draped place that took the diner back to the era of white linen tablecloths, black waiters, and creamed chicken.

"What do you have for us, Henry?" Gus had demanded of the tall waiter who was hovering over his table. "I don't suppose Miz Jackson has made any of her delicious vegetable soup today. I really recommend it, Heck."

"Yes suh, she has. Can I get you a bowl?" The waiter bent slightly at the waist as if heat were emanating from Gus Bussard, and he wanted to warm himself. It was a relationship established by their great-great-grandfathers, slaveowners and slaves. In more than a hundred years nothing new seemed to have developed.

But . . . vegetable soup? Hecklepeck was asking himself. Why did the rich often insist on food that only elementary schoolchildren ate, when they could presumably have anything? Was it some needy longing for mother, something they missed when they were children? Hecklepeck felt certain he could make predictions about the soup: While it would be homemade, it would taste for all the world like Campbell's.

"Salad," he said firmly. "I think I'll have a salad."

The waiter nodded with slightly less deference than he reserved for Gus and left.

Gus took a sip of his Maker's Mark. "The father of waters," he murmured. "The king of rivers. The one and only, the mighty Mississippi. The open water." Gus's armchair had all but swallowed him up, and he peered out of it like a toad from his hole. His thick, convex glasses heightened the amphibious look by pulling his eyes into bulges.

Hecklepeck tried not to be irritated by the string of platitudes coming from the mouth of this basically unlikable man. He had been adopted by Gus, taken up at a reception at the St. Louis Art Museum for reasons he had no illusions about. Gus had a use for him. Whatever it was it had nothing to do with common interests or male bonding; Gus's intent was to exploit. If it weren't for the steamboat, Hecklepeck would have had nothing to do with him, but he too could maneuver for the right prize. "Well, when are we going to hit it?"

"Heh. Heh. With a stick?" The monogram under the belt loop on his trousers betrayed the expense of Gus's custom-made suit. But no tailoring on earth could fit him. He was wide at the waist and dangly about the legs. Any suit, and Gus had hundreds, was going to hang oddly. The result of the thousands of dollars he spent on haberdashery was a look once again reminiscent of the scion of Toad Hall.

"No." Hecklepeck's irritation temporarily got the better of him. His salad consisted of iceberg lettuce and cardboard tomatoes. "Embark. Set forth. Launch the, uh . . . What are you going to name the boat anyway?"

Gus wrinkled his brow. He was probably looking at Hecklepeck. But his astigmatism and the glasses that compensated for it were such that his eyes never seemed to take in whatever it was they were aimed at. Therefore, although his corrected vision was close to 20/20, Gus had the slightly sinister appearance of a man who focused on nothing. "I got a list of suggested names from the PR department. Some of them are quite clever. Cardinal Virtue, for instance, after the baseball team. But let's face it, it's too buschy."

"Buschy", Hecklepeck knew, came from Anheuser-Busch, the beer brewery that owned the Cardinals and the stadium where they played. "Auggie Busch is, heh, heh, a friend of mine, but it is not my intent to use this boat to sell his beer." Was Gus really looking over Hecklepeck's right shoulder or did it just look that way?

"Then there was the Spirit of St. Louis II, a name that would do a super job of promoting the city. But what do you think of when you hear 'Spirit of St. Louis'?"

"Lindbergh and his flight across the Atlantic," prompted Hecklepeck, remembering Gus's distaste for airplanes. Since his father's death by plane he never flew.

"Right. You don't think of soap at all. I want to do this for the city, I do. But in order to deduct the boat as a business expense, and that just makes good economic sense, I've got to demonstrate that it has a business function. So on my own I conceived the idea of naming the boat after the corporation, the Bussard-Dusay." Gus paused and Hecklepeck nodded, trying not to think cynical thoughts. "But you know Albert Dusay sold out his share of the company to my father thirty years ago. My father made it what it is today. And really it's the spirit of my father that's behind this project and his father and so on back to the founder of the company. So I've decided to name the paddle wheeler after the entire paternal line. Hence the *Gustavius Bussard.*"

Hecklepeck couldn't help the suspicion that Gus was really naming the boat after himself as much as his father and the four Gustavius Bussards that came before him. "Hmmm," he said, "very, uh, distinguishable." He garbled the last syllable in the hopes that Gus would hear the word as "distinguished."

Gus smiled a little self-satisfied grimace that looked creepy in the absence of any expression from his eyes. "The *Gustavius* is being towed up from Louisville next week. We'll have a christening down on the waterfront when it arrives."

"Great! So, we'll get started when? The beginning of October?"

Gus smiled again, but this time it was an I-regret-this-as-much-as-you-do-but-we-have-to-keep-a-stiff-upper-lip smile. "I'm afraid *Gustavius*'s maiden voyage . . . perhaps I should say inaugural voyage . . . will have to be put back a little. I've had a request to hold a fund-raiser on the boat. Tom Honigger called from Public Advancement." Hecklepeck nodded to himself. Public Advancement was a group of wealthy St. Louis businessmen who did things for the city. These things flew under the flag of public service since the organization had been formed to demonstrate that St. Louis's wealthy did care about the city's vast underclass. But its membership came from that closed, rich portion of St. Louis society that respected only itself. Thus, many Public Advancement projects, while indisputably good for the community, tended also to have a strong scent of self-glorification. There was the Public Advancement Riverfront Gala, a Public Advancement parade, and, on every major civic issue, the Public Advancement opinion.

Gus, Hecklepeck knew, was a member of Public Advancement; his grandfather had been one of the founders. "The cause is so genuinely deserving I felt I just had to say yes. Besides, if we were to go right away, the cargo wouldn't be ready."

"Cargo?"

"Well, yes." Gus's eyes were still holes, but his smile was now self-deprecatory. "In keeping with the back-in-time tone of our journey, our little odyssey, I was planning to take on a cargoload in New Orleans just as a real steamboat would have done in the good old days. Cajun spices and French Market coffee. The trouble is I'm having some tins made up, ten thousand of them—souvenir type things with Gustavius-the-boat on them in maroon and gold. But they're just not ready, so the spices and the coffee can't be packed in them."

"What are you going to do with 10,000 tins full of spice and coffee?"

"Give them away." Gus made a gesture like he was throwing coins to beggars. "Business contacts, potential customers, friends. The tins are quite tasteful, the kind of thing that could used . . . ," Gus made a few circles in the air with his hand; he was having a hard time thinking of uses, ". . . for paperclips or something after the coffee and spices are gone. If I take them on as cargo on our little jaunt to New Orleans, it becomes a business trip and I can write off some of the expenses. Simple as that!"

Hecklepeck nodded. It *was* simple as that. Business expense here.

Tax deduction there. Gus had it all worked out, and he was going to get credit for promoting the city through his boat at the same time.

"So if I wait for the tins and do the fund-raiser, then we won't weigh anchor (Do steamboats weigh anchor?) until after the third week in October."

The third week in October! Well, if they got going the week after that or even the first week in November, it would be all right. It was a seventeen-day trip from St. Louis to New Orleans, and Hecklepeck wasn't really worried about cold weather until after Thanksgiving. In any case they would be going south. He said all this to Gus. "I've talked to my news director about it," Hecklepeck added. "He's going to free up a photographer for the trip."

"Oh, wonderful. Perhaps you could do a little something on the fund-raiser as well? It should be quite fun. We're going to get the *Gustavius* up like a gambling boat and cruise up and down the river in front of St. Louis. People will buy chips to bet, but the big winners will be rewarded with prizes, not cash. The money will go toward charity, a really good cause and . . . a timely one: drugs, drug abuse prevention. Tom Selleck will be there. By a stroke of luck the fund-raiser coincides with an opening in his schedule."

Hecklepeck raised his upper lip and then tried to pass it off as a smile.

Later that afternoon Hecklepeck stared at the script for the five o'clock news and felt each of the four walls surrounding his cinderblock cubicle take a giant step inward. The doorless recess that sheltered him from the newsroom and served as an office was claustrophobic to begin with. It was small and pale green and filled with the piles of trash and junk that he had used to decorate the place, his editorial comment on the news business.

But Hecklepeck had never viewed his office as small and stuffy before. He liked the place. He had launched into many pre-news show daydreams there, taken many comfortable naps, and he had emerged renewed. He had never noticed the walls closing in before.

He closed his eyes and took a deep breath and another, trying to drive the feeling away from himself. At some point he was going to have to take time out and figure out why he had these panic attacks. He was going to have to deal with them. But not now. Now he had to get ready to go on the air in half an hour. Hecklepeck took another deep breath.

"Ex . . . cuse me." Jennifer stood in the doorway, uncertain about interrupting.

"Yes," said Hecklepeck in a tone that advised against it. He did not open his eyes.

"Jim said you would help with this story on glue-sniffing." Jennifer forged ahead even though common sense was telling her not to bother a temperamental anchorman who appeared to be resting.

"What. help. do. you. need?" Hecklepeck's tone said that only an idiot could possibly need help.

"I just want to be sure I'm covering all the bases. This is the first big story like this that I've covered."

"I see." Hecklepeck opened his eyes and swung around abruptly to face Jennifer. "This is the eighteenth-largest television market in the country and you're just getting around to covering stories." He was in no mood to be merciful. Nor did mercy enter into it. This was a lesson any reporter had to learn.

Jennifer opened her gray eyes, wide and hurt. "I've just started."

"That's just it, isn't it. You just started. But you started here, almost at the top. Why is it that people like myself who have spent years . . . decades"—Hecklepeck once again saw black fuzzy material at the outer edges of his vision. He squeezed his eyes shut and willed it away in an instant before going right on with taking his anger out on Jennifer—"in this business have to start all over regularly with novices. Can you imagine what it's like after paying hefty dues to be confronted with coworkers who haven't? Who think they should get a free ride for no better reason than their pretty faces?"

Jennifer shook her head. There was a hint of tears in her eyes, unnoticed by Hecklepeck.

"You start," he said, laying a hand on his telephone receiver, "with the police. Always with the police. Have you called homicide?"

"No." Jennifer hadn't seen any reason to call homicide. The deaths she was investigating were not murders. But now she could kick herself for not having done it. She was trying so hard to be thorough.

He sighed and dialed a number. "Lieutenant Berger," he said when the phone on the other end was answered. "It's William Hecklepeck."

After an exchange of pleasantries Hecklepeck asked, "What do you know about these drug OD's that have been reported in the newspaper?"

"What overdoses?" Lieutenant Berger sounded apprehensive. He was wondering if he had missed something. But that was only a small part of his foreboding: For a man in his position Mike Berger was preternaturally affected by reports of death.

"One was in August, and one, last week."

"August 20th, September 17th," supplied Jennifer. Hecklepeck repeated the dates to Berger.

"What was it?" asked the Lieutenant. "Cocaine?" He named the drug with great sadness; it did such harm to people.

"No. Glue. Glue-sniffing."

"That's unusual." Berger lost himself momentarily in contemplation of it. "Well, nothing like that here. Accidental fay-talities don't come in here. Only homicides." Hecklepeck brought his open palm down onto what little surface of his desk was not trash-covered. Of course. He knew that. In an instant all his good humor bounced back. He wanted to laugh at himself—the expert showing the novice how to do it and doing it wrong.

". . . cahroner usually rules 'em accidental at the scene," Berger was saying. "Not even autopsied unless there's something suspicious." He had sounded almost cheerful when he first came on the phone; now he sounded depressed. "How old?"

Hecklepeck told him how young the glue-sniffers had been.

"Ohhhhh." Berger's groan came from deep within his troubled soul.

Hecklepeck hung up the phone and turned to Jennifer. "Nothing there," he said blithely. For the first time Hecklepeck noticed that Jennifer looked sad, almost tearful. He wondered why. Had she been expecting a big story from that one phone call and been disappointed? There was something so young and vulnerable about her. And something attractive. Definitely attractive.

Hecklepeck looked at his watch. "I've got to go on the air here shortly. But let's go out to dinner and see if we can't work out a plan of attack for your story."

A smile broke through the gloom on Jennifer's face, and it was radiant.

5

Pᴇᴛᴇ ᴄᴏʙʙ ᴀᴘᴘʀᴏᴀᴄʜᴇᴅ with Ben Howell, walking a little bit behind him as if he weren't quite able to keep up with the drug
counselor's brisk pace. But nineteen-year-old Pete was taller and his
legs were longer.

His pants flopped above the ankles, and he wore a short-sleeved
blue shirt that looked like something a much older man would wear
to a church meeting with a white tee showing at the neck. It was
not tucked in.

Jennifer couldn't help but look first at the area under Pete's nose
to see if there were long, red streaks. However, the area above his
upper lip only looked dirty. A thin moustache was trying to grow
there.

But Pete had given it up, Ben Howell had said. He had
stopped sniffing glue when his eight-year-old brother overdosed
and died in mid-August. That meant he had been clean for more
than a month now.

Jennifer shook his hand. The gesture showed forthrightness on
her part, a willingness to give the interview subject a straight hearing. "How do you do." Besides, shaking hands was only polite.

"Hi," Pete Cobb responded with great affability. Howell then
introduced him to Art, who began to explain the functions of various pieces of camera equipment. He was unpacking it for an interview in one of the gazebos that Tower Grove Park was famous for.
Howell had suggested Tower Grove because it was next to but out
of the Benton Park neighborhood where Pete lived. Pete, he had
felt, might give a better interview without the inhibitions of his
friends and neighbors.

36

Jennifer looked at her hand to see if it showed signs of contamination. Of course it wouldn't. That sort of thing was invisible. She chided herself for even thinking it. In any case Pete Cobb didn't look dirty. His clothes were cheap perma-press yet looked respectably clean. Pete himself, his head cocked as he listened to Art, had an unhealthy pallor under the dull black of his hair. Which didn't mean he didn't shower. The poor might not know about nutrition, but in the twentieth century they had running water. Jennifer felt certain about that and somehow reassured by it.

"I think he's back on the tulio." Howell was sweating around the edges of his face although it wasn't a hot day, Warm, rather, with cool edges.

"He is?"

"Yeah. I had a session with him yesterday that was . . . I don't know. I just got the feeling he was back on it. But maybe I'm wrong; I hope I am." Jennifer looked over at Pete Cobb, looking again for some hideous growth, a visual manifestation of his disgusting habit. But no, his brother had died from sniffing glue. Surely that was enough to keep Pete off the stuff forever. She said as much to Howell.

He shook his head, his cheeks jiggling. "You'd think so, but addiction is a powerful thing. Also you're assuming that Pete sees the same connection between his brother's death and himself that you do."

"But he has to. There isn't any other way to look at it."

Howell smiled. "Don't bet on that. He comes from a background where cause and effect often don't get hooked up but exist separately and distinctly . . . and are accepted without question. It's very hard for someone from the middle class with ordinary common sense to understand. But you'll see.

"If you don't mind, I'm going to stay out of this. I think you'll get a better interview if I'm not here. And I'll be interested in what you get from him."

Jennifer thanked Howell profusely for getting her in touch with Pete Cobb. Howell dismissed it with a gesture. "Maybe the publicity'll help." He walked up to Pete and put a hand on each shoulder. "Remember what we talked about? They're just going to ask you some questions. You answer any way you want to."

Pete pulled away, as if he found the therapist's touch distasteful. Jennifer thought Howell looked a little . . . what? Miffed? Hurt?

Either way it was ungrateful of Pete to treat his therapist, possibly the only person who cared about him, that way. She felt for Howell, but maybe he was used to that kind of treatment from his clients.

"They're awgona grill me." Pete's announcement came out of nowhere. It was as if he were on 20-second delay from the previous conversation. Everyone was surprised into laughter; Jennifer, because she was relieved.

"Naaaw," said Art. "Only if you don't answer the first time around. Then, we threaten to pull out your fingernails and lay you out on a bed of nails."

Pete looked confused. "He's kidding," Howell was quick to interject. "You don't have to answer anything you don't want to."

"That's right," said Jennifer reassuringly. "Just wave your hand or something and I'll ask you another question. We can edit, that is cut out, the questions you don't answer."

Pete was happy again. He batted at something in front of his face.

Howell backed away toward his tawny-colored Plymouth. "I'll be in touch. I think I've got a nine-year-old for you to interview, but I'm not sure yet. I'll let you know." Jennifer thanked him again.

She turned back to Pete with that slight clutch she got in her stomach when it was down to her and an interview subject. But this wasn't going to be difficult; Pete was willing enough. "Nice day, isn't it?"

"Yeah skina day I lak." Pete's words drooled out of him while he chewed around the edges.

It took Jennifer a moment. Then she nodded in understanding rather than agreement. It was the sheer nasality of Pete's voice that so obscured his words. Maybe that's what came of glue sniffing. "Just a moment," she said brightly, "and we'll be set up and ready to go." She looked at Art. "How are you doing?" Why did photographers always have to spend so much time playing with their equipment?

It was customary to use the time to preinterview subjects before putting them on camera, but Jennifer had just decided not to. She would have Art record every utterance of Pete's rather than risk losing any three words together that might be airable. Besides, the camera was a comfort; she had a reluctance to establish any kind of one-on-one contact with Pete Cobb. In spite of her story and her job, she just really didn't want to know about him. He looked normal; she would have been happy to leave it at that.

"Art's still setting up." Not that it wasn't obvious. "I like this weather too, except you know this morning . . . I get to work around five in the morning . . . I couldn't tell if it was going to be hot or cold so I couldn't really decide whether to wear a light dress or go for a suit with a jacket . . ." When in doubt rattle on about oneself. At the very least it was filling in the dead air. Pete was nodding, as amiable as ever. "I ended up with the suit, but now I'm a little warm . . ."

It seemed forever before Art intervened. Then he fussed for another eternity getting Pete situated for a good shot under the roof of the gazebo—out of the sun but not too shaded.

Jennifer started out with easy questions, although she could feel Art's disapproval behind the camera for wasting his time and video-tape on what amounted to no more than electronic notetaking. When had Pete started doing Tulio? At nine. How old was he now? Nineteen. Did he work? Some. How did sniffing glue make him feel?

"Good. Real good."

Could he characterize that? No, not characterize. Could he explain that a little more?

"Werll. Sorta high." Pete Cobb was obviously enjoying the attention, bouncing a little on his buttocks like a congenial hot-dog-shaped balloon. "I lak it." Jennifer had to find a way to release something coherent and properly sober for a former drug user. About 20 seconds worth, enough for a sound bite. Had he tried other drugs?

"Yeah."

Which ones? Why didn't he like them? Didn't he know tulio was bad for him? Did he know why?

"Yeah. It eatsit yer brain." Pete was reciting words that he had been taught, but they obviously held no real meaning for him. Jennifer suddenly understood what Howell had said about not connecting cause and effect. Pete knew tulio made him feel good because it did. But since he couldn't feel the drug hurting him, all warnings were meaningless. "I know zzwhy I gotta stop."

But he had stopped, hadn't he?

"Yeah." Pete was still imperturbable. "Ben Howell'z bin helping me."

Jennifer took a deep, impatient breath. One-word answers were a TV reporter's nightmare, and she had no repertoire of tricks to elicit more. "How," she snapped, "has he helped you?"

39

Pete grinned suddenly and for no apparent reason. "Ze talksa me. Bout my family. Bout . . . bout howz bad fer me."

"*He* thinks you've taken it up again, the tulio."

For the first time consternation showed through Pete's punch-drunk expression. He gaped but no sound followed.

"Have you?" Jennifer waited until she could hear Art shift his weight impatiently behind her. Pete showed no compunction to answer her question. "How could you start doing it again after Mike, your brother, died from it? How could you?"

"Mikes got zum bad stuff."

"What do you mean?"

"Not tulio. Tulio don't do'at."

"But they found some right next to his body!"

"Not tulio. Mikes bin stealin' tulio down by zzriver. Got zumpin else."

"Tulio . . . toluene *can* kill you. It can give you a heart attack. The police say that's what happened to Mike."

Pete shook his head, showing signs of being upset. "Not tulio."

Jennifer dropped it; it wasn't advancing her story. "How did you feel when Mike died?" she asked, carefully aiming each word to get through to Pete.

"Bad. Real bad." But the response was punch-drunk amiable again; Pete was obviously back in the realm of conditioned response.

"He was your brother. Wasn't there something special about him?" Jennifer could just imagine how she would feel if one of her sisters died of a drug overdose.

"Yeah. Mikes m'brother. Zwe hang out together."

"Used to, you mean. Used to hang out together. Don't you miss him?"

"Yeah, yez I miss'im." But Pete appeared just as dumb and happy as ever.

Jennifer asked the questions over again and in different ways until she was satisfied that she had enough, if not twenty-second, then ten-second sound bites for her story. She thanked Pete and wished him away, but he stayed on, leaning up against a peeling white column of the gazebo while Art packed his equipment.

"Whazat?" Pete pointed to the light meter hanging around Art's neck.

Art pulled the instrument off over his head and showed Pete how

40

it was used. Pete showed no signs of understanding, but he seemed to be getting some pleasure out of the movement of the indicator needle. Jennifer no longer thought he looked normal. Since the interview she had become aware of how vacant his eyes were and that behind them lay strange responses to things.

"Do you have a job?" Art put the light meter back around his neck and resumed packing.

"Naw now. ZI useta paint, work for a painter . . ." Pete shrugged.

"These are tough times." Art was coiling a cable thumb to elbow. He seemed to be able to talk to Pete in a way Jennifer could not. "How're you making it?"

"Jobz, here . . . there. Pick up bottles. Chicken work, sometimes."

Jennifer would have missed it, passed it off except that Art looked up sharply. "Does Ben Howell know about that?" There was a certain tension in his voice.

Pete nodded, and his grin, impossible to attach meaning to, reappeared. "Zee knows. Ben Howell knozit all."

It made no sense to Jennifer. But once she and Art were back in the car, watching Pete stride away toward the park exit, she received an explanation.

"Chickens are male prostitutes."

"Prostitutes? For whom?"

"Other men. Drive through here on a Friday night sometime. You'll see a lot of them." Art knew about chickens and was eager to elaborate. "Tower Grove Park is their hangout. I covered a bust here one time. The guys looking for action—chicken hawks—cruise around in their cars until they find someone they like. Then they pick them up and go to a hotel room, or they just drive to an isolated place and, you know . . ."

Jennifer didn't know and didn't want to. "Pete does that? He's too dumb."

"Brains have nothing to do with it."

"But . . . he's not at all attractive. It's gross. Really gross."

Art grinned. "It's free enterprise. Supply, demand. Demand, supply. But you'd better make a point of checking it out with Howell."

Hecklepeck was in Turnbull's glass-enclosed office, asking for a photographer to shoot the christening of the *Gustavius Bussard*.

Unerringly Turnbull put his finger on the weak spot. "The *Gus-*

41

tavius Bussard? Where did Gus Bus go for the name? His public service manual?"

"His genealogy tables. He's named it after his progenitors, a kind of paternal steamboat line." Hecklepeck grinned at his own cleaverness.

"His ancestors weren't steamboats." In contrast Turnbull didn't smile when he joked.

"I don't know. I bet Gus could play a calliope with all the hot air coming out of his mouth. But you're right. I think he named the boat for himself."

"It is going to be part of the riverscape," Turnbull mused. "Significant meetings may take place there. I think we ought to give it some play, and you should do the reporting, that is, if you're still planning that . . . uh . . . trip." There was a faint hint of hope in Turnbull's voice that maybe Hecklepeck wasn't.

"Yep." Hecklepeck had not yet figured out how to tell his boss that the trip had been postponed until the November ratings period. Anchorpeople were not supposed to be away from their desks during ratings, but he had a vision of anchoring live from the boat's pilothouse all the way down the Mississippi. He just had to sell it to Turnbull. That it would be a nightmare of microwave and satellite hookups did not bother Hecklepeck. "There's also going to be a fund-raiser cruise in late October. Gus has asked for coverage on that."

Turnbull dismissed that as a decision for another day. "Put it in the file." He studied the back of his hands as if meeting notes were written there. "I noticed you talking to Jennifer the other day. How's her series going?"

"Fine. Oh, fine." Had they even talked about the series? Hecklepeck couldn't remember. They had had dinner at Sebastion's, not a long dinner, short because Jennifer had to get home and sleep in order to get up for the morning news. He had been back in the station in plenty of time for the ten o'clock show.

What they had talked about was each other. He was impressed at how picture-book perfect her upbringing had been: she and her two sisters swooshing through the leaves on their way to the neighborhood school in one of those beautiful old upper-middle-class suburbs while their mother waited at home and father worked a dependable nine to five. It was so different from his own solitary upbringing. His father had been in international development in the

42

heady days when it was believed the lot of the world's poor really could be improved with a little monetary interference on the part of the rich. With his missionary's zeal and a hefty travel allowance, George Hecklepeck was almost always in African jungles or Indian villages. His son stayed home with his mother or, when she traveled too, a hired person. Later he had been sent away to school. The loneliness had all scarred over, had developed into indifference and then his grown-up insouciance. But for some reason Jennifer's description of her background in the snug glow of candlelight had taken the cap off an old emptiness.

"Are you giving her some help?" Turnbull stuck with his strategy to get Hecklepeck interested in the story.

"Help." Hecklepeck mulled that over in contemplation of just what he was giving Jennifer. She had liked the Porsche, been impressed by Sebastion's, and listened eagerly to everything he had to say. Yes, the benefit of his experience. He nodded.

"Good, good."

6

I‍T WAS AWFUL." Jennifer twisted a long silky strand of her ponytail around her finger. Women didn't wear ponytails anymore, but somehow on her it didn't look dated, just. . . very pretty.

Hecklepeck and Jennifer were waiting for their coffee, after another dinner together. Was it an accident that she was still at work after the early shows when her workday ended at three in the afternoon? Could she have been waiting there in the middle of the newsroom until he finished anchoring the news? Hecklepeck told himself not to be silly. Adolescent stuff. But the possibility gave him an absurd lift.

After describing her interview with Pete Cobb, Jennifer was finally getting around to the subject that was most on her mind. "He just didn't get it. His own brother died from sniffing glue, and he couldn't fathom what it was doing to himself."

Her earnestness was, no other word for it, cute. Hecklepeck cleared his throat. "But how is that different from people who smoke cigarettes? They have to know what the bad effects are, but they don't stop because they think those things only happen to other people, not to them."

"With Pete it's more than that . . . I don't know exactly." Jennifer looked around Sebastion's for inspiration. It was an elegant place, lots of green marble and gilt-framed pictures. However, Jennifer liked it more for its warmth and comfort than its opulence. "I don't think he can understand how bad glue-sniffing is because he can't see the dangers or taste them or feel them. It's like he can't process anything abstract . . . even the death of his brother. It's creepy."

"Be careful now. You interviewed this guy under artificial con-

44

ditions with a camera rolling and a microphone in his face. You don't . . . can't know . . . what effect those things had on the answers he gave you. Be cautious with your interpretations." Hecklepeck didn't hear his own words; he was falling into a pair of big gray eyes that seemed to be as soft and inviting as a feather bed. "It's quite possible to hear something one way when something entirely different was intended. I've done it many times. The trouble is you . . . and I . . . come to the interview with our own backgrounds and our own sets of prejudices."

"But I'm the reporter. I have to draw conclusions." Jennifer was defensive. She had heard Hecklepeck say that what she found wrong with Pete was really something wrong with her reading of him.

"Of course you have to draw conclusions. All I'm saying is be flexible, don't do it now. Wait until you're ready to sit down at the typewriter, having gathered all the information you're going to get and done all the shooting. Things could surprise you."

Jennifer was, or had been, sure about Pete. He affected her strongly, and she had thought about him a lot. Yet Hecklepeck had raised a good point. She had gone into the interview intending to feel sorry for Pete because he was poor and disadvantaged and had a drug habit. Instead she had been utterly repelled and was appalled at her own reaction. Wasn't it just possible that she was making Pete into a monster to justify it?

Hecklepeck twisted lemon rind into his espresso and watched Jennifer. He ate at Sebastion's almost everyday, but the place was taking on a new glow in the light of the appreciation in her eyes: the fat happiness of painted cherubs, the shine of glass against polished mahogany, and the dignified dark green trim. It was such a fresh new way to look at tired old surroundings. He was glad he could share them with her, glad he could also give her the benefit of his expertise. Maybe this was what was missing from his life. "What's next on your shooting schedule?" Hecklepeck asked to draw her back to him. His voice was gentle.

"I don't know."

"Don't be discouraged. I think you have a good story here, although not an investigative story. There's no mystery, nothing to ferret out. But what you do have is a chance for some really good expository work. You can bring this whole segment of society that nobody knows about into the public consciousness." Hecklepeck waved his coffee cup as he prepared to take a sip. "That's not insignificant."

Jennifer perked up a little. "What about all that stuff about Pete being a chicken?"

"You should follow it up. It'll add to your insight about Pete. Also, if these glueheads are having to resort to prostitution to support themselves, that's a big part of the story."

"But how do I follow it up?"

"Go down to Tower Grove Park one night and see." Hecklepeck saw Jennifer was about to object. "Not by yourself. Take Art with you. Get him to arrange for an infrared camera so you can shoot in the dark. And, obviously, go in an unmarked car."

"Won't it still be dangerous?" Jennifer was twisting the whole ponytail now.

"I don't think so, not to you. All those guys want is to transact a little business and the privacy to do it in."

"Yuck."

Hecklepeck chuckled. "Not to them. See how things are interpreted differently by different people? It raises the question, What is Truth?"

Jennifer dropped her ponytail abruptly. When it came to men picking up young boys in Tower Grove Park she had no doubts about the truth. The practice was disgusting and that was it, period. She had no desire to go and observe it.

"Would you like to come up to my apartment and have some brandy before I have to go back for the late show?" Hecklepeck lived a few blocks from Sebastion's in the Chase Park Plaza Hotel.

"I'm exhausted. I have to get some sleep or I'll never get up at four tomorrow for the morning news." For the first time it dawned on Jennifer that Hecklepeck might be interested in something besides dispensing story advice. She was too tired and discouraged to know what she thought about that.

Gus had hired a barbershop quartet! The wrong era entirely. But Hecklepeck thought he understood what was intended. Barbershop quartets were common at political rallies. They were supposed to evoke bygone eras when life was simpler, as if the outcome of an election could turn back the clock. As if politicians hadn't been crooked then. What Hecklepeck associated with barbershop foursomes was Tammany Hall and Teapot Dome. He had an innate distrust of politicians who hired them.

Gus was not a politician, of course, but he was eminently untrustworthy. And what was interesting was that he apparently viewed his boat as a political instrument.

The boat was there, docked at the downtown waterfront next to Eads Bridge. Understated and elegant, she took Hecklepeck's breath away. Gus had had her painted entirely white. He had avoided gingerbread trim, and her lines were clean. In the garden she would be more Greek Folly than Victorian Gazebo.

A stern-wheeler like the *Delta Queen,* this boat was smaller. There were only three levels: the functional boiler deck on the bottom, the hurricane or main passenger deck with rounded arches and pediment-capped supports, and the texas deck on top. The texas! Hecklepeck could see Gus intended it as a place for passengers to take in the air and the view. Thus, the pilot house was not large, but it was perfect, encased on all four sides by windows with many lights. Hecklepeck just knew they all cranked open to let in the river breezes. When the tall black chimneys were pumping out smoke and water was crashing from the boards of the paddle wheel and the shoreline below was moving back as if in deference, a man could be a king in a place like that. A boy could be a pilot.

He had to resist the impulse to head for the pilothouse right away. The christening came first. A platform had been lowered from the hurricane deck to a place on the bow of the boat where canvas had been draped over the name. A larger area of the stern over the paddle wheel was similarly covered.

On the ground the St. Louis press corps was setting up. The photographer who had came with Hecklepeck was already taking shots of the lunchtime crowd. Pans and zooms, muttered Hecklepeck to himself. Music video stuff that dragged the viewer all around his television screen but never really revealed what was going on. Young Rick could get it out of his system now. He'd have to settle down when it came to shooting the story.

"What are you doing here?" a reporter from one of the rival stations demanded of Hecklepeck. The anchorman covered only major, investigative stories, not boat christenings. "Isn't the artillery a little hefty for the target, or is there more here than meets the eye?"

Hecklepeck smiled a smarmy little smirk that said nothing more than Wouldn't you like to know?

"And the band played on . . ." harmonized the barbershop quartet in the background.

Gus and the mayor were coming out onto the hurricane deck, along with members of the board of aldermen, local business leaders, and Tom Honigger, president of Public Advancement. They stood and chatted for a few minutes so that their pictures could be taken and importance established. Gus looked short and bent, particularly in contrast to Honigger, who was tall, fit, and self-assured.

Gus stepped forward and introduced the mayor, who made the first of a series of dull speeches, all to the effect that Gus had made a fine contribution to the city. Then the white-uniformed boat captain swung himself over the railing, down a short rope ladder onto the platform. Far less gracefully the fat mayor was hoisted over the rail and maneuvered down the ladder to the platform.

"I got a great reverse zoom, starting on his butt and widening out," Rick whispered to Hecklepeck. Not for the first time Hecklepeck wondered at the ability of people like Gus to get politicians to perform the silly trick while they received the applause.

A bottle of champagne streaming with ribbons was being passed down to the mayor. It was attached by rope to the ceiling of the hurricane deck so all he had to do was swing it against the side of the boat.

Balancing precariously on tiny, inadequate ankles he flung the bottle in the direction of the ship's side. But it glanced off intact, dangling in midair. The mayor made a swipe at it and almost went into the water, to the delight of several among the press corps.

" 'Mayor's popularity plummets'," quipped one of them. "Oops, no, that's 'mayor plummets'."

The champagne bottle was being hauled up from above by a crewman so that it could be repassed down to the mayor. Looking over the rail, Tom Honniger said something that must have been a joke because his neighbors at the rail laughed. The mayor's smile, even from a distance, appeared forced.

He tried again, and this time the bottle never even came close to the side of the boat but swung wildly in the wrong direction. Once again the dignitaries made some jokes among themselves. But their laughter seemed less than wholehearted.

The mayor got it the third time. The bottle hit the boat hard enough to knock a small chink out of the bottom, and a dribble of champagne flowed out of the hole into the river. Never mind that not a drop of liquid actually touched the vessel. The Mayor didn't hesitate. "I christen you the *Gustavius Bussard,*" he yelled.

While the champagne bottle continued to piss away its contents, crewmembers raised the canvas coverings on the boat's bow and stern, and its name was revealed. Hecklepeck saw it and groaned. He was echoed by a chorus of snickers from the rest of the media.

Forgetting that the letters formed "Gustavius Bussard", it was possible to see the name was handsomely scripted in black letters edged with gold. That wasn't what set the reporters off. What they were reacting to was the Bussard-Dusay ermine, which was wrapped in and around the lettering, its chin resting on the first 'u' and its big black eyes staring out over the crowd with mixed pathos and adorableness.

Hecklepeck thought the painting was a shameful defacement of what promised to be a dignified, noble vessel. It was no credit to the poor ermine either. The animal was being exploited, its features exaggerated and painted up on the side of a boat. Gustavius Bussard was showing almost as little regard for the ermine's animal rights as his fur-trading ancestors, who had no compunction about slaughtering it.

But the Bussards had always picked on the ermine. In the last several generations it had appeared on boxes of Bussard-Dusay soap flakes, promising to make whites "ermine white". Hecklepeck supposed the marketing ploy was aimed at housewives who fancied but couldn't afford fur coats. Instead they were supposed to luxuriate in laundry soap.

An ermine was a weasel, for Christ's sake. Literally a weasel, a not-very-clean and somewhat smelly animal, related to the skunk. Evidently the public didn't know that. In the winter weasels turned white and that made them ermines. But "weasel white" had an entirely different ring to it.

It was at that moment, staring at the weasel, that Hecklepeck felt a sharp sense of misgiving. He ignored it of course.

The news media trooped up to the hurricane deck for a follow-up press conference in what Gus referred to as the grand salon. It was a large, gracious room with a parquet floor and a whole wall of arched windows.

The windows had been cranked open, and through them Hecklepeck caught a hint of river breeze. It stirred something in him, and he immediately took note of the grand salon's exits.

49

Rows of red plush chairs had been set out for the press corps, and on each one was a press packet. Hecklepeck took a seat in the far corner of the back row and opened the packet. It was full of press releases about the construction of the *Gustavius Bussard,* as well as pictures of the boat and a gold metal key chain.

The newspaper reporter next to Hecklepeck was examining his key chain. "Plate, nothing but plate," he griped. "The gold'll probably wear off in a week."

"How do you know that?" Hecklepeck inquired in spite of himself.

"Well, Honigger made it, didn't he, his company? What do you expect?" Tom Honigger's company, Korporate Keepsakes, produced executive souvenir items, things that could be imprinted with company logos and handed out to clients or customers. His extensive catalogue included pens, hats, and mugs as well as clocks, ID bracelets, metal paperweights, tie pins, and, of course, key chains.

"Cheap shit." The newspaper reporter removed the key chain from the press packet on the chair next to him and slipped it, along with the one he already had, into his jacket pocket.

Gus was walking toward the podium. Hecklepeck gathered up his packet and walked down front to where Rick was set up with his camera. "Roll on the first five questions," he told him, "and then shoot some cover."

Rick looked at Hecklepeck with a troubled expression. This was not the way most reporters covered news conferences. They sat by his elbow and tapped him when they wanted to record sound bites. How could Hecklepeck be sure that all the important stuff was going to be covered in the first five questions? But there was no time to protest. The first question was already being asked.

". . . the *Gustavius Bussard* is going to be traveling up and down the river in front of the city, and it's going to be running on coal. Won't that add to our air pollution?" The question came from a competent female reporter working for one of the other TV stations.

"We think we've addressed that problem." Self-satisfaction emanated from behind Gus's glasses. "The furnaces have been fitted with specially designed catalytic converters. We reached this solution after much . . ."

By the time Gus finished answering the question Hecklepeck had reached the pilothouse and was shaking hands with the boat captain.

7

T HE DARK COULD be so disorienting when you were tired. Tiredness just obliterated night vision. Absolutely did away with it.
Riding toward Tower Grove Park in the front seat of Art's news car,
Jennifer decided it was like being old: Every movement became
unsure and unsteady, and you could never trust either yourself or
the objects around you.

The twenty-four-year-old had had ample opportunity to observe
the effects of dark on the tired person. For almost a year she had
been rising at four in the morning and by five was racing to the
station for the morning news. At least racing was the intent. For all
her expenditure of frantic effort she never seemed to crank up more
than slow motion.

Because in the summertime she went to bed when it was still
light, this was the first time in months she had seen the dark from
the other end, the end that was closer to dinner than breakfast. But
it didn't seem any different. She had gone home and napped first so
it was just like getting up for the morning news. Only it was earlier,
eleven P.M. If possible she was tireder.

What was so difficult to relate to was that most people, members
of the normal society she was no longer part of, were just going to
bed or settling in for the last half-hour of Johnny Carson or, on a
Friday night like this one, going out on dates. It was the end of their
day and, here, the beginning of hers. But at least she could go home
when the shoot was over and sleep, sleep, sleep.

Then there was William Hecklepeck, the man on whom the sun
never seemed to set. He had been at the station, full of his usual
energy, when Jennifer got there to hook up with Art. She had been

glad to see him because the truth was she didn't at all want to sit in a dark car and observe male prostitutes at work. And if she had to, she wanted to do it with a maximum amount of company and protection. She had suggested that he come with them.

He had declined. It was her story; he didn't want to take it away from her.

That was okay, she averred. She was so tired, she could use some help.

No, he didn't want to intrude. As if he were doing her a favor sending her out into a park full of sick, perverted men.

Heck had laughed at that, a laugh that showed he thought she was appealing. They weren't interested in her, he said. Then he sobered up and started talking about dues again, about how lucky she was to cover a story like this in a major market, what good experience . . .

Riding in Art's dark car on the way to heaven knew what unspeakable horrors, Jennifer felt anything but lucky. She didn't see why she had to pay dues as a reporter when she wasn't sure she wanted to be one. Jennifer had never set her sights on a television career; it had just happened to her, and now she was beginning to wonder if it was worth it.

More and more she just wanted a good night's sleep. She was tired of being tired, of having to sleep most of the weekend, when everyone else was awake, of being alone. Her girlhood, college, the short internship at the Philadelphia station all seemed like other lives lived by another person, an innocent, playful person. When she went back home, as she did whenever she could, it was impossible to explain what a dreary struggle her current existence was.

"I hope they're out there tonight." Art was full of cheerful enthusiasm, as always. "I don't want to have to make a habit of hanging out at Tower Grove Park for twenty seconds of voice-over tape."

Art's face, lit by streetlight, looked to Jennifer like a mask. "Twenty seconds?"

"Yeah, well what else are you going to use it for? This is a report on glue-sniffing. You're going to say that some glue-sniffers have resorted to selling themselves to finance their habit. That's all. Period. Unless you see somebody with a glue bag in one hand, taking money from a chicken hawk with the other. But come on, that's unlikely. So twenty seconds, less probably."

"Then why are we even bothering to come down here and shoot this?"

"Because it's something. One more piece of the puzzle to show that you really did your job. Besides, people eat this stuff up."

"People . . . ?" She was risking her life to appeal to television viewers? No, there was more to it than that. She was, she reminded herself, doing this because of the public's right to know. If she could just focus on that . . .

A few blocks from the park entrance Art stopped the car and collected his gear. He gave the car keys to Jennifer. "We'll do a few drive-through shots. Then we'll park somewhere and see what develops."

The car was a fat Oldsmobile, much bigger than Jennifer's Honda, and she felt as if she were behind the wheel of a snowplow or street sweeper. But there was a secure feeling in that. The wide expanse of white hood she saw over the steering wheel stood between her and whatever menaced.

In contrast the car handled with little more than a touch of the finger. She turned it into the park entrance. Immediately they were in another world. It was as if the volume had been turned up on the sense of unreality that Jennifer already had.

The park was bathed in theatrical pink from anticrime streetlights, and to Jennifer the rotary ahead looked like a preset stage, bushes and trees like painted scenery. What was troublesome was that the actors weren't going to come out of the wings and perform. Instead Jennifer and Art were driving under the proscenium arch, right into the play itself, and any awful, weird thing was possible.

She turned onto a park road and tried to confine her mind to her driving, keeping it slow and even so that Art could balance his camera. "Nobody will notice us," he said, "because everybody cruises through here, only they're looking over the merchandise; we're photographing it."

Whatever terrible thing Jennifer was expecting didn't immediately appear. What she saw when she glanced away from the odometer and the road ahead was nothing more than cars parked intermittently along the side of the road and, beyond them, people standing at the periphery of the park. People. They were all men, some in groups of two or three, some alone. Smoking. Jennifer could see out of the corner of her eye that a lot of them were smoking cigarettes.

Nothing worse than that. One was leaning into a car window and talking. Jennifer had the impression he was wearing a blue-jean jacket. She took a breath and felt relief filter down through her body. She was so tired that it was all sort of surreal and weird, especially knowing that the casual bystanders were really offering some kind of horrible illicit sex out there in the open under the anticrime lights. But at least they weren't performing it in the road or advertising in some lewd fashion. Was that what it was that she had feared?

Jennifer drove up and down the park's main thoroughfare several times until Art declared he had gotten enough rolling shots. Then he directed her to a side street, into the shadow of some trees. From there they could see the main park road and some of its traffic. "I don't think anybody'll see us here," Art opined. He chuckled. "They don't go around looking too closely into cars around here anyway."

"Now what?"

"Now we wait. I want to get a shot of an actual transaction, somebody getting into somebody's car or something . . ." Art was looking out over the dashboard.

On the far side of the street two men were standing on either side of a young tree. Men. It was too far away to tell, but Jennifer could guess they weren't any older than she. Younger probably. Maybe only sixteen or seventeen. They looked ageless, somewhere between puberty and thirty, which was where youth ended in Jennifer's shortsighted view. She could not see the color of their skin but guessed they had the same unhealthy pallor as Pete Cobb. They certainly had his thinness, so apparent in the set of their shoulders against the early morning chill.

Art raised the camera to his shoulder. From the whirring sound, Jennifer could tell he was taping the two by the tree. He lowered the camera to his lap and time passed. Jennifer, her nervousness behind her, wished she could sleep. Every now and then a car passed. One or two slowed in front of the self-promoting pair.

Jennifer's eyelids were actually getting heavy when a shiny fawn-colored sedan pulled up and stopped there. Art picked up his camera. She hoped that he would get whatever he needed so they could get out of the park and go home.

She made a sleepy survey of the car and decided it was what law-enforcement people referred to as a "late-model" vehicle. The car didn't look old, but it was big and clearly American in make, the kind of car that sheriffs and salesmen and beer distributors drove. It was nothing Jennifer aspired to, and under the circumstances she found it impossible to imagine the occupant. The driver was invisible, obscured by the streetlight reflected off his window.

The two who had been hanging out by the tree were approaching the car. Jennifer imagined the invisible driver pushing the window button with a lazy finger of his left hand and then leaning across the passenger seat to say . . . what? Her imagination failed her there, just as it did when it came to his face. No matter, the car itself was beginning to take on all the faceless connotations of evil that Darth Vader's mask had. She shuddered and found herself awake. The being, the thing behind that car window was out to prey on young men, to take them with him and . . .

Art lowered his camera slightly. "I wish they'd come around to this side of the car. Oh, good."

The two were walking around to the driver's side of the car. Their walks were not deliberately provocative like a female prostitute's would have been, but they were self-conscious as if the two boys—Jennifer could see now that they were boys, or very close to boyhood—knew they were being scrutinized.

They stopped in front of the driver's window, and Jennifer saw in the crack between them that the driver's window was coming down. She moved her head around to try and see him, but all that was visible was a pudgy hand with a cigarette in it and the arm of a suit jacket. The boys were evidently chatting with whoever the owner was.

One of them laughed. It could have been three buddies shooting the breeze, and that's what it would look like on the air, but everybody would know it wasn't because of what Jennifer would narrate. The tone of her voice would tell the story.

She still couldn't see the monster in the car. Every once in a while she caught a glimpse of thick shoulder or the curve of his head. At one point she flashed on a black rectangular thing that must be his wallet. However, the whole man kept escaping her.

At last one of the boys made a step backward, and it became clear the interview was over. He headed back to the tree while the other boy walked around to the passenger side of the car and got in.

As soon as the boys moved, the window on the driver's side glided upward, reshielding the man inside. But not before Jennifer got a good look at him. She gasped. "Did you see who that was?"

Art was letting the car drive out of frame. He finished the shot before replying. "I hope you don't care about your sound track; you just ruined it by talking."

"That man. In the car. Did you see him?"

"Not really. I was paying attention to my shot."

"It looked . . . an awful lot like Howell." Art looked blank. He was tired too. "Howell. You know, the drug counselor."

Hecklepeck was waiting by the two-way radio in the newsroom. He was not so cavalier about Jennifer's safety as he had seemed. In fact he liked looking out for her. Art would pick up the two-way and call if there were any problems.

It was approaching two in the morning. Hecklepeck sat in the assignment editor's chair with his feet propped up on the assignment editor's desk next to the radio. It was his favorite time, after the news, when almost everybody else was asleep and he owned the world. When he had something to think about, this was when he did it.

Now he was wondering if he didn't need a mentor/protégée relationship in his life. Well, more than mentor because he was rapidly becoming obsessed with Jennifer's person, dwelling constantly on the silk of her hair and the frankness in her eyes. Perhaps it was the obsession part he needed. Or the combination. Probably the combination.

In any case he hadn't had a panic attack since he first took note of those qualities of hers. So maybe what he had needed all along was someone to care for. Maybe he had just been in some advanced stage of loneliness. And maybe now for the first time he should think about making an adjustment in his life that would forestall the panic permanently. Hecklepeck was amazed that he was thinking such a thing. Marriage (he had to admit it was marriage that came to mind) had always seemed like a bad bargain to him, a leash with a woman at the controlling end. He had come close to it once or twice, not because he wanted it but because the person he was in love with did. The last serious brush with marriage had been thirteen years ago in Washington, D.C. He had avoided it by moving to St. Louis. Most of the time he was relieved.

Now he had this vision of himself making coffee for Jennifer in the morning and seeing her off to work with some words of good advice. It was an image that would have sickened him in other years. But maybe now the timing was right and he, Hecklepeck, was finally reaching adulthood. Timing was supposed to be all when it came to . . . long-term relationships. (For some reason he felt better postponing use of the "m" word.)

Why wouldn't the timing be good for Jennifer as well? She was young of course. There could be things she wanted to do before getting involved with somebody. But many of those things would go better with his guidance, and he'd give her plenty of space; he needed it himself. So . . .

A key turned in the lock of the newsroom door. Art shouldered his way in, followed by Jennifer with two videotapes in the crook of her arm. The look on her face brought Hecklepeck to his feet, although he kept his arms firmly clamped to his sides rather than obey the impulse to hug her. "What happened?"

Jennifer shook her head as if she were beyond speech and sat down at somebody's desk. "She thinks she saw the drug counselor, who's been helping us with this story, pick up one of the chickens," volunteered Art.

"But . . . that's great." Jennifer looked at Hecklepeck, incredulous. "That's a great story. Did you get it on tape?"

Art nodded. "I think so; let's go back and look."

In an editing room he loaded one of Jennifer's tapes into a machine and rewound it slightly. Jennifer watched him apprehensively. Hecklepeck leaned against the wall, jiggling the change in his pocket.

Art froze the image solidly on the man in the car window. "It is him," he breathed.

"Zippedy do dah," crowed Hecklepeck. "Now you know what you do?" He wheeled on Jennifer. "You pretend you're Mike Wallace. You walk into his office with the camera rolling and the mike open and you ask him what he was doing in the company of male prostitutes on Friday, September yaddy yaddy yaddy. And you've got him, baby."

Jennifer reached for her upper arms and hugged herself. "I don't want to." She didn't want to see Ben Howell ever or even call him to mind. She'd like to forget that he and the whole glue-sniffing story even existed because everything she had learned was awful.

"Why not? This guy's in the business of counseling boys with drug problems, and there's evidence he may be taking advantage of them for sex. You can't just drop it."

"He was helping me. He was"—Jennifer was aware how lame it sounded.—"going to get me an interview . . . with a kid."

"So, okay, let him. Shoot that part of the story and then go in later with the cameras rolling."

"Yea . . . eah," seconded Art.

"That's dishonest. That's stooping to his level."

Hecklepeck stepped away from the wall he had been leaning on. "It's not the same thing at all. This man's a . . . could be a . . . pedophile. All you're doing is postponing the confrontation with him. Remember, if it's true, you have a significant story here, one that deserves to be aired."

"Maybe he was just trying to help, taking that boy home or somewhere to counsel him."

Hecklepeck chuckled. "Two A.M. counseling sessions? I doubt it. But you're right not to draw any conclusions. Confront the man and find out."

Jennifer's spirits sank lower than before. What had she gotten herself into?

8

Late afternoon. the light told her that, and she noticed for the first time that it was fall. There were big blue-black clouds on the horizon, the kind that promised cold air rather than rain, and the occasional leaf drifted by her window. Jennifer felt a stab of melancholy that she had only now seen fall coming in and hadn't tracked it bit by bit the way she usually did, savoring every little change of season.

She reached over to her white-painted bedside table and picked up the clock. it was almost five. She had lost another entire day in sleep, a full twelve hours, since it was close to five in the morning when she had finally gotten home. Hecklepeck and Art had insisted on a celebration breakfast, and she had gone along, allowing herself finally to be swept up by their enthusiasm for her story.

She tucked her flowered sheet firmly under her armpits as if she were naked in bed, and only the sheet protected her modesty. So seductive, this gonzo approach to life where reporters galloped in in white hats and cleaned up Dodge, if not with six-shooters, then with 3/4-inch videotape. Jennifer could almost see herself as one of them.

Except that what had to be cleaned up smelled so bad, and she doubted her ability to do the job. When she interviewed Ben Howell she had been impressed with his knowledge and the care he had for his glue-sniffing clients. One glimpse in a darkened park and all of that was disquietingly suspect.

Hecklepeck had been right. Her impressions were not always to be relied on. He evidently coped with that knowledge by having supreme confidence in the eventual outcome. When the chips fell,

Hecklepeck seemed to believe, the pattern would delight and amaze him.

Jennifer had no such assurance. Just the opposite. If she did prove that Ben Howell picked up male prostitutes in Tower Grove Park, the result would be anything but positive. Local glue addicts would lose their only advocate and, while Howell would certainly be fired, there would be nothing to prevent him from continuing to pick up young boys wherever he found them.

What she hoped was that in all his years of experience—like most young people, Jennifer did not have much regard for experience—Hecklepeck had picked up some little thing that informed his blind trust in the future. Because she saw nothing to cleave to but that, the reassurance offered by him. Or was that his attractiveness? Oh, dear, what if she were deluding herself about his abilities because she found him attractive? Jennifer had to admit she did. So much so she had agreed to go on some kind of evening steamboat cruise with him in a few weeks. She felt misgivings when she remembered but, damn it, the only time she ever went out anymore was when she went home to Philadelphia, and she didn't get to do that as often as she would have liked. She just wanted to have a little fun, and Hecklepeck, if nothing else, was an adventure.

When Howell called the next week to give her the name of a nine-year-old boy with a habit of glue-sniffing, she merely wrote the information down and, ethics notwithstanding, mentally postponed her confrontation with the drug counselor.

Benton Park, to Jennifer's surprise, was a wonderful old neighborhood. It reminded her a little of the historic district in Philadelphia, not in appearance or age but in feel. A hundred years ago Benton Park would have been a thriving middle-class community. Jennifer longed to know the people who had lived there: who they were, what they did, how they felt. She could sense their clamor and feel the wind of their passage on the sidewalks.

Their houses were still a handsome red-orange brick, not the dull, maroon-black of so many of their St. Louis contemporaries. Nor did they repeat themselves block after block. They were varied and interesting, from handsome row houses to stand-alones with ornate iron railings.

Because the buildings had been so solidly constructed, because their brick had not faded and there was a minimum of painted surface to chip and peel, because hardly any were boarded up and a few were being fixed up by the first urban pioneers, it was hard to believe in the poverty of Benton Park. Jennifer had seen urban slums at home in Philadelphia and in other parts of St. Louis. They looked like slums. Benton Park did not. But she had learned by now to be wary of appearances.

Nine-year-old Jimmie Smith lived in a row house, the end one of three. There was a fire escape on the side of the building, and on the second-floor landing a woman in a tank top and cheap nylon jacket pulled on the back of a toddler's diaper. She looked down at Jennifer, the skin on her face pouchy, her hair uncombed. Jennifer looked away, embarrassed, as if she had been seeing through the walls of the woman's house, into her living room, and had caught her naked.

As she knocked at the front door, Jennifer noticed that the first-floor window was covered with a torn paper shade. The woman who answered her knock had no front teeth and was no taller than Jennifer's chest, shrunken and sack-shaped in a faded cotton shift. Jimmie's grandmother? "Uh, I'm looking for the Smiths. Jimmie Smith's family?"

The woman opened the door wider and shuffled in heelless slippers into the house ahead of Jennifer and Art. They followed her into sudden gloom.

There was no vestibule, and Jennifer had come directly into a room. What she saw when her vision cleared was that it was full of beds. No less than four, two double-sized and two twins. They were fitted together so that one could not walk between them, and the only open space in the room was a semidiagonal path from the front door to a door at the far left of the opposite wall.

The woman had seated herself in the room's one chair, a torn vinyl easy chair, drawn up to a TV set on top of a dresser. The set was on, but the woman was watching Jennifer out of colorless eyes that matched her equally colorless hair.

"We're here to do an interview with Jimmie about glue-sniffing," Jennifer said, her voice drawn as tightly as a violin string. "I'm the one who called."

The woman opened her mouth and yelled something so thick Jennifer couldn't discern the words. From the open doorway of the next room came the sounds of movement, and a boy emerged. He seemed small for nine, thin, with dark eyes and hair that stuck up in places. Obviously not combed, Jennifer thought. "I'm Jennifer Burgess with Channel Three News. I'm here to interview you . . . to put you on TV." The boy nodded and rubbed against the inside of the doorway, half shy, half flirtatious. "Is it true that you sniff glue?"

Jimmie left the doorway and flopped onto one of the beds. "Sometimes."

"Don't you know it's bad for you?" The question tore up out of Jennifer, and she wished it hadn't. She didn't want to scare him out of doing the interview. Perhaps if there had been a place to sit down she would have had more control. It was awkward standing in the middle of the room.

Yet her censure didn't faze Jimmie. "Yeah." He wriggled on the bed like a specimen delighted to be viewed under the microscope.

Jennifer swung around to Art as if it were up to him to decide what she should do next. Art had been looking around the room with disfavor. "Let's interview him outside. It's too dark in here."

"Okay, but I'd really like to try and talk to his mother first." Jennifer turned back to Jimmie. "Is your mother or father here?" The boy giggled and raised his hand to point at the woman in the chair.

His mother? But the woman had seemed too old to be the mother of a nine-year-old boy. Jennifer swallowed. "Mrs. Smith? I'm sorry. I didn't realize. I was wondering if you might be willing to do an interview . . . on camera . . . with pictures." Jennifer was acutely aware that she was asking this woman to go on television and talk about the fact that her son sniffed glue. If she were in the woman's place, she would never have consented.

But the woman was nodding. From the paste of her speech emerged the words "Don't mind."

Once again Jennifer looked at Art. "It's okay." Art was ready to accommodate. "If we turn off the TV, we can tape her right in that chair. We just need a chair for you," he said, looking around.

The woman spoke again, and Jennifer understood that she was telling Art to get a chair from the next room. Her ears were adjusting to the woman's speech just as her eyes had become accustomed to the darkness of the room.

Art came back with an old oak straight chair. Jennifer zeroed right in on its wooden seat. For a moment she worried that she would have to conduct the interview from one of the beds, which were unmade except for fitted bottom sheets. Dirty looking covers lay on top as if they had just been thrown off by whoever had been sleeping there.

Art's face was a study. He came close to Jennifer and whispered. "Wait till you get a load of the guy in the kitchen." A muttering had started up with Art's foray into the other room, and it was getting louder, indicating the approach of someone. "I think he's Jimmie's father."

A figure appeared in the doorway. "Jennifer Burgess," said Jennifer immediately. She would have held out her hand to shake but thankfully could not get around Art. "From the television news. I'm here to talk to your son about glue-sniffing."

"Didja come by ta' narragate?" Art set the chair down and squeezed past Jennifer. Homer Smith had fewer teeth than his wife and the same gray-brown colorless hair. But what stood out about him was the look of soul-deep anxiety in and about his pale eyes. He wore suspenders over his undershirt and gray work pants.

"Narragate?" Jennifer was confused. "I don't . . ." It was a weekday morning and this muttering man was not at work. His son was not at school. Jimmie was squirming around on one of the beds.

". . . narragate outta hell. Hellfahr!"

The sudden eruption made Jennifer jump. Navigate out of hell? He was some kind of religious fanatic. Jennifer made a wordless noise by way of reply and sat down in the chair Art had produced for her.

". . . many oner road . . . bill co-lecter, mailman, thiefs oner road, POLEEZMAN. . . . poleezman truda wadgate. . . . many oner road, marchin, marchin, marchin. . . ."

The sound of the mad, shrill voice grated on Jennifer like fingernails on a blackboard. It was expressing some emotion, some pain entirely unfamiliar to her, and nothing in her background provided her with the correct response.

Fortunately Art did a quick set-up. For once he seemed willing to sacrifice visual quality for expedience. Instead of setting up all the stand lights, he used only the light on top of his camera and a battery belt.

"We're going to do an interview with your wife about the glue-sniffing Jimmie does," Jennifer explained as succinctly as she could to Homer Smith. "That means we need quiet, so if you could . . ." She didn't want to say shut up. But Homer did. He plopped himself down on one of the beds and, wrapping his arms around himself, began to rock.

"Do you know that your son sniffs glue?" was Jennifer's first question to Betty Smith. The woman nodded. Looking at her directly Jennifer saw that she wasn't necessarily old after all but somewhere indeterminate between thirty and sixty.

"But don't you try to do anything about it?"

The woman shrugged. "When I ketch him I whup him."

"That's all? You don't try to stop him?"

"I cain't do nuthin'. I cain't do nuthin' about them boys. Not Jimmie, not his brothers neither."

Jennifer tried asking the questions again in a number of different ways, but the mother still seemed unconcerned. It was impossible to understand how any mother could care as little for her son as Betty Smith did. The only emotion she betrayed was dumb pleasure at being interviewed. Nor did she show any signs of reflection as Jennifer took her back and forth over the same ground.

"That's great." Jennifer finally lowered her microphone. In the background Homer Smith had begun to moan, and the moan was building. "You do a good interview." The woman smiled toothlessly, pleased with the compliment.

". . . lookin fer sarvation," her husband burst into speech, "marchin oner road . . . poleezman marchin, prezdent marchin, telev'sion people marchin . . . marchin . . . inna hellfahr . . . Hep em outta ther . . . HELLFAHR . . ." And he subsided into his mumble from which Jennifer could catch only an occasional word. Had this man been a glue-sniffer, and was this what happened after years of practicing the filthy habit? Pete Cobb had obviously been mentally impaired, but Homer Smith, possibly the next step in the progression, had no mind left.

Art was moving his equipment out to the car as quickly and expediently as he could. When he was down to the last piece, Jennifer stood up and beckoned to Jimmie. "Well, thank you very much. We'll just interview Jimmie walking through the neighborhood, and we'll have him home in an hour, no more than an hour."

Jimmie's mother nodded with the same dumb, happy expression she had assumed when Jennifer had complimented her. It was as though she'd been handed a lollipop and was still sucking on it. Jennifer wondered why she was working so hard to reassure Betty Smith about her son.

Art picked up his light belt and followed Jennifer out into sunlight. From behind him rose the voice of Homer Smith. "Mayor's oner road . . . marchin . . . marchin . . . marchin . . ."

Jennifer turned to Jimmie in a burst of relief. "Let's just walk for a little while and Art can take pictures of us. Then we'll find a place to sit and do an interview."

It turned out to be a glue-sniffing tour of the neighborhood. "See 'at?" Jimmie pointed to a plastic bag that lay up against a fire hydrant. His arm and hand showed streaks of dirt, but his dark eyes danced. "Tulio bag." He picked it up and showed it to Jennifer.

Before the walk was over she would see many such bags, discarded in alleyways, left in gutters, thrown down alongside housewalls. The detritus said everything about Benton Park's current residents. In another hundred years archaeologists might sift through backyard soil for bits of pottery and metal that depicted the lives of the Park's first inhabitants. But no matter how many years went by, nobody would look for traces of the present group. Its lives were passing through the neighborhood as fleetingly as a plastic bag in the wind. "What's inside?"

"Mattris stuffin' and tulio. Ain't no tulio no more. Jist mattress. Ah show you." Jimmie led them down a block and over some to an empty lot between two houses. Someone had put a chain-link fence across the front of the lot, but the door swung open and there amongst the rubble was a discarded mattress in midevisceration.

In one sense, Jennifer thought, Jimmie showed considerable ingenuity. He was using the materials he found in his environment for play, just as a country boy explored the woods for sticks and rocks. In each case the play was really the work of shaping a man. But in Jimmie's case, what would that man be? Not a park ranger, that was for sure. Not even the urban equivalent. Jimmie was going to turn into Pete Cobb and, if he lived long enough, into his father. His engagingness would become unreasoning and then vanish completely behind a vacant stare.

Jennifer forced it out of her mind. "And where do you get the tulio?"

"Ah show you." Jimmie was off, eagerly answering Jennifer's questions as he went. He was impatient when Art stopped them to get ahead for a shot.

They were heading down toward the river. Jennifer was conscious of that but not much else because she was so focused on

Jimmie. "What about your mother and father? Don't you feel . . . uh, bad about sniffing glue when they don't like it?" Jennifer wasn't at all sure this was true, but she wanted to sound Jimmie out on his parents.

Jimmie shrugged. "They don't bother me none. Ma mother cain't catch me. Ma father—"

"What about your father?"

"He got religion." Jimmie was matter-of-fact about it. "Ah doan see 'em much; he ain't never home—out walkin' the streets."

"Oh. Jimmie, does your father or did he ever sniff glue himself?"

Jimmie shrugged, a gesture that seemed to be one of his primary conversational tools. They rounded a corner and he stopped, "Here's whur it's at. Whur ah get th'tulio."

She looked up in surprise. They were standing in front of a big industrial plant. Several factory buildings sat behind a twelve-foot chain-link fence. At the entrance was a guard shack. "In there?"

"Yeh. Thur'ur bahrels in thur. White ones is tulio. Not yella. Gotta stay away frum yella. Tulio is th'white ones. Jist turn't on and fillup your jar. S'easy." Jimmie grinned. "Ah climb that thur fence. At night when them guards ain't watchin' too careful."

"Aren't you worried about being caught?"

Jimmie swaggered slightly. "They cain't do nuthin but yell. Anyhow ah ain't niver been caught. They got Mike wun time in th'spring. Not thur, some uther company. After that we cum up to this place."

"Mike? You mean Mike Cobb, the boy who died in August from glue-sniffing? He was a friend of yours?" Jimmie nodded vigorously. "And you still do it? How can you do it when your friend died from it?"

Jimmie's eyes got large, and he lifted his shoulders up around his ears in an oversized shrug as if he knew the reprimand was not a serious one, and his behavior, really cute. Jennifer grinned at him in spite of the deep disturbance she felt about his answers.

She made a note of the plant's name: Metalcote, Inc.—Electroplating. Then she directed Art to take some pictures of it.

"You should have seen the kitchen," Art said when they were driving back to the station. "It was a pigsty. Food all over the place . . . dirty dishes and piles of trash: tin cans and glass jars. There were only the two rooms. No heating, they had a space heater, and I don't know about a bathroom. I didn't see any signs of one.''

Jennifer wasn't listening. She was consumed with the terrible dilemma of Jimmie. Nothing now seemed as important as saving him, and nothing she was doing was going to help at all. Showing an interest, interviewing him, putting him on television—those things wouldn't discourage him from sniffing glue. On the contrary, they were rewards he had only received *because* of his drug habit. No disincentive at all.

So where was the good in her covering the story? Was some charitable soul supposed to see Jimmie on the air and come to his rescue waving adoption papers? Jennifer could only hope so.

9

THE *GUSTAVIUS BUSSARD* loomed out of the almost darkness at them. Although wire and electric current had to have a part in it, the stern-wheeler seemed to glow with ectoplasmic light. She was a huge, luminescent, almost terrible presence on the waterfront. The ermine on her bow, cartoony in daylight, appeared knowing and slightly sinister.

From the top of the street William Hecklepeck looked at the vessel as if her gangplank were the gateway to the rest of his life. She was the promise of adventure still to be had. Implicit in that promise, although Hecklepeck wasn't aware of it, was that the adventure came without accountability. *Gustavia,* as he called her, would take charge, breasting uncertain currents and shrugging off autumnal squalls. All Hecklepeck had to do was go along for the ride.

The only thing better than that was that with Jennifer. Hecklepeck looked over at her next to his right shoulder and wondered if she saw the same thing he did when she looked at the steamboat.

But Jennifer's woman's vision was darker. She felt a shiver curl down her spine, half anticipated pleasure, true, but half something else. She took the pleasure out of her mental drawer and closed the rest away in the bureau. It was seven o'clock on a Thursday evening, getting close to her bedtime, but for once she wasn't going to think about the time or her lack of sleep or her work. She would just enjoy herself and cope with Friday morning when it came.

As they walked toward the boat Hecklepeck noticed the big banner strung along the texas deck. The banner, which promoted "Riverboat Gambling and other various entertainments" in pseudo-nineteenth-century script, looked like clothes that didn't fit, a mini-skirt on a grande dame.

He deplored it. With complete disloyalty he also disapproved of the video crews lined up on either side of the gangplank. Had it not been for the klieg lights he could have squinched his eyes together and seen the crowd in nineteenth-century dress. Well, maybe not. The problem was that in the twentieth century, women's evening wear clung too tightly in the rear. One never saw the shape of a butt a hundred years ago.

"Do we have to go through there?" Jennifer asked.

"Yep. Looks like Oscar night in Hollywood, doesn't it?"

Jennifer nodded. "I don't understand. There are only four TV stations in town but I count five . . . no, six crews down there."

"That's because two of them are production crews. The two three-man crews running around getting in everybody else's way as if they are more important, they've been hired by somebody to visually record this event. It's a wealthy version of home movies."

"It must be expensive."

"It is. Very. And it raises the question, Is the cost coming out of the $500 ticket price and therefore out of revenues that are supposed to help drug addicts . . . or is somebody footing the bill?"

"Why would anybody want to pay for it?"

"Who knows? Gus might, in order to have it as promotion for the boat, which he may want to lease out in the future. I suppose Public Advancement could see it as a way to boost the city. But if you want my most cynical opinion, I think the money is ultimately coming out of revenues and that they're really doing it to enhance their own sense of self-importance."

"But if the money's supposed to go to charity, somebody ought to do a story about it."

"And accomplish what? These people do this kind of thing all the time. As I say, they'll have some lofty reason for it and a private source of funding. Then they'll repay themselves under some other heading like printing costs or catering. It's difficult to track down, and no public official wants to take on this bunch if he can help it."

But to himself Hecklepeck admitted that Jennifer was right. It was a legitimate question to ask how much money was going to charity and how much to a party for rich people. That didn't mean *he* had to ask it. There were lots of other reporters in town.

Most of the television lights went out when Hecklepeck and

Jennifer approached the gangplank. Only one, the KYYY crew, was interested in getting their pictures. The competing stations didn't want them, and obviously the hired crews had a list of VIPs they were supposed to shoot that didn't include a local anchorman.

"Hey Heck," taunted somebody from a competing station, "is this what they mean about newspeople getting too close to their sources?"

Hecklepeck grinned. "This is what they mean by 'getting the story.' Where are you going to be when this crate"—he mentally begged *Gustavia's* pardon—"hits a snag and goes down?"

"Alive and able to cover it. You can't deliver an eyewitness account floating face down in the river."

"I could do a live remote from the river bottom, and you'd still be looking for a way to get there." Hecklepeck reached into his breast pocket for his complimentary tickets.

The captain of the *Gustavius* was greeting guests personally. He looked like a captain in a black dress uniform, festooned with gold braid, and shameless muttonchop whiskers. " 'Tis a fine night for it," he said to Hecklepeck in an assumed Irish brogue. The two men looked at each other through half-closed lids and Hecklepeck nodded. He pulled Jennifer forward and introduced Captain James McNiff.

"Welcome aboard." The captain winked, and Jennifer had the feeling she had just participated in some secret ritual that she didn't understand but both men did.

Another officer collected Hecklepeck's invitation, and they were ushered through to the cloakroom, where Jennifer surrendered her red wool coat. To Hecklepeck it looked wholesome among the furs and glistening evening coats. Jennifer herself wore a black cocktail dress with no jewelry to speak of, and she looked . . . well, like Jennifer, only more so—radiant. Hecklepeck was no longer able to think of her in generic terms like beautiful or attractive. The only word that described her was Jennifer, and it evoked a response in him that was all its own.

He had bought a new black tuxedo for the event and with no trouble convinced himself that he still looked thirty-five, which wasn't that much older than twenty-four, closer to a ten-year spread than the truth, which was over twenty.

They moved through to the big ballroom where Hecklepeck had attended the press conference, and Jennifer gave a gasp of delight.

The big room had been set up to look like a nineteenth-century casino, the kind that appeared in so many movie westerns. Green felt and polished dark wood prevailed. The roulette wheel had been set into a steamboat wheel, and a female croupier pulled it by its handles to set it in motion. She had feathers in her hair and a bustle in the back of her skirt. Male croupiers and bartenders wore black armbands that puffed up their upper sleeves and string ties. A piano player was playing honky-tonk in an area set off for a stage.

The room was dusky under simulated gaslights. Guests were already gaming and, if there was any part of the whole that disappointed Jennifer, they were it. She had expected the rich and powerful of St. Louis to be as magnificent as the setting. But they were actually a rather dowdy looking crowd: older women in sour colors, hung with yellowish stones that were probably family diamonds; middle-aged women who seemed to be basted into their strapless gowns and were terribly afraid the stitches might break; and Jennifer's age group, looking like unmade beds, as if that were the privilege of wealth and status. The men were somewhat better, but then it was harder to go wrong with black tuxedos and white dinner jackets worn with complete confidence.

Hecklepeck, as he steered her into the receiving line, was having similar thoughts. This crowd knew where it stood, and that was on top of the pile. Most of them had been up there for generations. They had no appetite for risk, too many banana peels. So they shopped in the places their ancestors had shopped and lived in the same houses and vacationed in the same places and wore the same diamonds in the absolute assurance that all those things were *right*. Hecklepeck felt a stab of gratitude to his own grandfather for having slipped decisively off the pile decades ago, leaving him free to roam.

"By heck, Heck!" Gus had made the joke before. It was clearly aimed at Tom Honigger, standing next to him in the receiving line. Honigger smiled, a weak two-thirds smile that did not threaten to shatter his tan.

Gus was wearing a formal white vest under a black jacket that seemed calculated to bring out his chest, but didn't. He was holding a pair of brass-rimmed pince-nez in front of his eyes. They hung around his neck on a black satin ribbon.

"No need for a fuss, Gus." Hecklepeck's tone was dry. He shook hands and introduced Gus to Jennifer.

Gus looked at her for a moment through his lenses, then, tucking them into his vest pocket, he took Jennifer's hand in both of his. "The morning girl," he murmured, still holding her hand. "I see you, you know, from time to time. Has Heck told you about our little trek down the river, a first voyage for my little *Gustavius*? I hope you will come too, although I'm not just sure when it will be. It depends on when my cargo is ready." Gus's inability to set a date for the trip to New Orleans annoyed Hecklepeck.

"You can see how you like it tonight. We'll be weighing anchor at eight-thirty, in another fifteen minutes." Gus dropped Jennifer's hand at last and, pulling out his pince-nez, addressed Hecklepeck. "Isn't this thrilling? I don't mind telling you, and I know you will understand, that this is the dream of a lifetime. My life's work, my legacy."

"I can see that," Hecklepeck replied.

"Hello." Tom Honigger, Jennifer noticed, had a weak handshake for all his tanned, fit appearance. He was wearing a plaid dinner jacket with a black cummerbund.

"This is quite a gala," Hecklepeck observed when it was his turn.

"Yes," and then, as if Honigger had been goosed, "Yes" again. "The St. Louis Community is very generous when it comes to causes like this one." A bland quote for the media as embodied by Hecklepeck. There wasn't a hint of anything real behind Honigger's words. "It would have been more newsworthy if Tom Selleck could have made it. But I think we'll be able to donate just as big a check as if he had come."

"Whatever's left over after expenses."

"Yes, whatever's left over." There was a hint of irritation in Honigger's voice now.

"Have you thought about how you're going to allocate the money you raise?" Hecklepeck couldn't help it. Prying was the habit of a long career.

"Public Advancement is sponsoring this event in conjunction with St. Louis Without Drugs. After we take out our expenses, we're going to present the check to them." Honigger turned to the woman on his left. "Let me introduce Marion Honigger, my wife and chairwoman of St. Louis Without Drugs."

Marion Honigger bowed coldly and maneuvered Hecklepeck and Jennifer down the receiving line. But Hecklepeck had picked up one piece of information: Public Advancement and therefore St. Louis's power brokers weren't more than nominally interested in drug abuse prevention. With Marion Honigger serving as chair of St. Louis Without Drugs, the issue had been relegated to the auxiliary level, which meant the point of the evening really was partying on Gus's new boat.

Fall had cut into the nightlife in the Benton Park neighborhood. It wasn't cold, no frost predicted, but a chill dampened the air, and concrete stoops no longer held the warmth of the day. Outdoor life had been almost but not completely killed off by frost. The occasional swoop of a cigarette or glint of a bottle revealed loiterers in the shadows.

Jimmie Smith patted the front of his jacket and was rewarded with the crinkle of a plastic bag. The tulio inside was drying out, but he could probably get another hit off it.

Jimmie swaggered a little as he walked up Arsenal Street. He was wearing only a light jacket. Nor did the empty calories in his stomach do much to warm him. But he didn't feel the cold. Chemically fueled heat burned through his system and he felt good.

Hecklepeck picked up the last three chips and held them up, two silver and one gold. "This is it, brother Bart," he drawled. All we have left in the world. Forty dollars. What are we going to blow it on?"

Jennifer considered the green felt spread in front of them. Hecklepeck had bought twenty chips to begin with, ten of each color, worth 300 dollars. It had seemed like a lot of money to Jennifer, but she reminded herself that Hecklepeck earned a lot and the cause was a good one.

Chip by chip they had proceeded to lose all but the last three. In spite of herself Jennifer was a little disappointed. She had had visions of accumulating a large pile of silver and gold and then cashing it in for the porcelain bowl. She was not really interested in any of the other prizes to be purchased with game winnings—silver trays, etched leather desk sets, gold pens, stainless steel thermoses fitted with shot-glass caps, cashmere throws, garden sculptures, and more, many of them engraved with the name of the boat and the date. The yellow porcelain bowl covered with birds and flowers had stolen Jennifer's heart.

She wasn't going to get it unless the last three chips were winners in a big way. The bowl cost 450 dollars worth of tokens.

"My pappy"—Hecklepeck tucked his forefingers and thumbs into his vest pockets riverboat gambler style—"always said that if you don't have the hot hand, find the person who does and follow his lead."

Jennifer didn't need to look around the roulette table to see who was winning. Sitting directly across from them Marion Honigger had piled up a little mountain of metallic chips. She was playing the game with total concentration, and winning.

Mrs. Honigger had all the outward characteristics that Jennifer associated with the rich-woman type. Her hair was blond, shoulder-length, and back off her face, carefully trained to be casual. She was scrupulously thin, wearing strapless rose satin and substantial gold jewelry, all of which made the grim look of determination on her face that much harder to understand. None of the prizes could have meant that much to this woman.

She was weighing her chips, a stack in each manicured hand, one silver, one gold, and studying the green felt in front of her. With sudden determination she swooped and put both stacks on the three.

Hecklepeck nudged Jennifer. "Shall we?" Jennifer acquiesced. She didn't have any better ideas. Neither apparently did a young man with a white scarf around his neck who put five of his gold chips on the three.

As the croupier looked around for any last bets, Hecklepeck whispered to Jennifer, "I have a feeling about this one. We have three chips left and we're playing the number three. Good things come in threes."

"No." Jennifer suddenly felt the chill of misgiving. "That's bad things. Bad things come in threes."

The wheel was in play. Marion Honigger watched it intently. Her husband came up behind her and murmured something, but she did not answer. To Jennifer they looked like two halves of a glossy magazine photo.

The steel ball was slowing, and it came to rest finally on twenty-eight, about as far away from the three as it could get. Jennifer stared at it, thinking good-bye to the yellow porcelain bowl. She became aware then that the woman in the rose gown was staring at her and Hecklepeck. The expression on her face was angry and accusatory. When she saw that both Jennifer and Hecklepeck had gotten her message, she turned on the man with the white scarf. He immediately gathered up what remained of his chips and left the table.

"Whoof," declared Hecklepeck, "big mistake. Marion Honigger obviously thinks we jinxed her."

"Huh?"

"Well, we're losers and she's a winner. So, if the three was a losing bet, whose karma prevailed? That's how she seems to see it anyway."

She appeared to be telling the story to her husband, who listened impatiently. He reached into his jacket pocket for his wallet and pulled out several bills. "Go get some more chips and buy what you want." This didn't seem to satisfy his wife. "Well, okay, buy some more chips, parlay them into a fortune, and then go buy it."

Hecklepeck took Jennifer's elbow and guided her away from the table. "We shouldn't have done that," said Jennifer. "We ruined it for her."

"Bullshit. People always bet with winners. That's not what turns them into losers. That woman—I've run across her at a lot of charity functions, fundraisers—is pretty tense. Don't let her ruin your evening."

Hecklepeck squeezed Jennifer's elbow and steered her toward the eating section. "Well, brother Bart, I guess we'd better take advantage of the free food because we sure as hell can't afford to buy any."

Jennifer sat at one of the white-linen-covered tables while Hecklepeck went to the food tables. She wondered if Marion Honigger were interested in the yellow porcelain bowl. Because she would win whatever she set her sights on. It might cost her thousands of dollars in gambling losses, but it would be hers. As much as Jennifer had wanted the bowl, she couldn't see sacrificing a week's pay to buy it, much less gambling more money to win it. But of course the money was going for a good cause. Maybe at the back of her mind Marion Honigger was thinking about all she was doing to prevent drug abuse.

"Gus Bus!" An elderly woman in a lime-green dress proffered her cheek, but her expression did not change. Jennifer suspected the skin on her face would have cracked if it had. Everybody seemed to know everybody else here, and they greeted each other with displays of eagerness, as if they had been saving up something to share with each other and were delighted to have the opportunity at last.

Right in front of Jennifer the woman in lime green scrabbled for Gus's hand with one of hers. He let her have it but steadied his pince-nez with the other. "Your father once said to me, 'Betsy, make no mistake, the size of the gesture is everything. If you're going to make a statement, make a big one.' Well, Gussy, you have made a big one!"

"Betsy." Gus dropped the pince-nez and shook his head back and forth. "Betsy. You don't know how much that means to me. It's my mark. My mark on the city."

"I only hope I'll still be seeing you on Harbor Island this winter . . ."

So as not to appear to be listening, Jennifer reached into the silver bowl beside the table's centerpiece and pulled out a gold key chain. She was used to getting attention for being young and pretty, but here nobody showed an interest in her. Even when Hecklepeck introduced her, they barely paused to nod. The nascent cynic in Jennifer whispered that Hecklepeck was a longtime St. Louis celebrity with corporate-sized earnings and she wasn't.

Her salary didn't count here, and even if she earned everything Hecklepeck did, it still wouldn't count. She had to have been born into this crowd or, failing that, married in. That much she had learned from a few forays into society at home.

What society still respected in a woman was ability to contract a good marriage. Maybe they were right. Not that Jennifer was interested in marrying into St. Louis society. Not in the least. Marriage didn't interest her at all. Nothing like a good night's sleep did.

Hecklepeck set two gold-rimmed china plates on the table. "The food went on for miles and was surrounded by sharks."

Jennifer could see why. There were huge shrimp and caviar and big pieces of lobster on her plate as well as savory looking sculptures that she could not identify on sight. Clearly no expense had been spared on the food. She put the key chain down beside her plate and picked up her fork.

"After we eat I'd like to show you the pilothouse." Hecklepeck felt he had already spent more than enough of the evening below decks.

Sucking the sweetness out of a piece of lobster, Jennifer examined the key chain. A steamboat replica, rather finely drawn. She picked it up and felt its weight. It would balance well against her keys.

On the back was some tiny writing. She looked at it closely and let out an exclamation. "Weird. This key chain was made at the same place where all those glue-sniffers break in and get tulio."

"How do you know?"

"It says 'Metalcote, Inc.' on the back. That's the same place."

Hecklepeck held out his hand for the key chain and looked at it. "It's an upgraded version of one they were handing out at the christening press conference a few weeks back." He leaned back in his chair. "You know Honigger makes these. His company, Korporate Keepsakes."

"Then what's Metalcote?"

Hecklepeck shrugged. "I don't know. Subcontractor? Subsidiary?"

Jennifer took the key chain back and weighed it in her hand. Honigger's connection didn't matter. What struck her was that the gold-covered trinket linked two different worlds, symbolized by discarded Wonder Bread bags filled with old mattress stuffing—and the gold-rimmed, food-laden china in front of her.

10

J ENNIFER CAUGHT THE scent as soon as they stepped out onto the
deck: the Mississippi, fresh and funky and teeming with biology,
even when the wind blew with the threat of winter. Hecklepeck's
hand in the small of her back was a circle of heat that sent warm
shoots out into various parts of her.

But the hand was hustling her along the deck and into the pilothouse. Hecklepeck was a man with an agenda.

Captain James McNiff swung around. "Yo ho, Heck and lady, uh,
lady friend. Welcome to the crow's nest, or what passes for a crow's
nest on this ell-ee-gante vessel." The man had a manic intensity
about him, as if he had embraced a character not his own and was
acting it for all he was worth. But then being a steamboat captain
in the latter twentieth century was probably as much a theatrical
proposition as a serious command post.

"Jennifer." Absently, Hecklepeck reminded Captain McNiff of
her name. "How's it going?"

"Smoothly. Smoothly. She's smokin' like a teakettle." It was hard
to separate the gray in McNiff's hair from its original color; both
were overwhelmed by the floridity of his complexion.

"Where are we now?"

The captain beckoned him over to the chart on the deck in front
of him and pointed. "Just below Jefferson Barracks, headin' up . . ."

The desk lamp was the only light in the room, but it was enough
for Jennifer to see there were big glass windows on three sides, and
out in the dark a distant sprinkling of lights: more on the Missouri
side; hardly any on the Illinois bank. Another man in uniform

swung the steamboat wheel, keeping the *Gustavius* to the channel in the middle.

From the hushed consultation between Hecklepeck and the shorter, rounder captain, Jennifer caught words like "current", "shallows", and "channel". After a few minutes McNiff looked around, his muttonchops casting long shadows on his face, and addressed the man at the wheel. "Take a break, Cork. G'down and get yourself some of that gooermett grub. I'll take over for you." Captain McNiff moved toward the wheel.

He exchanged more words with his subordinate, who then left with a smile and a salute to Jennifer. The door closed behind him, and for a moment nobody moved. Hecklepeck remained bent over the map, and the captain peered out into the darkness ahead.

All of a sudden they burst into life. "Get on over here and get your hands on this thing." Hecklepeck was across the room in two big steps. The captain moved aside, and he took the wheel in his hands, carefully at first, as if he were taking up the most revered of dance partners, but then more firmly as romance deepened.

Jennifer was awed. This was Hecklepeck standing in a whole new light: that of some dark, dashing movie star of the past. Errol Flynn. Clark Gable. All he needed to do was take off—there he *was* doing it—his jacket . . .

Jennifer caught the jacket as Hecklepeck tossed it to her with a grin. He bent his head to roll up his sleeves. A shock of hair fell down over his right eyebrow, and Jennifer found herself hugging the jacket in her arms. For the first time what she felt about Hecklepeck was simple desire, unmixed with disparaging thought.

"A light touch. Just a light touch. That's all she needs." Captain McNiff was exhibiting as much pride as if he had invented the steamboat and built this one in his backyard.

"You're not kidding. At the same time she seems to be cutting right through the current."

"That's technology mow-derne. These boats weren't as brisk in the early days. The catalytic converter produces a secondary combustion. Gases created by the first burn reignite. Not only cleaner but hotter."

"Jen, come here." Hecklepeck called over his shoulder. *Jen. He called her Jen.* "See those lights?" Hecklepeck gestured toward the Missouri shore where there were groupings of lights down along the waterfront. "The bright light that seems to be sitting out on the water is the Coast Guard base. The lights on either side belong to private companies with docks along the riverfront. We're slightly favoring the Missouri shore right now because there are a lot of underwater hazards along the Illinois side."

"Here. You can see it on the chart." McNiff handed Jennifer a thick spiral-bound book, which had already been flipped open to the appropriate map. "The lights he's talking about are here, and those red dots are the submerged features." Jennifer let herself be maneuvered onto a stool McNiff had placed next to Hecklepeck. She laid Hecklepeck's jacket carefully across her lap before looking at the map. The lights were marked with steamboat-wheel-shaped symbols that were filled in, in red for the Coast Guard, in black for the private companies. They were also labeled. Jennifer noted that the companies were Pioneer Chemical and Maquette.

She looked back out over the water and saw that the lights were behind them, and the bank, once again, was lost in darkness.

"Nothin' along here," McNiff commented. "The railroad runs right up against the bank, and they've built up some bank protection. Without it the river would take it away piece by piece until it snatched up a railroad tie or two. See all this on the Illinois side? Those're levees. They go on for miles and miles. The river's inundating them and nibbling away at us over here."

"Surely not." Hecklepeck pretended to be shocked. "I thought they had locked him and dammed him until they had old man river right where they wanted him."

McNiff chuckled. "Never happen. Ja-may. No man, nor even a member of the smarter sex, can tame that river. He may not do quite the roamin' he used to, but he's still got plenty of jew-ah de vivra, and every so often he kicks out. All the years I spent busting drug runners off the coast of Florida and I can tell you, the open sea's got nothin' on Mr. Mississippi." He eyed Jennifer. "Don't ever treat him with anything but respect."

All three looked out into the black expanse in front of them and thought of the Mississippi roiling below. For the first time Jennifer understood the river's romance. In school her teachers had either anthropomorphized it, placing it in plodding human ranks, or, worse, they had characterized the great river as man's tool, a conveyer belt for the products of capitalism. What Hecklepeck and the captain were saying was that for all the farm crops, for all the nasty barges she—to Jennifer the river was a she—consented to carry, the

Mississippi was not just an ugly, muddy stream but some sort of nurturing-destroying life force. A watery . . . earth mother.

McNiff broke the spell. "You're all right for a stretch here. I'm goin' to step out and have a smoke before my pilot comes back and we have to prepare for docking. Keep an ear on the radio. I'll be right outside the door if you need me or if anybody comes. Some of these tuxedos might get nervous at the idea of a nonuniformed man at the wheel. Or worse, they might get the idea to take a turn at it themselves."

"Aye, aye, sir." Hecklepeck did not look around. It felt like the big stern-wheel was dropping in his soul and he wanted to keep it there as long as he could.

Except for the hum of the engines it was quiet. Jennifer felt exhaustion in the offing. Given a chance it would creep over her and take her. But she wasn't ready yet and could still hold it at bay.

On the Missouri side they were passing another cluster of lights. Jennifer looked at her map. Texaco's dock. Now they were passing over a submerged cable or pipeline and then there was a whole stretch of dock lights. She began idly to match them up with the companies on the map. Gulf Barge Mooring . . . a street dock . . . River Cement . . .

The companies appeared to be nothing more than hubs or transfer points, sandwiched as they were by the river on one side and the railroad on the other. Jennifer stared at the symbols on the map. Barges docked. Their cargo was offloaded and immediately put into railroad cars. Or the stuff came in by rail and was transferred to barges. Jennifer knew that at one time the railroads and the river traffic had competed. Trains had put steamboats out of business. They in turn had been supplanted by trucks. But the oil crisis had brought back both rail and river traffic, this time in obvious partnership.

Jennifer looked back at the bank, at the steadily burning dock lights, and at one that appeared to be blinking at her. Well, not blinking. It wasn't regular like that, but sort of irregular, as if it were dancing to some ponderous, syncopated beat. She tried to follow it and gave up. "Why is the light on that dock blinking like that?"

"Where? Oh. Maybe it's got a short." Hecklepeck looked again. "No. It doesn't look like a short."

"It looks like a signal, like Morse code." Jennifer had seen similar flashing in the movies.

"It does sort of." Hecklepeck did not want to be diverted from his steering.

"But why would they need to signal? These companies are marked on the map. All a towboat captain has to do is read it." Jennifer demonstrated with her map. "That's the last dock in this group of docks. It belongs to a company called"—She brought it closer to her face to read the small print.—"Metalcote. Oh! Metalcote."

The door of the pilothouse banged open and the boat pilot, Cork, burst in. He put both hands on the steamboat wheel, and Hecklepeck stepped quickly aside.

". . . thought I'd come up and see how you fellows do it." The sound came from the other side of the open doorway.

"Glad to have you. Always glad to have visitors in my pilothouse." McNiff stepped in first and looked around. Ascertaining that Hecklepeck was no longer at the wheel, he ushered in the person behind him. "On-trez. On-trez."

Tom Honigger stopped in the doorframe. Did he want all eyes upon him as he stood like a figure in a cruise ship ad? He was gazing into the night over Jennifer's shoulder. She turned and saw the blinking light. Was that what was riveting him? Honigger has, she reminded herself, some connection to Metalcote. He was at the very least a customer.

Suddenly Honigger moved. "So this is where the proverbial action is. I see I'm not the first to find my way here." He put a hand on Cork's shoulder. "And you're the man behind the wheel. Literally hands on. Is that Eads Bridge up ahead?" He pointed upriver, inviting them all to look. Almost as if he wanted their attention there, Jennifer thought, rather than on the blinking light off to the left.

"No, sir. That's Douglas MacArthur. Then we go under Poplar Street. Then Eads."

"Ah, yes." Honigger remained in rapt contemplation of the distant bridge lights for a moment before turning to Hecklepeck. "Is Channel Three doing a story on steamboat navigation?"

"Like you. Just visiting." Hecklepeck's tone was bland.

"Yes, ah. Isn't this something, ah . . ."

"Jennifer," amended Hecklepeck.

"Jennifer. I hope you see with the addition of this vessel just how much St. Louis has to offer. This is an accessible city. Very very important for companies that might consider relocating here." Honigger was giving Jennifer his Chamber of Commerce spiel. Hecklepeck had heard it before. Even when the man was making an effort, his voice had an undertone of irritation. "Moving materials in and product out. This little boat trip illustrates what an asset the Mississippi is. It's . . ." Honigger paused. For effect, Hecklepeck decided. Whatever he was about to say would hardly be spontaneous. ". . . a hydro superhighway—with no potholes. The Army Corps of Engineers sees to that."

McNiff, who was once again poring over his charts, made a sound in his throat like growling.

"There's plenty of space for new companies along the riverfront here . . ."

Like Metalcote, Jennifer wanted to say. She looked at the Missouri bank and realized the company and the flashing light had been left behind. The bank was dark again.

". . . and Public Advancement wants to talk to anybody who's interested." Honigger followed her gaze into the night. "We have a great city here. It's just a matter of getting the word out. Well"—He was edging toward the door now. Was it just a coincidence, Jennifer wondered, or could Honigger have wanted to divert them from scrutiny of the flashing light on the shore?—"I have to get back to the roulette wheel. My wife is about to lose her, actually my, shirt. Heh heh." The door closed behind him.

The four remaining each breathed a separate sigh of relief. "Let's cut back on the steam. I don't want her coming in too fast." McNiff was all business.

Hecklepeck and Jennifer edged away from the wheel. But they stayed and watched the captain bring the *Gustavius* neatly into berth. It was just after 9:00 P.M.

Jimmie Smith had been fooling around with a couple of friends on the Arsenal Street side of Benton Park. When they went home he took his last hit of tulio and threw the bag onto the ground. The breeze picked it up, rattling the plastic before sending it up against a tree.

Jimmie hadn't stayed to see the bag's fate. He was walking across the park, in the opposite direction from his home. He had been cold, but the chemical once again warmed him. Until it ceased to give him pleasure there was no reason to turn around. Home was only a place to sleep. No use going there until he was tired enough to overcome the sound of the television and his own underfed restlessness.

The nine-year-old boy picked up a pebble and threw it, realizing that he would have to break through the chemical haze to hit a particular target. Delighted, he accepted the challenge, aiming another pebble at a nearby trash can. It fell short and he tried again, tossing small rocks at an overflowing waste receptacle as the sound of footsteps grew closer.

The party on board the *Gustavius* continued well after the boat docked. But Jennifer and Hecklepeck did not stay. They thanked Captain McNiff warmly and disembarked.

Jennifer nestled into the leather cradle of the Porsche seat, letting tiredness descend over her like a weighted curtain. It was not an unpleasant feeling, relaxed rather, as if she had accomplished something and deserved the restful reward that was coming to her.

Hecklepeck's ringless right hand played with the radio buttons. It was a good hand. Too tired to detail why, Jennifer just accepted her own impression that the hand had strength and character.

Hecklepeck gave up on the radio, put his hand back on the gear shift, and applied it to driving. The steering wheel felt puny and tight in his left hand, and for all its deadly pick-up the Porsche was still a small, steel-encased vehicle that felt every bump in the road. *Gustavia* had nowhere near the speed but what she did have was power—massive, majestic power—the kind that met the most elemental forces head-on and persevered. Hecklepeck was too knowledgeable to believe the river couldn't just lick out and swallow the handcrafted vessel. All the more reason to admire the partnership and to want to be testing the ever-shifting boundaries.

Some tiny voice urged him to talk. Yet he was reluctant to express his feelings. Jennifer had been there with him. Tacitly they had shared the experience. Hecklepeck didn't want to risk their rapport with words. Anyway she was falling asleep, poor kid.

He pulled the car over to the curb in front of the house where her apartment was and switched it off. Jennifer struggled a little to sit forward. He put a hand on her shoulders to help and left it there. With the other he smoothed away a lock of hair. Her face was moon-colored in the light from the streetlight. He knew there were none of the lines he found in the faces of women his own age. It wasn't just that the dark obscured them; they weren't there. Heck-lepeck kissed Jennifer lightly on the lips. Soft, the lips of a child.

Jennifer was dimly aware that she should be paying attention. But her monitoring eye was shut tight and sleeping.

Maybe Hecklepeck knew. In any case he didn't push it. He got out of the car and ushered her to her door.

11

J ENNIFER RUBBED HER eyes vigorously in an effort to get them to focus on the morning newspaper. Since her arrival at the TV station at five A.M. she had had several cups of coffee and some sugary pecan rolls. These had given her enough energy to peruse the thick rolls of overnight wire copy, write scripts for the early morning shows, and read them over the air with something like her usual perkiness.

But now it was eight-thirty and, with the news behind her, all adrenaline had drained away. This was her free half-hour, her chance to read the newspaper in comparative quiet before the rest of the staff stormed in and the second half of the day began.

Jennifer's eyes slid over the front page, unable to hook into anything. Had the late night with Hecklepeck, the steamboat ride, been worth this exhaustion? She was too tired to assess it.

She flipped over the first page and several others, focusing in and out but assimilating nothing. She had the question wrong. She should have been asking herself, was it worth it to get up at four in the morning day after day? For what? But no, Jennifer was incapable of putting together the answer to that one either.

She came back to the newspaper on page A8, which was mostly taken up with the advertisement for a Famous Barr shoe sale. An awake Jennifer might have skipped over the page entirely because the news items were small and inconsequential. But in her tiredness she found herself reading one of the headlines over and over until finally it penetrated. She sat up then, suddenly awake:

GLUE-SNIFFING DEATH

(St. Louis) The body of a ten-year-old boy was found in a South St. Louis Park about 11:30 P.M. Thursday night. A second shift brewery worker on his way home from work spotted the body of Jimmie Smith, lying near a wastepaper receptacle in the middle of Benton Park. Authorities say the boy apparently died from an overdose of a chemical associated with the practice of "glue-sniffing". Smith lived with his parents in the vicinity of Benton Park.

"Oh. Jimmie." Jennifer's face turned flat white. She had predicted a short, sad future for the boy but nothing as brutally curtailed as this. "Oh, no."

She reread the bare facts a second and third time. How had it happened? Had he so broken down his system with tulio that that last inhalation was all it took to push him over the edge? Had he somehow gotten some "bad stuff"? Was there bad stuff when it came to glue? And then, like a knife wound in her lower abdomen, why hadn't she seen it coming and somehow prevented it?

"I see you had a rough night." Richard Markowitz was on his way back from the coffee machine. He had come to work early. "Don't you look outside before you do your morning weather forecasts? It's not raining."

Unthinkingly Jennifer handed him the newspaper and Richard read the article. "Yeah? So? Another gluesniffing death."

"It's the third one." In her grief over Jimmy it was a fact Jennifer had not yet contemplated. But it had hit her almost immediately.

"That's right." Richard whistled under his breath. "August, September, and now Mr. October." He regarded Jennifer, wondering what she was going to make of it. Not much was his guess. Richard found Jennifer attractive, which meant categorically she was not too bright.

He ventured a guess. "Did you . . . know that guy?" Jennifer nodded. "How. did. you. know. him?" Richard mouthed the words as carefully as if he were addressing someone who was hearing impaired.

"I"—In a rush of sadness Jennifer realized it didn't matter how

Jimmie died. It was the hopeless pathos of his life that should be mourned. He had never lived and, even if he were still alive, would have no future.—"interviewed him."

"On camera. You interviewed him on camera?"

Richard's intensity brought Jennifer to really look at him. "Yes."

"O-oh kay!" She had just moved up a fraction of a notch in his estimation. "Turnbull'll want you to break out a piece of that for the news tonight. It'll make a great tease for your series next month, show that we're really on top of things."

Jennifer felt like she was going to throw up.

William Hecklepeck gave his shaggy black cat a final scratch under the chin before leaving for work that afternoon. As soon as he stopped, Colonel Chambers let his head drop and his purr lapse. Nor did he stir when his master left their hotel suite. He needed his sleep.

Riding the elevator down to the parking garage, Hecklepeck reached the same conclusion about Jennifer. She needed her sleep. That was why he had spent the previous night alone. He himself did not sleep much. He hadn't when he was Jennifer's age either. But he could well believe that she did. The child in her obviously needed it.

It was the child who aroused such warm feelings in him. The child he wanted to protect, to take care of, to teach. For the first time since his interest in Jennifer had begun, Hecklepeck felt the distant choking sensation of approaching panic. When the elevator doors opened he all but raced for his Porsche.

By the time he reached the station the car had had its usual effect, and anxiety was driven off. But Hecklepeck could not help feeling a little unnerved by its recurrence. He strode across the newsroom without greeting anybody. Jennifer, he noticed, was not at her desk.

Richard trailed him into his office as he almost always did, full of newsroom gossip and talk about the evening's news stories. Today he had the morning newspaper in his hand.

"Can I say it? No, I mustn't. But I can't help it. It's coming out: I told you so. Oh, bite my tongue. Put a noose around my neck. Here it comes again: I told—"

"Cut the crap. What are you talking about?"

"Oh, nothing." Richard rolled his eyes. "No thing. Just a little ne-ews story."

"Awright, what?"

"This." Richard dropped the newspaper in front of Hecklepeck. "Read the item at the bottom of column one."

There was silence for a moment while Hecklepeck did. "Another one?"

"Yep. Now aren't you sorry you didn't take a little interest in the story?"

Assuming a mystified expression, Hecklepeck handed the newspaper back. "No. Why?"

"August 20th. September 17th. October 15th. It's like overdose-of-the-month club. Doesn't it make you curious?" Richard dangled his paper like bait.

"Coincidence. Sheer, random coincidence."

"It gets even better. Jennifer interviewed the victim before he died."

"I trust she's doing it on the news."

"A set piece. She's gone home to take a nap, but she'll be back."

"Well, then." Hecklepeck leaned back in his chair. "It sounds like you have it under control."

Richard took a step toward the door and stopped. "What the fuck is wrong with you? You never used to be like this. You used to care about the news. Now everything is . . . Porsches and steamboats. Grown-up toys."

Hecklepeck shrugged. "I just don't see any reason to get involved in this one. Jennifer's doing a fine job."

Since Jennifer had managed to interview the boy before he died and became news, Richard couldn't argue with that.

As soon as he left, Hecklepeck picked up a pen and wrote down the three dates, August 20, September 17, October 15, before he forgot them.

He wasn't going to say so to Richard, but there was something intriguing about a third overdose. Something that niggled in the back of his brain. Of course, if . . . if he were to give the matter a little informal thought, it was because of Jennifer. He really wanted to see her succeed with her story. He had after all been helping her all along.

August, September, October. Three successive months. 20, 17, 15. Three dates with an overall spread of only five days. Was it something about the moon? Could a full moon or whatever it had been—Hecklepeck didn't remember seeing a moon the night before—somehow enhance the effects of toluene on a small boy, giving an extra tug to his heart muscles?

Of course not. Ridiculous. But under that same moon he and Jennifer had been cavorting around on a latter-day riverboat, gotten up for mock gambling. They, who were the only people anywhere with a reason to be interested in that boy, were playing with gold and silver chips when he took a deep hit off a chemical-soaked rag and died. Happenstance, but how methodical fate seemed sometimes. They could have been passing by when it happened, only a short stretch of water away.

Hecklepeck reached for his calendar and turned back to August. There was no mention of the moon on Thursday, August 20th. He leafed backward and then forward until he found the new moon listed on August 24th. Four days earlier it would have been waning, just a sliver in the sky. The moon would also have been a sliver on the 17th of September, five days before the new moon on the 22nd of that month. But last night, had Hecklepeck seen it, the moon would have been bigger, closer to the last quarter phase.

No pattern there. Even assuming there was, Hecklepeck would have had a hard time coming up with some demonstrable connection between new moons and drug overdoses. He flipped around until he got so irritated with the calendar—great for keeping track of appointments, horrible for looking at the bigger picture—that he went through and ripped out the pages for the days when the three deaths occurred.

Sweeping aside much of the trash on his desk, he laid them out side by side. August 20. September 17. October 15. Three rectangular sheets of paper with torn-out holes, representing three different dates. Then he saw it. They were all Thursdays. Each boy had died on a Thursday night.

Jennifer was already sitting on the news set when Hecklepeck came in for the six o'clock news. She was bent low over her script paper doodling something small and tight in one corner.

"Hey," said Hecklepeck as he assumed the main anchor chair he always occupied. "I hear you got quite a scoop. Congratulations."

Jennifer raised her head. Deep circles cut into the tennis-ball shapes of her cheeks, which also appeared to have a tennis-ball texture. She hadn't blended in her face powder.

Hecklepeck warned her about the powder. While she fixed it, he wondered, had she slept? Maybe she had, but not enough. "You're the lead story tonight."

Jennifer snapped her compact shut. "Yes."

Hecklepeck pulled out his own mirror to shield himself from the intensity of her feeling, whatever it was, and began to flip aside a shock of hair that was forever falling onto his forehead and getting in his way.

Under a blanket of pancake make-up his features looked flat. But his examination of them was merely technical. Had the stuff (Hecklepeck didn't like to refer to it as makeup) been evenly applied?

Weatherman Irwin Samuels pulled out the chair on Hecklepeck's left, taking his place for the opening shot. "It would take more than six inches deep of that stuff to make you look good. Have you considered a paper bag?"

Hecklepeck scowled at him. Irwin never seemed to wear more than a light dusting of face powder, yet for some reason his muted brown face always looked earnestly handsome on television. "Are you going to bring me some good steamboating weather at the end of next month?"

"Will you never learn?" Irwin pursed his lips. He hated the conceit that weathermen were responsible for the weather, and besides, "I forecast five days in advance. Not a week. Not two weeks. Not a month. Anything more than five days is voodoo."

Hecklepeck smiled with satisfaction. He knew how to get to Irwin. That Irwin had gotten to him first didn't occur to him.

"Stand by," warned the floor director.

Within seconds Hecklepeck was reading the lead-in to the first story, Jennifer's story. He was well aware that it had been taken from the back pages of the morning newspaper and turned into lead material simply because KYYY had an interview with the victim. The argument could well be made that airing it at the top of the newscast was mere self-promotion. For proponents of that view Hecklepeck added a gruffness to his reading, a take-this-seriously-tone, because he was beginning to have the feeling that there was a story buried in the deaths of three boys. He had no idea what it was, just a hunch that there was something there.

". . . and here with more on the story is KYYY reporter Jennifer Burgess. Jennifer, you talked with Jimmie Smith just last week. What was your impression?" In the two-shot Hecklepeck looked over at Jennifer and was taken aback by the grim set of her face.

"Yes, I interviewed Jimmie as part of a special series I'm doing on the problem of glue-sniffing." Jennifer turned to her camera and continued.

Off the air Hecklepeck watched her deliver her report. She was being much too solemn. Serious was one thing. A newscaster should be serious, but dispassionately so. It was critical to stand aside from the story, to maintain objectivity. That he himself usually stood chin-deep in the news he reported did not enter into his judgment.

Jennifer's voice was somewhat flat, and her face in the monitor looked hard. There was discernible anger behind her eyes. You, audience, are responsible for this, she seemed to be saying. Her words were bludgeoning.

Hecklepeck recollected himself just in time to read the lead-in to the next story. As soon as he was off the air again, he turned to Jennifer. "Go and sit in my office. I will be there as soon as I am through with this newscast. I want to talk to you."

"A glass of white wine and a Beck's." Hecklepeck placed the order with the waiter at Sebastion's without consulting Jennifer's preference. A drink would be good for her, he reasoned, and what she drank was white wine.

The very set of Jennifer's shoulders in her houndstooth tweed jacket was angry. Hecklepeck had half expected her not to be in his office after the news, but there she was, sullenly playing with his typewriter keys. He had swept her up and away to Sebastion's.

"All right. Now what the hell has gotten into you?"

Jennifer looked at him, incredulous that he didn't know. "He died. Jimmie Smith died."

"Yes?" To Hecklepeck, Jimmie Smith was the subject of a news story. They died frequently. If he failed to maintain his dispassion while reading the news, Hecklepeck did disassociate from the actual people who were the news. He had had to.

"He was just a little boy. He never had a chance." Jennifer's voice was tight.

"Little boys die all the time. The tragedy about this one was that he wouldn't have had a chance even if he'd lived."

The waiter brought the drinks and Jennifer took a big gulp of hers. "But he died. I interviewed him a week ago—a little more than a week ago—and then he died."

Hecklepeck suddenly understood. "Hey, it's not your fault. The fact that you interviewed him didn't kill him." It hadn't, had it? There was no connection between Channel Three's interest and the apparent overdose of an admitted glue-sniffer. The third one in as many months. All on Thursdays.

Juxtaposed like that, the facts sent a thrill through Hecklepeck's gut. However, the television station hadn't gotten involved until after the second death.

"But you, and everybody, said it would help. You said that if I did this story, I would be helping, letting the world know about a serious problem and, thus, getting somebody to do something about it. Instead, he died." Jennifer spoke fiercely, grasping her wine glass.

"Yeah, but Jen . . . Jen. The boy died because he had some bad stuff or because there was something wrong with him or because he got too much toluene in his bloodstream. Not because you stuck a mike in his face."

"Really? You think he got some bad stuff?"

"Well, no . . . maybe. It's possible. There is a pattern about these glue-sniffing deaths that is worth investigating." He explained about the Thursdays, concluding, "If there is something going on here, then it's as important as ever to get to the bottom of it, more so in fact."

Jennifer was intrigued in spite of herself. "Like what? What do you think is going on?"

Hecklepeck shrugged. "I don't know."

"So how would you go about finding out?"

Hecklepeck almost said, Call the police, but he caught himself. He wasn't going to get into that trap again. "Okay, let's assume that these three deaths, each a month apart, each on Thursday, are not drug overdoses."

"Ben Howell, the drug counselor, said they weren't."

"He did?"

"When I interviewed him, just after the second death. He said toluene wouldn't do that. It had to be something else. I didn't really take him seriously—"

"Well, maybe he was right. He would know." A practicing psychologist specializing in solvent abuse would seem to know, even if he were overfond of young boys. "If the police had just done an autopsy, we'd all know. They'd have found traces of whatever it is.

93

But since they didn't, we have to cast around for other means to figure out where and how those boys got what killed them."

"Metalcote," breathed Jennifer, remembering that Jimmie had taken her there to show her his source of drugs.

"Metalcote does come to mind, doesn't it? There are lots of chemicals there, and that's where those boys were going to steal toluene. Maybe they got something else instead. And if . . . if those boys were climbing over the fence and stealing something besides toluene, something lethal, wouldn't that be a lovely case of corporate liability? Toluene would be bad enough, but something poisonous would be much worse."

"But Jimmie knew, he was very adamant that the toluene was stored in white barrels. He said to stay away from the yellow barrels."

"That proves it. They do have lethal stuff there."

"But if he knew which barrels had the bad stuff he wouldn't have taken it."

"Maybe they switch the contents of those 55-gallon drums around. Maybe . . . a whole of number of things. What we have to do is get inside and take a look around."

Jennifer raised an eyebrow. Up until now it had been "her" story. Now there was this "we".

"If we can find out what poisonous chemicals are lying around at Metalcote, then all we have to do is prove they took one of them." Hecklepeck let out a rush of air. That was the difficult part. "Maybe we could get the police to do an autopsy on one of the boys. It would show what substance killed him, and we could match that up with what we find at Metalcote. But the police won't do a damn thing if we don't present them with some evidence first."

"So, how do we get into Metalcote?"

They thought it over for a moment or two. Jennifer reached into her purse and pulled out her keys with the steamboat key chain attached. She held it up to Hecklepeck. "Didn't you say Tom Honigger has some connection with the company? Maybe he'd let me come in and shoot some tape."

"He owns a company called Korporate Keepsakes. I don't know what his relationship to Metalcote is. Anyway he's the kind of guy who regards the press as an annoying insect species. All we have to do is tell him we're interested in relating his company to glue-sniffing in the community and he'll have the number of security guards at the gate doubled, tripled to keep us out. No, if we're going to get inside Metalcote, we have to do it another way."

The waiter had been waiting patiently at Hecklepeck's elbow for an order. Suddenly aware of him, Hecklepeck waved a hand to indicate another round. He leaned back in his chair and thought out loud. "We could do what those kids do and go over the fence at night, but of course that's illegal and we wouldn't want to risk being caught."

There was the "we" again, Jennifer thought, like she and Hecklepeck were working on the story together. Yesterday it had been *her* story. Today there was this *we*. She had welcomed his help a few weeks back, but now she wasn't so sure about it.

"Hey, we could take them by sea." Hecklepeck's face lit up at the prospect.

"What?"

"Board them from the river. Of course that would be trespassing too, but there probably wouldn't be any security guards on the river side so we'd be less likely to get caught."

"You're crazy."

Hecklepeck sighed. "Maybe you're right. How to get into Metalcote . . . how to get in . . ." He stared down the neck of his new bottle of beer. "Oh! I know! Come on!"

He propelled Jennifer out of the restaurant without even giving her time to put on her coat. The waiter stared after them, wondering if they were going to come back to finish their drinks of if he should just add the cost to Hecklepeck's account and forget about a tip.

Jennifer was still carrying her coat when they arrived back at the station. She followed Hecklepeck across the newsroom to his office. There he immediately began to sift through the pile of trash on his desk, opening each balled-up wad and shaking it out, dropping each scrutinized piece onto the floor.

Attracted by the activity Richard Markowitz stuck his head in. "What's he on? Some kind of rampage?"

Jennifer smiled. "Just rearranging the furniture."

"Yoo hoo, Heck. Cleaning out the bat cave?" Hecklepeck did not reply. Since he was not to be diverted, Richard lapsed into silence.

When he was ankle deep in the trash, Hecklepeck suddenly dove and came up with a business card. "That's it!" He held the card to his chest and addressed Jennifer. "I got this at, of all places, a

Rotary Club meeting back . . . last month. Can you believe it? This guy . . . this guy did not have the common courtesy to listen to my speech . . ."

"Ooooooo," Richard mocked.

"He got up and asked a question that I had already covered in my talk, but he didn't know, since he obviously hadn't heard. Then . . . then this little guy has the unmitigated gall to come up afterward and ask me to do a story on his company. I promptly filed his card under 'never happen'." Hecklepeck gestured at his desk as he handed the business card to Jennifer.

She looked down and read "Frank Sempepos, Plant Manager, Metalcote Inc.—Electroplating." "Woooo, Metalcote."

"As I recall," Hecklepeck continued proudly, "he wanted me to do a story on what good environmental beavers they are at Metalcote. They got a jump on the presidential ban by starting to phase out their chlorofluorocarbons early. Call me a cynic, but I have a hard time believing Metalcote really cares about the ozone layer. Still, a story would give us a good excuse to ask about whatever chemicals they have there."

"Far out." Jennifer locked eyes with Hecklepeck, and understanding passed between them.

"Yeah," muttered Richard, "sounds like the story of a lifetime. Real lead potential." But it killed him that he didn't know what was really going on.

ART AND JENNIFER pulled up to Metalcote's front gate and stopped. In front of them the chain-link fence rose twelve feet above the ground. From a guard tower a security officer gestured to them to stop and wait while he picked up his telephone.

"Do you suppose they do something connected with national security here?" Art asked with great innocence.

"What? Like what?"

"I don't know. Put metal coatings on neutron bombs? Electroplate missiles? It's just that they have enough security here to protect an army base."

"They sure do." Jennifer regarded the fence and the guard post with some trepidation. Both gates, a small one for pedestrians and a much wider one for vehicular traffic, were shut tight. How did a ten-year-old boy get past all this? Then how did he go about stealing chemicals out of barrels that were not in all probability lying around in the open? "Why do they have so much security?"

"Companies are always like this. They're paranoid about industrial sabotage of all their trade secrets or they're in violation of some standard or other. These guys could be worried about liability because of dangerous chemicals they have lying around."

Not worried enough, thought Jennifer, but it did seem like Metalcote had done everything in its power to keep trespassers out. She wondered what else the company could do. Dogs maybe?

The guard appeared to be reading off their license plate number into his phone. Jennifer looked down at her hands to avoid staring at him. "It makes me feel scuzzy, like I'm not who I say I am."

"Like you're here under false pretences?"

"Hmm-hmm."

"Well, that's about right, isn't it?" Art grinned at her.

It *was* right. Ostensibly Jennifer was doing an environmental story. Hecklepeck had called that guy, Sempepos, and asked if feature reporter Jennifer Burgess could do a story on Metalcote's "program" to phase out its chlorofluorocarbons. Surprisingly, Sempepos hadn't grabbed at it. It had been his idea in the first place; he had waved his business card in Hecklepeck's reluctant face, but when it came right down to it, Hecklepeck had to argue forcefully about the value of "good news" stories for local businesses while Sempepos hemmed and hawed and consulted with his superior and laid out ground rules and finally gave a weak assent.

Beyond the fence Jennifer could see little: a squat concrete building, a stretch of railroad track, and a boxcar. Somewhere over there, she thought, are the barrels that Jimmie and his friends tapped. Somehow she had to get over there and take a look at them.

"Finally," said Art, as a guard emerged from the door-sized gate in the fence.

He came over to the driver's window and asked to see their identification, noting their license numbers on a form attached to his clipboard. "When the main gate opens, drive through and wait on the other side. We'll direct you to a parking place."

"And don't sneeze unless we tell you," Art muttered, as he followed directions and drove through the electronically opened gate. On the other side he waited and was conducted to a parking space about thirty feet away in front of the squat concrete building. "Thank heavens they were there to point this out. We would never have found it on our own."

"Shhh." The little man approaching Jennifer's open window was bald on top. Only a few strands made the complete journey from one side of his head to the other. He wore a brown suit, made out of some shiny synthetic material.

"Miz Burgess? I'm Frank Sempepos. Welcome. Welcome." He talked very fast, like a snake oil salesman on whom the posse was descending. "Listen, the way we're going to operate here is you get all your equipment together, bring it in, and set it up in the conference room. When you're done, our board chairman will come in and do a sound bite, give you an overview, let you know what we're all about here. Then I will take you on a tour of the premises."

Fifteen minutes after Art had finished setting up his equipment they were still waiting. It was more of a conference cell than a room. The windows were high, and the walls, cinder-block. They were hung with some glass cases containing various gold-plated objects, mostly electronic components, obviously products of Metalcote. There was a glass jar full of pens and pencils in the middle of the plastic-laminated conference table.

Jennifer stared at it and fidgeted. She wanted to get the interview over with since she was more interested in the unofficial questions that had brought her to Metalcote than in drumming up false ones for official purposes.

Sempepos pulled open the metal conference room door and ushered in Tom Honigger, thus answering all Jennifer's questions about his relationship to Metalcote. Honigger was the chairman of the board.

A few steps into the room he stopped and held out his hand, making Jennifer walk over to take it. His tan seemed to have deepened since she had last seen him, or maybe it was seeing him in daylight. "How do you do?" he asked and turned to shake hands with Art without waiting for an answer.

Was it possible Honigger didn't remember her from the boat trip? Yes, Jennifer admitted to herself. He was so stuck on his own importance that he would only register people who fed it. She could not have been more insignificant. But for some reason that didn't bother her. She had a feeling Honigger's attentions would be more degrading than his slights.

"You people certainly don't travel light." Honigger seemed to be more comfortable with Art, as the photographer ushered him to the designated seat and clipped on a microphone.

"Well, it takes a lot of equipment to take a good picture. You want to look good, don't you?" It was Art's standard line for making interview subjects comfortable.

Jennifer sat in the chair, catty-corner to Honigger. Did he do all the interviews at Metalcote? It seemed like he would have better ways to spend his time. Maybe he liked to see himself on TV. Jennifer took her wallet and keys out of her purse in order to get to the pen at the bottom.

"Where did you get that?" Honigger indicated the steamboat key chain attached to her keys. When she told him, he raised an eyebrow in surprise. "Oh. Well, that's another story for you. We're going to be making an announcement about that next week. Public

Advancement will be donating a considerable amount of money to combat drug abuse in this community. We'll have final figures next week.

"That key chain, you know, is one of our products." Jennifer nodded. "Metalcote is a subsidiary to our parent company, Korporate Keepsakes. We acquired it because so many of the corporate mementos we were making were metal plated. Strictly speaking, you should be doing a story on Korporate Keepsakes, but I can appreciate that an office building down town does not make for good visuals. Also, Metalcote is interesting in its own right. We plate a lot of electronics components here—the wave of the future."

"Rolling," announced Art.

Jennifer spoke into her microphone. "Your company, Metalcote, began phasing out its use of harmful chlorofluorocarbons several months ago. Can you explain how that came about?"

"Yes, certainly, uh, ah Jennifer." Jennifer suppressed a smile. She had never understood why corporate executives felt they had to include the reporter's name in their interviews. Was it meant to be friendly or intimidating? The practice was always stilted and in Honigger's case condescending because he couldn't remember who she was. "It has been obvious for some time that the future of CFCs is not too bright. So this spring we began to look around for an alternative."

"What exactly does—or did—Metalcote use fluorocarbons for?"

"Uh, Jennifer, degreasing. Before we electroplate something it has to be thoroughly degreased, cleaned. Otherwise all sorts of stuff would show up in the gold coating we're applying. Fortunately there are a lot of agents that can do this sort of thing, and we've been able to promptly phase out our use of CFCs. We believe in taking a strong proenvironmental stance here at Metalcote. We are a local company and have the long-term future of this community at heart. The risk to the ozone layer is, we believe, substantial and real . . ."

Tom Honigger had memorized it. The speech was too pat to be coming off the top of his head, and his delivery, too uniform. Jennifer waited politely for him to wrap it up before asking, "What did you replace the CFC's with?"

"Replace? With . . . Oh, I don't know. You'll have to ask, uh, Frank. Something . . . benign. We care about the environment at

Metalcote. That's because we're here for the long haul, productive members of the St. Louis community. Committed . . ."

Honigger barely sat still for the set-up shots that Art took afterward. As soon as the camera was lowered, he pulled off his mike and got to his feet, giving the impression that he was an important man with pressing business. "Well, is that everything?"

Jennifer assured him it was and thanked his back since he had already turned around to leave. Sempepos held the door for him and followed him out.

Art and Jennifer were subjected to another long wait before the plant manager finally returned. By that time Art had packed up most of his equipment and was prepared to go portable with the camera on his shoulder.

Sempepos was wearing a belted leather coat and carrying some yellow hard hats. These he passed out, putting the last one on his own head. Because he was a slight man, only as tall as Jennifer's shoulder, his hard hat looked a little like a yellow mushroom cap. His eyes underneath had a harassed, nervous look. "Well, hey. That sounded like a good sound bite to me; lots of good stuff in there. What we're going to do now is take a brief tour of our operation here so you can get some visuals. I must ask you to limit your shooting to what I indicate is permissible."

Sempepos led them outside, around the front of the office building toward another, larger building. There in the middle of a stretch of blacktop were the barrels. Fifty-five gallon drums, five rows deep. Some of them were yellow; most of them were white.

Jennifer felt excitement in the pit of her stomach. Could those be Jimmie's white barrels, where he had gotten tulio?

Sempepos stopped and gestured toward the barrels. "There's your first visual. Because this is a phaseout we still have some CFCs here in stock. They're represented by the yellow barrels. The white barrels contain the replacement chemical, toluene." These *were* Jimmie's barrels! "We're slowly using up the chlorofluorocarbons in those yellow drums and, as we do, we're bringing in more of the white drums. This phaseout process has been going on since late May and will be completed in the near future."

Chlorofluorocarbons in the yellow barrels. Could they have been what killed Jimmie and his friends? Jennifer copied the label off one of the barrels before asking, "Are the chlorofluorocarbons dangerous? Could they hurt or, say, poison, somebody?"

Sempepos had been watching Art take pictures of the barrels as if he didn't want to miss a move the cameraman made. Now he did a slow turn on Jennifer, looking as if he didn't like or understand the question. "No. Not dangerous. We wouldn't keep them out here in these drums if they were dangerous."

His answer disappointed Jennifer, who was so wrapped up in her problem that she failed to notice how thin Sempepos's pleasant demeanor was. She pondered a little longer. "Do you ever get these barrels mixed up?" In any case Jimmie had known to avoid the yellow barrels so he wouldn't have mistakenly tapped one for tulio. But what if one of the white barrels had something else in it, something other than toluene, something lethal?

Sempepos once again withdrew his gaze from Art. Jennifer noticed some old acne scars on his skin. "Mixed-up. Why no. How could we? They come to us like this directly from the distributor by barge, and we haven't had any problem with them. Is this part of your story?"

Jennifer assured him no, that she was just curious. She looked off in the direction of the security fence. If a person could just get over the fence and past fifty yards of blacktop, the office building and the boxcar would protect him from the guard tower. But he would still be out in the open—unless he ducked down behind the barrels. A small boy like Jimmie, who was small for his age, could do that. "Wouldn't Metalcote be liable if someone did get hurt because of the chemicals in these barrels?"

Sempepos let out an audible sigh. Why wouldn't the reporter let it go? "These here are not that dangerous. If they were, we wouldn't leave them out in the middle of the yard like this. Our people handle this stuff all the time and they don't suffer. Which is not to say we don't have some really lethal stuff here. We do. But let me tell you we take very good care of it. Very good." There was a clear warning in Sempepos's voice now, and Jennifer heard it. Against what? Discussing chemicals in a story about chemicals?

"Oh, let's go see that . . . I mean the rest of the electroplating."

Having finished shooting, Art was waiting with his camera balanced on a barrel. He picked it up and followed the others toward the plant.

"Do you know how electroplating works?" Sempepos was asking. "The same way as a battery basically. The object to be electroplated is put into a bath . . ." Still talking, he pulled open a metal door and conducted them up a flight of steps to another metal door. This led to a long, narrow observation deck that overlooked a lot of industrial equipment below.

Art made an irritated sound and Jennifer guessed it was because he was going to have trouble shooting down through glass windows. "Can't we go down there and tape it?" she asked brightly.

"Not allowed. For liability reasons." Sempepos tucked his chin and looked up at Jennifer, implying that if she wanted to talk about liability, this was the time. "You mentioned poisonous chemicals. The acids used in the electrolytic baths are highly toxic. Any contact, any contact at all with that stuff would kill you."

"Really?"

"You betcha. That's why the system is entirely closed and we bring visitors in behind glass. Double protection. Now, if you look—"

"What is it exactly? The stuff in the baths."

"The metal being electroplated, of course, and hydrogen cyanide, also known as hydrocyanic acid." At the mention of cyanide Jennifer felt her heart skip a beat. "We mix it right in the system itself so that nobody had to get anywhere near the acid. Now look down to your right . . ."

Sempepos explained at length and in detail about electroplating, and Jennifer nodded along with him to show she was taking it all in. But she wasn't. She was wondering if there was any way somebody could get hold of a container full of hydrogen cyanide at Metalcote. She knew enough to know that an acid would eat through a plastic bag but maybe it could be carried off in a jar or something. The question was how to get hold of it.

"What happens to the bath solution, those acids, after you're finished with them?" Jennifer asked as they headed back outside the same way they had come in.

It was too much. "Miz Burgess, I brought you here on the understanding that you were going to do a story about our phaseout of CFCs. What is the relevance here?" She must have pushed too hard with all her inquiries about chemicals. Or was it that question in particular that made Sempepos so sensitive? "Metalcote is the kind of public-spirited company this community needs. We care about the environment. I thought you'd see that. But you're asking about disposition of hazardous waste. Is that really relevant?"

Hazardous waste? Was she asking about that? She hadn't thought so, but it was clearly time to back off. "Curious. I was just curious."

"We dispose of it in accordance with EPA guidelines." The look in Sempepos's eyes had distilled into something like salt crystals.

"Yes. Of course." She hadn't meant to imply that they didn't.

They were walking toward the office building, and it dawned on Jennifer that the tour was over. Had she seen everything? No. "May we shoot your dock while we're here?" Sempepos frowned, no longer, it seemed, willing to give Jennifer the benefit of the doubt. She searched her mind frantically for a reason to visit the dock and miraculously came up with one. "You said the barrels of that chemical that you're replacing the chlorofluorocarbons with are delivered by barge. The barrels of toluene. I thought it would make a good opening shot. Pretty. Environmental."

A hit! Sempepos nodded. "That sounds nice, very nice. But it wasn't on our agenda this morning. Let me just stop in here at the office and check it through with my superiors."

Sempepos reemerged from the office building after making Jennifer and Art wait for twenty minutes and took them down to the dock.

It was an ugly industrial area. Rusting gas pumps stood like tired sentinels along a concrete pier that stretched out into the water. Flanking the pier and an area of blacktop was an office building made out of corrugated metal. It didn't look like property that belonged to an environmentally conscious company. But it was a quiet morning at the Metalcote dock, and nothing was happening to actively harm the environment.

Jennifer took up a position in front of the office building where she would be out of the way. Intertwining a finger with one of the curls at the end of her ponytail she looked beyond the concrete jetty to the river. Hard to believe it was the same black, black water she had watched Hecklepeck navigate only days before. In the late morning sunlight Ms. Mississippi was buckskin brown. Her skirts, lapping against the dusty shoreline, were trimmed with the shiny blue and purple of oil.

Out on her broad back a wide fleet of barges passed, drab and toilsome. But Jennifer had been bitten by the romance of the river, and she knew that when the barges passed downriver, the vista on the opposite shoreline would come into view.

She watched until they did and saw more industry on the Illinois side. But even that didn't discourage Jennifer. She wondered if her soaring feelings had anything to do with the man who introduced her to the river, William Hecklepeck. It was possible. He had been so courteous and gentle with her that night. So respectful of her feelings. Jennifer set some store by respect since she didn't always get it from the men she dated.

Hecklepeck had also backed off when she told him that this was her story and she wanted to cover it. Another form of respect, and one that was particularly sweet because Jennifer had never experienced it before. Maybe later, when the story was done and had aired, they could pursue . . . well, whatever.

"Do you know," Jennifer said to Sempepos in her excess of good feeling as they walked back toward the main building, "that the last time I saw your dock was less than a week ago from the water? When I was on that steamboat cruise."

"Yes, well, that's quite possible. You probably passed right by here."

"We did. I was referring to the Army Corps of Engineers chart so I picked yours right out. Besides, it was blinking."

"There's a string of industrial docks along here, and at night they have lights just like ours, so you may have passed us but I doubt you saw us. The river at night—"

"I was ticking off lights against companies so I'm pretty sure I identified yours. Besides, the blinking really stood out."

"That sounds like a short, a malfunctioning light, and it couldn't have been ours." Jennifer winced at the tone of the man's voice. There was something defensive, almost angry about it. Yet she had just been making conversation, not getting at something in particular, the way she had been with the chemicals. What could he be reacting to now? "We haven't had any problems with our light recently, I assure you. In my position I would know." Sempepos looked directly at Jennifer as he said this, and the glint in his eyes struck her as dishonest.

13

O KAY," SAID RICHARD, flopping into the extra chair in Heck-lepeck's little office-cave, "you tell me. Why did we air that piece?"

"Which one?" Hecklepeck knew exactly which one.

"The one about that company on the river that is phasing out its chlorofluorocarbs. That story is a month and a half old. We didn't do anything when it happened. I don't see why we're doing it now."

"Well," Hecklepeck reached for a reason, "the ozone layer is being depleted as much now as it was then. And that's a serious, serious problem."

"Yeah? Then why didn't we do it right? Why didn't we find out how many St. Louis companies use chlorofluoroflpppbbbs and what kind of plans they have for phasing them out? Because I will bet you anything that they aren't doing a fucking thing. They can't. They need all their little chloroflops for their air-conditioning systems and their refrigeration, and here's a sticky little point that didn't surface in our story: THERE IS NOTHING TO REPLACE THEM WITH. So, I fail to see why we are doing a story on some tiny company that was using chlorofluoroflops for metal polish and has now switched to something else. It's misleading. It misrepresents the problem and it leads to the nasty, suspicious question: if they are so environmentally conscious at Metalcote, why didn't they phase them out a long time ago?"

"Well, sometimes consciousness has to be raised a baby step at a time. At least we did something."

Richard frowned at him. It wasn't like Hecklepeck to take a bad story so calmly. "You see what I mean about Jennifer. She can't report her way out of a paper bag. She ought to be out in Podunk,

Idaho, earning her stripes, not here in a major market, airing shit like that."

"I don't think it was shit," said Hecklepeck, needling Richard. "The story had merit. Information. Interest."

"Shit! Shit, shit, shit. And if you think that's bad, just wait until she does that story on glue-sniffing. Three boys dead from deliberate inhalation of industrial solvent. Now *that's* a story. But she can't handle it. No way, no how."

"She'll do fine." Having gotten a good rise out of Richard, Hecklepeck was ready to quit the game. Besides, the mention of the glue-sniffing story made him wonder what Jennifer had really found out at Metalcote. He had not had a chance to talk with her before she left for the day. For the first time in a long time Hecklepeck felt the thrill of the chase rise up in him.

Richard was looking at Hecklepeck with suspicion. "What was all that about in your office last week? When you were tearing through the trash in here? Did you put her on to that story? All those river shots. Does it have something to do with steamboats? Is that why you're being so laid-back about it?" Lost in his own thoughts, Hecklepeck merely shrugged.

Richard stood up. "I can't believe this. You used to have . . . integrity. You used to care about reporting the news. You should be helping Jennifer; instead you're using her to promote your own petty little schemes. Oh, God, is this what happens to people when they go through male menopause?" Richard cocked an eye in Hecklepeck's direction to see if he was getting a response. No.

From the doorway he fired his best, last shot. "I can tell you one thing. I'm not putting that story on the ten o'clock. It's not going on my show."

In his office the next morning KYYY news director Jim Turnbull had a similar conversation with Jennifer. That is, it arose out of concern about the direction of her glue-sniffing story. Where it ended was somewhere else.

"How's it going?" Turnbull looked out over the newsroom as he asked the question in the most casual of voices.

"Fine." Jennifer could be forgiven for interpreting this in its general sense. A year ago Turnbull had hired her. Then he had neglected her. Only once had he come out of his office to offer guidance. That was when she wore her hair down for the morning news cut-ins instead of in its usual ponytail. He suggested she tie it up again. What Turnbull appreciated in hairstyle was consistency, nothing to cause comment or distract from the news.

"What I'm looking for is a status report on this glue-sniffing series you're doing. I'd like to schedule it for the second week in November as one of our ratings grabbers. That gives you"—Turnbull consulted his calendar—"the rest of this week and two more weeks to get it together. Will you be ready?"

"I guess so." Jennifer sounded less than sure.

Turnbull looked at her keenly for a split second, then out and away again into the newsroom, where his employees were beginning to filter in for work. Turnbull, who never had a problem waking up in the morning, thought they all looked dopey and unpleasant. He hoped the vending machine with coffee in it was working. "Tell me what you have."

Without hesitation Jennifer did, glad to have somebody besides Hecklepeck to confide in. She felt rather than knew Turnbull was listening, since he continued to scrutinize the newsroom. Perhaps he was able to function on two levels at once, take mental notes about what was going on out there and listen to her in here at the same time.

Jennifer wouldn't have put it past him. She admired the man even though all she had to go on was what she had observed, and that was mostly him watching them. He did it a lot. It was the way he did it. Totally impassively, true. Without comment but also without censure, which to Jennifer implied a sort of benevolent paternalism. As tired as she always was in the newsroom she took some comfort there.

". . . and so Heck and I are still trying to see if there's anything to tie those three deaths together." Jennifer folded her hands in her lap and waited for Turnbull to comment.

He did not. Instead he let the silence grow until she wondered if he had heard her after all. Out in the newsroom one of the reporters tossed an empty pint-size styrofoam coffee cup into a trash can and launched into a dramatic argument with the assignment editor, presumably about his story assignment. The editor drew back, and his ears seemed to flatten against his head like those of a threatened cat. Sometimes he stood his ground, sometimes he didn't. It was the usual newsroom negotiation.

Turnbull reached for his calendar. "I can put it off for another week until the third week in November. That's the last full week of ratings. Best I can do."

Jennifer hadn't asked him to do that much. She had merely presented the facts, hoping he would tell her exactly how to proceed. Not that Hecklepeck wasn't already giving plenty of direction. It's just that Turnbull was the boss. He would know what was right because he was the final arbiter.

"I can't let you out of the morning news," Turnbull added. "I've got no other body to fill the slot. But I can relieve you of some of that feature reporting you've been doing." He let his mind wander back to the report he had seen the night before on the six o'clock news. Something about some local company and PCBs. No, another chemical. Jennifer's features were usually a little more . . . complete than that. Turnbull hoped the glue-sniffing series was not too much for her. "Is Heck giving you some guidance?"

"Yes, he is."

Of course, what did that mean? The anchorman had seemingly retired from reporting. The old pique rising, Turnbull reminded himself that it had been a long time since he'd seen Hecklepeck in action. "Well, weigh his advice carefully. Follow only what seems right to you. Remember, in the final analysis this is your story and you are responsible for it."

It was a guideline. Except for the thing about not changing her hair, Turnbull's first tenet. Jennifer nodded solemnly and took it very much to heart.

Later that afternoon Turnbull poked his head into Hecklepeck's office. "This . . . this steamboat trip. Down to New Orleans. Are you still planning on it?" There was trash all over the floor. "You ought to clean this place up."

Hecklepeck did not lower his long legs from where they were resting amid the papers on his desk. "Yes."

"When?" Turnbull turned so that he could see out into the newsroom. A reporter was strutting in front of the producer's desks like a winning prizefighter. Turnbull hoped it was because he had brought back a good story.

"It keeps getting postponed. Gus has a shipment of cargo he's waiting for, souvenir tins. Now we're looking at a weekend departure, the fourteenth of November. But it depends on the weather. If the weather doesn't cooperate, we'll have to postpone again."

Turnbull handed Hecklepeck a press release. "Since you've put yourself on the steamboat beat, I want you to cover this." It was the Public Advancement press conference to announce the money it was going to donate to combat drug abuse.

Hecklepeck skimmed the release and looked speculatively at Turnbull. The news director seemed lost in the newsroom scene. Impossible to tell from his shoulder if he were hinting that it was inappropriate for a newsman to make steamboat trips with major news sources. But Hecklepeck didn't want to test this. "Okay," he said, cheerfully bland.

Jennifer had written all the elements of her glue-sniffing series on various three-by-five notecards and was trying to organize them. It was very difficult to know what she had, since she was continually finding out more that she didn't know. Maybe it was her little talk with Turnbull. Maybe she was more tired than usual, but in all candor she had to blame Hecklepeck for this. His directions seemed to take her down new avenues, broad avenues, which tended to end up at four-way stop intersections. The truth was that every time he helped she got more lost.

So where did she go now? With a deadline to consider, she wanted to have a plan. She moved her three-by-five cards around strategically until she had a pile thick enough to be the first segment of her series, an introductory piece that would explain what glue-sniffing was and why it was such a big problem.

Of course right there she ran into trouble because all of that depended on the explanations of Ben Howell, drug counselor and expert. The last time she had seen Howell he was waving his wallet around in front of a male prostitute in Tower Grove Park. She was either going to have to find another expert or confront Howell. If he could exonerate himself, fine. Otherwise she would have to make his guilt part of the story.

Jennifer noted the alternatives on a piece of scratch paper and attached it to the pile of index cards with a rubber band. One of the remaining three-by-five cards attracted her notice and she picked it up. In her own neat handwriting she read, "I don't know. Maybe work in the brewery. But them jobs is hard to get." Most of his vernacular had not been transcribed, but the words were Jimmie's, part of his interview in response to her question, What did he want to be when he grew up?

Poor Jimmie! The only thing more pathetic than his aspiration was how out of reach it was. Jimmie had no more chance of becoming a brewery worker than a foreigner did of running for president. Less, if his father was anything to go by.

Jennifer's heart ached all over again for Jimmie. A profile of him should be the second part of her series. She picked up the three-by-five cards pertaining to Jimmie and arranged them in order.

But here she was at a dead stop again. She could assume that Jimmie died from too much toluene or from suffocation and just write the story. But to do so was to ignore the possibility that he had gotten something else, maybe that hydrogen cyanide, from Metalcote. However limited her knowledge of chemistry, Jennifer knew that cyanide was a killer. When Sempepos said cyanide, bells had started ringing.

Besides, if there was any chance at all that Metalcote was in any way culpable, the company should be hung out to dry in front of the whole world. Jennifer was surprised at her own vehemence about this. She meant it. Not because her reportorial instinct had been awakened at last (Jennifer was determined not to have a reportorial instinct.), but because of Jimmie. Avenging his death did seem to be the least she could do.

Of course, assuming that Jimmie had somehow inhaled hydrogen cyanide, she had to come up with proof. How in the world was she supposed to do that? She could always ask Heck . . . But there she was, back where she started.

"So, Jen-Jen, how did it go at Metalcote?" And here he was, pulling around a chair from an unoccupied desk nearby and wheeling it right in next to her. If Jennifer had been less preoccupied with her own thoughts, she might have noticed the lack of preamble. There was no Hello, how are you, no How's it going, only the similar but entirely different-in-meaning "How did it go?"

"Fine." For a moment or two Jennifer kept up the pretense with herself that she would tell him nothing.

"Well, give me a report."

She did, eagerly pouring out descriptions of the toluene barrels and the enclosed electroplating system and, most of all, the hydrogen cyanide in that system. When she was done, she found Hecklepeck grinning sardonically at her. "So what you're telling me is that you think Jimmie and his friends somehow got hold of some of this hydrogen cyanide and sniffed that instead of toluene." Jennifer nodded. "How are you proposing that these boys transported this deadly acid?"

"It would eat through a plastic bag, wouldn't it?" Hecklepeck nodded vigorously. "A jar? A glass jar?"

"I love it. So what we've got here is some young boys tapping into a big tank of hydrogen cyanide, filling mayonnaise . . . peanut butter jars? with this chemical and taking them back over a twelve-foot fence and up several city blocks to Benton Park, where they do what? Take the lid off the jar, or maybe it's topless? Either way they sink their noses into it, inhale, and die. Think again, Sherlock."

Jennifer was aggrieved. "What's wrong with that? Hydrogen cyanide would kill them, wouldn't it?"

"Oh, yes, it would kill them all right. The problem with hydrogen cyanide is not that it's not toxic enough, it's that it's too toxic. That guy, Sempepos, meant what he said when he told you that they mix it in an enclosed system and keep it there. Otherwise it would endanger the very people who work at Metalcote."

"Yes, but"—Jennifer had gotten around the problem of the enclosed system—"he wouldn't answer when I asked him about the disposal of the hydrogen cyanide after they're through with it. Maybe they pump it outside into a tank. He seemed . . . evasive about that."

"There are federal regulations they have to follow for safe disposal of hazardous chemical waste. I guarantee you that at no time is that stuff accessible from the outside. Metalcote workers would have been dropping like flies. That stuff is so hazardous that you couldn't survive one whiff of it, much less the act of filling a jar with it."

Jennifer said nothing. This slapping-around of her theory made her angry.

Hecklepeck was too in love with his rebuttal to notice. "Besides, if those boys had died from cyanide-anything the police would have stumbled onto it. Haven't you read your Agatha Christie? Victims of cyanide poisoning give off the smell of almonds. Of course, I've never been able to figure out just what the smell of almonds is . . .

"Much more interesting to me is those chlorofluorocarbons. They're sitting out there in barrels so they're quite accessible. Maybe they're what we're looking for."

"But they're not poisonous. Sempepos said so," Jennifer was still piqued. "They wouldn't be sitting out there in barrels if there was a problem with them."

"Oh. That makes sense."

"And they're in the yellow barrels. Jimmie knew not to take the chemical in the yellow barrels. He said so." Jennifer couldn't resist driving another nail in the coffin of Hecklepeck's hypothesis.

"Well, it brings us to a dead end. We have one chemical, hydrogen cyanide, that's too toxic and another, a chlorofluorocarbon, that isn't toxic enough. We need something with the cyanide's deadliness and the fluorocarbons' handleability. Any ideas?"

Half way across the room Richard stood up behind his desk. Phone receiver in hand he yelled into Hecklepeck's office, "There's a call for you on line one, Heck." Seeing that Hecklepeck was not in his own office but sitting with Jennifer at her desk, he added in the same loud tone, "Helping Jennifer with another story? What's she doing now to further your self-interest? A survey of local Porsche dealerships?" Richard sat down again without pausing for a reaction.

14

GLARING AT RICHARD, Hecklepeck stabbed at the line button on Jennifer's phone. "William Hecklepeck."

"How did you know?" It was the voice of St. Louis homicide lieutenant, Mike Berger, and it was full of suspicion.

"Know what?" Hecklepeck's tone of voice was protesting his innocence before he knew what he was accused of.

Jennifer went back to her index cards, stacking them aggressively to demonstrate her still wounded pride.

"That there was something wierd about those alleged gluse-sniffing deaths."

"Something wierd?" Hecklepeck deliberately did not address the issue of his having known.

"I ahrdered an autopsy on the latest one, on that boy that died . . . what? A week ago. A little over a week ago."

"Yes?" Hecklepeck barely let out his breath. He didn't want to risk seeming impatient. Even more he didn't want the sound of his own breath to make him miss something.

"There was toluene in the boy's system all right. But it wasn't what killed him." At this Hecklepeck sent a meaningful look in Jennifer's direction, a look she had no idea how to interpret since she wasn't privy to the other end of the phone conversation. But she stopped playing with the index cards and listened.

"What was it then?"

"Nothing."

"What?"

"Nothing there. Now I know what yahr thinking. Yahr thinking a ten-year-old boy doesn't just die. There has to be something. A

114

blow to the back of the head. A congenital heart defect. Something. But this one did just die. His heart stopped. No cause. Just effect. So, how did you know? What have you been up to?"

"Wow. There was nothing there? No trace of ingested chemical?"

"I'm telling ya. Nothing." Berger seemed to take some pleasure in repeating the word for Hecklepeck's benefit.

"What about in the vicinity of the body? Did you find anything?"

"Nanh. There was a plastic bag containing a rag with traces of toluene a couple hundred yards away. And there was a jar next to the body."

"A jar? Anything in there?"

"Nothing. Whatever was in there, if there ever was anything in there, evapahrated. Gone to the high heavens. What we do know is that the boy, Jimmie Smith, handled the jar. His fingerprints are on it."

"Interesting. Any other prints?"

"Just the victim's." Berger choked a little over the word "victim".

Knowing the lieutenant's preternatural sympathy for the world's casualties, Hecklepeck ignored the sound. "But there was nothing in it? No trace of anything? No chemical?"

"Nothing but air."

"What kind of jar was it?"

"I don't know. A big one . . . a mason jar . . . like pickles come in or mayonnaise. Now you tell me something. What were you doing asking questions about these solvent abusers as long ago as last month? What have you got?"

Hecklepeck countered with another question. "Did you test either of the other two who died?"

"Can't do it. They've both been cremated. Of cahrse there are still tests that could be run on the ashes. But what am I testing fahr? Nothing? And what's the rationale? I've got a boy who died of nothing and I want to see if a couple others did too? On what grounds? This isn't a homicide, because the boy can't have been murdered with nothing. So you tell me why yahr so interested. What's going on here?"

Nothing, Hecklepeck started to say, but then he decided the use of the word might be ill-advised. "I honestly don't know," he said instead. "I called you on a hunch. Because at that time there had been two deaths in a row and that seemed a little odd."

"Fahrgive me if I don't kee-whhite believe you." Mike Berger had known Hecklepeck a long time, and he knew that when the anchorman was on the scent of something he was unlikely to lift his nose in order to bring in the police. When Hecklepeck was protesting his innocence was the time to be most suspicious.

Hecklepeck wouldn't have hesitated to lie if it served his purpose, but this time he was completely honest. "No, I don't have anything."

"Yahr grandmother," growled Berger. "Just let me know befahr all hell breaks loose. Please."

Hecklepeck was still protesting his innocence when the lieutenant hung up. He dropped his own receiver and turned to Jennifer. "Well, you were right about one thing. There was a jar."

"Was it mayonnaise or peanut butter?" Jennifer echoed Hecklepeck's words and tone when she had first brought up the possibility of a jar.

He threw her a look that said, 'ha ha.' "But it didn't have hydrogen cyanide in it."

"It didn't? What then?"

"Nothing. There was nothing in it."

"Well, that *is* a dangerous chemical."

"The police did an autopsy on your friend Jimmie. It revealed that he died of nothing." Hecklepeck related the rest of what Berger had said.

"People can't die of nothing," Jennifer observed when he was finished. "There had to be a cause."

"Yes. I would have said so. It stands to reason. Particularly since there are three deaths and we assume they all died of the same thing. That eliminates wierd congenital problems because they couldn't all three have had them. So there had to have been something else, something that just isn't showing up on the autopsy."

"Like what?"

Hecklepeck merely shrugged in response.

Their rancor forgotten, they were silent for a moment, keeping company in the difficulties presented by this new information.

"One thing is certain," said Hecklepeck finally. "There is a story here. Whatever killed those boys . . . however they died . . . is a major, major story."

"Yes. Now we know for sure it wasn't toluene. They didn't die from glue-sniffing."

116

Hecklepeck leaned back in his chair and hoisted his legs onto Jennifer's desktop into the position in which he mulled best. "It seems to me we have one new piece of evidence here. The jar. Of course that's assuming that the jar had something to do with all this and wasn't just a piece of litter that happened to be near the scene."

"Jimmie was pretty near—maybe twenty feet—from a park trash can when he died." Jennifer moved some of her index cards around absently. "The jar could have come from that."

"But his fingerprints were on it. They would seem to connect him."

"There wasn't any jar where the second one . . . Hoyt Jenkins . . . was found." One observation followed another as if they were sharing one thought process. But neither was aware of the intimacy that implied.

"No jar? How do you know?"

"I was there. He was found underneath the swing set, remember? Art and I went and shot it."

Hecklepeck looked at Jennifer in admiration. This was an observant woman. She was proving herself more than worthy of his interest. "But when did you go?"

"The day, no, two days after he died. It was all dirty and dusty around there. No jar."

"It could have been removed by then. We ought to find out. We could learn a lot from the presence or absence of a jar at the scene of Hoyt's death."

Jennifer picked it up. "Because if there was one then we know that whatever killed those two boys, and probably the third boy, was in the jars."

"Right. Then we can take it one step further and assume they were probably obtaining some chemical somewhere, sniffing it, and then dying from it. Now if no jar was found at the scene of Hoyt's death then it's a little more ambiguous. Then either Jimmie's jar is not significant and, like you said, came out of the park trash can or . . . the jar at the scene of Hoyt's death was removed by somebody."

Jennifer felt a shiver skip up her spine. Something about the way Hecklepeck said those last words. Anybody could have picked up a jar and made off with it, but that wasn't what he was implying. "You're saying somebody did it on purpose. Gave those boys some poisonous chemical in a jar and then took the jar away with him."

with a PIO officer. But this girl . . . was his wife's favorite news-caster.

The sargeant went back through the records to see who had answered the calls on the nights of August 20th and September 17th. Then he called a couple of young police officers up from the locker room.

They stood in front of Jennifer, neither they nor she suggesting they sit on one of the long wooden benches that filled the station's big reception area. One was brown-haired and the other blond, but both had the same pallor that affected Jimmie and Pete, that same translucence of skin that Jennifer assumed came from lack of nutrition or, in case of these guys, poor nutrition. It threw her.

She re-collected herself and shook hands with each of them before explaining what she wanted to know, giving them the same not-quite-truthful reason she'd given the sargeant. When she had finished, the two patrolmen looked at each other and laughed. "Them glue-sniffers'll never change. They'd about rather have their faces in a tulio bag than inherit a million dollars," the brown-haired one said by way of explanation. He thought carefully about whether he'd seen a jar at the scene of Mike Cobb's death in August. "He was lying on the corner just outside the park. We knew right away it was an OD because that glue bag of his was right next to him. So I cain't say we looked around too much. If we did, and there was some old mayonnaise jar there, I don't know's I would have noticed."

The other patrolman was more helpful. By way of preliminary he stroked on his almost nonexistent moustache. "My partner and I"—Jennifer realized the formality was in her honor and was touched by it.—"arrived on the scene around eight A.M. We were on first shift. Some waitress, who was cutting across the park to git to her job, saw the body and called it in. We didn't know what we had so we were real careful not to walk into that dust under those swings where the body was. Footprints, er, what have you." The patrolman paused for a breath. His forehead was wrinkled and his face drawn up in the dual attempt to remember and present the information properly. "There wasn't no jar there. I know that. I could swear to it. We walked around on the outside of that dusty area, and that's where we found his glue bag. We figured then we had another OD just like the one Bob had." He indicated the other patrolman. "I don't remember seeing no jar there on the outside either."

Jennifer let out her breath. She had gotten the information she had come for. "You really have a good memory. That was a month and a half ago."

The patrolman shook his head. "We don't get too many dead kids. It kinda stuck in my mind."

"Yeah," his companion concurred.

But you've had three in a row, one a month for three months, Jennifer wanted to say. Didn't that raise some questions in your minds? How can you be so uncurious? However, she was silent. In raising their consciousnesses she didn't want them to begin questioning her own interest in the matter.

15

CAPTAIN JAMES MCNIFF looked darkly out of his pilothouse, not at the Mississippi, pewter in the early November gloom, but at Laclede's Landing, where businessmen and conventioneers were going into trendy restaurants for lunch.

"I've been looking out at Green-witch Village there for weeks," he grumbled. "You could say the whole of humanity has passed by my eyes, every species of landlubber from the three-piece suit to the leisure suit to the don't-own-no-suit. It is not a pretty picture."

William Hecklepeck nodded. This sounded a chord with him. Maybe not exactly the same chord that set him off on his panicky solos, but the sentiment was similar enough.

"There comes a time when a man, a man in uniform like myself, has got to quit this vale of teeming humanity and ride the hard current down to the sea. 'The sea doth wash away all human ills.' "

"What?"

"Uuu-ripedes. The time for going"—The captain glowered at Hecklepeck—"came and went awhile ago, but I have been setting here looking at Sodom and Green-witch Village. Hear that?" Hecklepeck listened and heard nothing except the creaking of the boat. "The winds of autumn. Soon to be winter. And still that Gus Bus wants to wait yet another week and a half before putting out. Reesky policy. Very reesky. An early freeze could throw us off until spring and then what?" In answer to his own question he looked despondently out at Laclede's Landing.

Hecklepeck followed his gaze and shared his gloom. He wanted to go too. He, the starving man, kept getting tastes of the river. What he craved was the whole pie.

Not that he'd been exactly beset with the hunger lately. Rather, the mystery of three boys who died of nothing preoccupied him. After Jennifer's visit to the police station he could not discount the notion that that 'nothing' had been deliberately administered in a glass jar.

Jennifer's story. He had to keep reminding himself it was Jennifer's story. Well, here it was time to return it to her and get back to the place where man and the elements met. After all, what was really important in life?

"Trained animal acts. That's what he's got me doing. Luncheon cruises for soap distributors. Tours for furreign businessmen. Errands. Steaming downriver aways to pick up souvenirs."

"What?"

"On my honn-eur. We spent yesterday morning loading those," McNiff gestured toward an object on his desk, "into the hold."

Hecklepeck picked up the object. It was a maroon-and-gold tin, a copy of the kind of thing that might have been manufactured in the early twentieth century. Gus had gotten his eras mixed up again, Hecklepeck thought. Steamboats were long gone from the waterways when store shelves began to be stocked with tins like this one.

On one side was a steamboat, obviously the *Gustavius,* its smoke curling black and gold into a maroon sky. On either end of the tin snaked the Bussard-Dusay ermine, but it was the depiction on the last side that made Hecklepeck snort with derision.

"That's what you call amour improper," commented McNiff.

Hecklepeck chuckled and nodded. Gus had put himself on the side of his tin. Himself, in muttonchop whiskers with his gold pince-nez and a string tie, like some early twentieth-century proprietor of a dry goods business.

The tin felt heavy, and Hecklepeck opened it to find it was full of coffee. "I thought he was going to pick these up in New Orleans. This was supposed to be French Market coffee." McNiff shrugged. "My understanding was that that was why he was delaying the trip to New Orleans, because these tins weren't ready to be picked up down there."

McNiff dropped his eyelids to half-mast, and in the short silence Hecklepeck saw or thought he saw the former drug enforcement agent lurking behind them. "You know what I tell him. I tell him I got to keep the crew in shape and that we have to take practice runs. Day trips. Night cruises. When he doesn't need us to be sitting here so that he can serve lunch to a bunch of corporate suits or to do some circus tricks, we go." McNiff sighed. "Between here and Cairo I could do it blindfolded, but it keeps me alive. It does. Like old man river I gotta keep rollin' along."

Was McNiff changing the subject? Had he just picked up a thread of the former conversation and used it to stitch up a hole, or was he merely airing his grievances? Hecklepeck couldn't be sure. He looked at his watch. "I have to be rolling below. The press conference is beginning."

"The *Gustavius Bussard* is a wonderful addition to the St. Louis waterfront." Gus Bus had gotten the mayor to give an opening statement. This he was performing with more aplomb than he had the boat's christening a month before. "Last week I took a group of Japanese businessmen on a tour. These were people who are here to consider investing in our community. And let me assure you they were impressed. Of course I couldn't tell you exactly what they said . . ." The mayor paused so that everybody could share his chuckle, "but they were awed. You could see it and hear it in their tone of voice . . ."

In the audience, members of the news media squirmed. Whether measured in column inches or reading seconds, this was going to be a short story, simply a matter of letting the public know that X dollars had been raised and donated to fight drug abuse. The mayor was barely going to make the news. Maybe a line or two. Maybe a photo. It would really be better for all concerned if he shut up and stepped down. This was what the news media was trying to signal each time a member shifted another body part.

Since clapping was the only body language the mayor understood and no one was clapping, he trudged onward across a wide field to show that the *Gustavius* was a double blessing, not just a municipal attraction but also a fund-raiser. From there he took the long path to introduce "the man, not to be confused with his boat, who made it all possible—Gustavius Bussard the sixth."

Gus had apparently decided to keep the pince-nez. He took his place at the microphone and pulled them out of a pocket of his bright red vest. "This has been the dream of a lifetime . . . good feeling I get when I can help my own community . . . My father always said . . . man who really deserves the credit . . ."

Hecklepeck, who arrived just as Gus started to speak, heard only the occasional phrase and had heard each one before from Gus. He wondered fleetingly if anyone had ever kissed the multimillionaire to see if there was a prince under that froggie exterior.

Gustavia's salon was no longer a gambling den, and a good thing too, since it was too noble a room to be decked out for such a tawdry purpose. But it was still full of trespassers who had no true appreciation of the river. The press people clearly had none. They were a notoriously unsentimental group about everything except their own camera images or bylines. Roughly the same could be said about the politicians.

Gus Bus theoretically should have known better. He had built the steamboat and he had done it well. He just hadn't done it for even a sprinkling of the right reasons. Hecklepeck finally admitted to himself what he had known all along. Gus's boat was no tribute to the father of waters; he had no respect, not even a smidgen, for the muddy current. The *Gustavius Bussard* was nothing more than a shrine to Gus Bus himself. If it had been built of marble and placed in a public square, Hecklepeck wouldn't have cared. But on some level the wooden steamboat was a living, steam-breathing entity, and it deserved better.

As Gus Bus droned on from the lectern, Hecklepeck comforted himself with the thought that he and McNiff could carry on from the pilothouse, that they could take the boat to all honor and glory in New Orleans while Gus sipped champagne below.

Tom Honigger stepped up to the microphone. The man looked like a human golf course, he was so perfectly but somehow artificially groomed. In spite of his determination to keep mental fingers off Jennifer's story, Hecklepeck had to wonder if Honigger knew that chemicals were being stolen from his company. Toluene, anyway, and maybe something else. Something that killed boys without leaving a trace. Do you know that? Hecklepeck silently demanded of the man.

"It is with great pleasure"—The media came alive. After all that waiting Honigger was getting to the point without giving them enough warning to roll the cameras.—"that I give this check to Marion Honigger, chairwoman of St. Louis Without Drugs." In a Chanel suit that probably was a Chanel suit and not a knock-off, Marion Honigger stepped forward to accept the money. "When I hand out big checks like this, I like to keep it in the family,"

Honigger quipped to the press, his smile all but cracking his facial tan.

The joke seemed to irritate his wife. Hecklepeck could only conclude that she didn't care about the impression she made on people. Otherwise she wouldn't stand up in front of rolling cameras with that bad-tempered look on her perfectly made-up face. But she had played roulette the same way, as if the game existed for her benefit and the other players were trespassers.

Honigger held up a check. "It is with great pleasure that I present to you the proceeds from gambling night on the river. This is a check for 80,000 dollars." Marion Honigger grasped one end of the check and tugged until her husband released it to her.

Eighty thousand dollars! Hecklepeck couldn't believe it. It didn't seem like enough. Not nearly enough! For the first time he opened the press packet that had been handed to him at the door, scanning the releases until he got to the cost breakdown. According to Public Advancement, some 250 people had taken the riverboat trip and they had each paid 500 dollars a ticket. That came out to 125,000 dollars of which 80,000, or two-thirds, was being donated to combat drug abuse.

Hecklepeck looked around at his fellow reporters. They didn't have any problem with it. They were lapping up the numbers Marion Honigger doled out like a saucer full of cream. Why not? A two to one donation-to-expense ratio was not the best, but it was acceptable, and 80,000 dollars was a goodly amount of money. Carefully distributed it could help some people. So the reporters were proceeding, untroubled, with their little stories.

But they hadn't been there. They didn't know what he knew. About the gambling. About all the money that had been wagered on various games. Since winners got prizes, all of that money had been kept as proceeds from the fund-raiser. There must have been a lot of money too. Hecklepeck had observed a number of high-stakes players. The chairwoman of St. Louis Without Drugs to name a prime example. She who had been determined to gamble the night away until she won a prize and was now announcing figures like the gaming had never happened.

He scanned the press release again. Why wasn't the gambling money listed, and where had it gone? Hecklepeck could well believe the party soaked up some of it, considering the amount and quality of food, all the gambling equipment, the elegant prizes, the people needed to run things, and, of course, the film crew. Some of that had probably been donated. Even if it hadn't, there would have been money left over.

How outrageous! There had been more than 200 people on that cruise, including the mayor of the city and one of the city's top journalists. Were the organizers assuming William Hecklepeck was going to keep quiet about their unreported income? Not a chance. He almost stuck his hand up in the air then and there and demanded an answer.

Marion Honigger had announced she was ready to take questions and was now waiting smilelessly for someone to take her up on it. Nobody moved. Nobody had any questions.

Hecklepeck restrained himself. This was not the time. The room was full of competing reporters, and there was no point in making them privy to his exclusive information. He was too much the reporter for that, and he would get his chance another time.

Marion Honigger found an invisible spot midway up the far wall and stared at it. Nobody helped her out by raising a hand.

"Thank you all for coming." Gus trotted forward into the breach and ended the news conference.

Hecklepeck waited for his photographer to pack up and then followed him toward the door. "Less than two weeks now"—Gus Bus was ushering the press out—"and we'll be working up a traveling head of steam. Just as soon as my cargo shipment has arrived in that warehouse in New Orleans."

Hecklepeck raised an eyebrow. "This would be the shipment of souvenir tins that you're expecting?"

"Yes, my little momentos. I want to be sure they're safe in port before I head down there to pick them up."

"Yes, of course. Very sensible." What silly little game was Gus playing? Hecklepeck might have done a little judicious probing to find out, enough to make Gus jump without betraying McNiff, but his mind was preoccupied with more serious matters.

Once back in his own office he made yet another and more thorough review of the press packet he had been given. There was no mention anywhere of revenues from gambling. Maybe it was because gambling was still illegal in St. Louis? On election day Missouri voters overwhelmingly approved riverboat gambling, but a court challenge had been immediate. In any case this had been a private party and there were no winnings, only prizes. Besides, the mayor had been one of the gamblers that night.

No, Hecklepeck had to assume that the gambling money was not being reported because it was being used for something besides the public good. He turned to the last page of the press release. On it was listed the public agencies that would be receiving a share of the 80,000 dollars and the amount each would receive.

Predictably most of those listed were larger, better-known drug agencies in town. No surprises. Except for the last one. St. Louis Without Drugs was giving a whopping 10,000 dollars to the solvent abuse clinic at Malcolm Bliss Hospital. Not the biggest of the grants listed but disproportionately large. Too much out of too small a store for such an insignificant agency. It made Hecklepeck very curious.

He stuck his head out the doorway. "Hey, Jen, come here." She was getting ready to go home, looking forward to a nap. "Look at this."

Jennifer read the release. "Wow. That's Ben Howell, the guy I interviewed for my series. What a coincidence."

Hecklepeck nodded, his suspicion confirmed. "Coincidence is an understatement. The person behind all this grant money is Marion Honigger, whose husband, as you well know, owns Metalcote, the company from which Howell's clients steal the glue they sniff."

"Maybe it's hush money. Maybe Howell knows about the chemicals being stolen from Metalcote. So he put it to Honigger in terms of corporate liability and Honigger is paying him off through his wife this way. In a way it's fitting: money from the company that is the source of the drug being used to help the drug abuser." She leaned against the doorjamb as if all the thought to produce that speech had worn her out.

"Yes, but how interested is Howell really in helping his clients? Remember, you saw him forking out bills to a teenage prostitute in Tower Grove Park?"

"Yeah, but I think he cares. Well, maybe not. I don't know. I haven't had a chance to confront him about that."

"I would say now is the time."

"Wouldn't it have shown up in the autopsy if Jimmie was sexually abused?"

"Only if they looked for it."

Jennifer sighed. "Okay. I'll set something up."

When she was gone Hecklepeck cranked script paper into his battered manual typewriter. In the upper-left-hand corner he typed the story name, "DRUG CONFERENCE". Then he advanced the page about two inches and, punching the margin release, typed "ANCHOR/ON CAMERA" on the left-hand side of the page, which was divided down the middle with a black line. He moved the carriage back over to the right, the side that would appear on teleprompter, and continued, "THE CITY OF ST. LOUIS GOT SOME HELP FROM LOCAL BUSINESSMEN IN ITS WAR ON DRUGS TODAY . . ."

The story came so automatically to him that he hardly had to think about it. He had written so many similar pieces over the years, anchor voice-overs that filled the newscast but never caused a ripple in anyone's memory bank.

It didn't occur to Hecklepeck, but that was the kind of observation that had been launching his panic attacks. Nor did he notice that this time his office walls stayed where they belonged. While typing up the public version, Hecklepeck meditated on his private vision of what had happened at that press conference.

It had raised some fascinating questions: Why wasn't Public Advancement forthcoming about the money it had taken in from gambling? Why was an obscure substance abuse clinic getting a grant for 10,000 dollars when other agencies administered to tougher, more widespread drug problems? Fascinating questions. They were drawing the long-dormant reporter out of Hecklepeck with his heart pounding and eyes flashing.

Which was a good thing too because the press conference had also answered a question. It had settled an uncertainty that Hecklepeck hadn't even known he had. Or perhaps he was denying. Probably that. In any case he had now woken up to the fact that he could not possibly take a steamboat trip down to New Orleans with Gus Bus and his 10,000 commemorative tins.

Gus was part of a news story, and reporters did not hang out with the people about whom they reported. To do so would be unethical, a clear case of conflict of interest and a violation of his own personal moral code. Had the code been on a prolonged vacation? Hecklepeck did not choose to pursue an answer to that question. Instead he took a breath and noted how clean and fresh the air in his dusty office was.

16

J ENNIFER HELD THE microphone out in front of her as if it were a cross and would be preceding her into Dracula's lair. "Give me a second or two to get him in my shot and get focused," said Art from behind. "Otherwise I may miss something."

She put one hand on the knob of the door that bore Ben Howell's nameplate. He was expecting her. She wouldn't have been able to get by the guard at the front desk or the pool secretary at the end of the hall if she hadn't gotten clearance from Howell. But she hadn't told him why she wanted to see him. Nor had she informed him that she would be coming in with the camera rolling to record his first spontaneous reaction when she accused him of pederasty.

Jennifer was neither happy nor comfortable with the ambush approach, but people at the TV station had been almost unanimous in advising her to take it. In fact they got all lit up over it. "Just like 'Sixty Minutes' " was the most often heard rejoinder. But Jennifer didn't feel like a "Sixty Minutes" reporter. Those guys had producers and three-man crews and a whole country of TV viewers behind them. She had Art and his Ikegami camera.

Something else Mike Wallace and the other "Sixty Minutes" guys had was their own sense of righteousness. Jennifer didn't feel righteous at all. She wasn't happy or comfortable with what she was accomplishing. But there was no backing out. She had to flatten her ears, go forward, and do whatever was required to put together the series on glue-sniffing. Then . . . she would see what she would see.

Jennifer turned the doorknob handle and with some effort pushed the door inward. Howell was sitting behind his desk in some kind of synthetic weave jacket. At the sight of the advancing camera he involuntarily smoothed the side of his hair with his palm. Yet he could not then have realized what was about to happen to him. Art was still struggling to get through the door with his camera on one shoulder and tape recorder hanging from the other.

Jennifer turned and watched until the photographer and his equipment were at least all in the room. Then she took a step closer to Howell, held out her microphone and "We- saw- you . . . we- have- tape- of- you- at- Tower- Grove- Park- with- a- male- prosti- tute- and- want- to- know- what- you- were- doing- there- and- how- you- can- reconcile- that- behavior- with- your- role- as- drug- coun- selor." If the microphone were some sort of protective talisman, Jennifer's much practiced words emerged like an oft-repeated prayer. In fact she was internally begging Howell not to be angry with her for having to ask the question.

"What?" Howell's exclamation coincided with the coming on of Art's camera light, so it was impossible to know if he was reacting to that or to Jennifer's speech.

She took in a sharp breath and gaped. She hadn't expected to have to repeat herself. "We, uh, saw you, uh, trying to pick up a male prostitute at Tower Grove Park and we, uh, want to know about that . . . about how you can do that and still be a drug counselor."

Howell moved back in his chair and looked from Jennifer to the camera. The color of his face changed from rabbit-nose pink to deep red. "I wish you'd turn that thing off." But they weren't going to do that. "Well, all right. I . . . uh . . . Outreach. My clientele, as I've explained to you, is . . . scattered. They don't always come in to this office and plop themselves down in front of this desk and ask for help. Sometimes I go out into the field to find them, and that means hanging out at Tower Grove Park in the middle of the night be- cause . . . because . . . that's where the people are who need help."

"But you gave one of them money, and then he got in the car and drove off with you. We saw him. We have it on tape."

A drop of sweat ran down Howell's forehead. He wiped it off with a hand. "Yeah, well." With the same hand he rubbed his eyes, as if reluctant to make the next admission. "I do that. It's . . . well . . . not part of the therapeutic model, but sometimes it's the only way to get them off the streets and out of temptation's way. I . . . pay them to go home and get a good night's sleep."

Was that last a sudden inspiration or was he telling the truth?

Jennifer looked closely at him, but she couldn't be sure. "That's not part of your job," she probed.

"No . . . I'm sure my professional association would frown on it. But these guys have no steady jobs, no family structure, no real incentive to stay away from the drug lifestyle." This was safer ground for Howell. He had obviously trod it many times before. "I figure if I can be a caring presence in their lives, if I can be there and not just here on appointment days, maybe it'll help."

"It looked like you were trying to pick the guy up."

"For that reason I hope you won't air it." Howell saw the opportunity to make the request and pounced. "That, and the fact that I really don't want my . . . outreach efforts to be broadcast. I don't want my clients to get to expect it. Not good therapeutic practice for one thing—and, let's face it, my salary isn't that big." He offered Jennifer a sheepish smile.

She refused to be charmed but decided the matter was best pursued off camera and put down her microphone. "You can understand that I had to ask."

"Yeah." With the camera's eye off him, Howell pulled out a handkerchief and wiped his face. "Yeah. I just wish you could have done it without that camera going. It makes me feel like one of those crooks you see on 'Sixty Minutes' all the time."

Jennifer nodded. He had made the "Sixty Minutes" connection too. The trouble was there hadn't been a "Sixty Minutes" ending. The crooks on that show always looked like crooks, but Howell's behavior had been inconclusive. Yet the "Sixty Minutes" people had only reality to work with, didn't they? No more than she.

"Hey, man. Gotta do it. S'our job. Had to catch that first reaction just in case you were guilty." Ever genial Art stuck his hand across the desk and Howell shook it.

"Does that mean you won't be putting it on TV?"

"Don't know about that, man. It's not up to me." Art bent over his equipment.

Jennifer pretended to be absorbed in her notes so that she didn't have to answer the question, and then she changed the subject: "The St. Louis Without Drugs organization has announced that it's giving you a 10,000 dollar grant."

"Yeah." Howell reoriented himself. "Yeah."

"What are you going to use it for . . . outreach?" Jennifer didn't mean to be snide. It just came out.

132

A rice paper shade seemed to descend over Howell's face. It was the same face but somehow now veiled. Perhaps he felt he had not won much ground with "forthcoming" and was retreating to "guarded." "I'd like to hire another psychologist, like myself, possibly someone with a social work background who can get into some of the root causes of the problem. Part time."

"It's a lot of money," Jennifer probed.

"On the one hand it is; on the other it isn't. We could use more."

"Do you often get grants like that?"

"No."

"It's unusual then. Were you surprised?"

"Yeah, sure."

"Other agencies, bigger agencies didn't get any money. Why do you think you did?" It was almost harder, pushing him without the whir of the camera in the background. More personal somehow.

"Why shouldn't we? We perform a valuable service in this community, and when the grant money is passed out we get passed over. This time our number was up and we walked away with the prize."

"But aren't you curious about why it happened now? Do you know Marion Honigger, the chairwoman of St. Louis Without Drugs? Her husband is Tom Honigger, who owns Metalcote." That stopped Howell right in the middle of shifting around in his chair. "You know Metalcote, right down from Benton Park, near Anheuser-Busch. Where they steal tulio."

"So what are you saying?" Behind the rice paper shade Howell's features were pugnacious and mean.

All her life Jennifer had tried to please people. Parents, teachers, friends. This deliberate goading went against her nature. "I don't know. That it's a coincidence. That maybe they're afraid of being held liable for those boys who died or something like that so that's why they're giving you the money."

"And if they are, how is that my fault?" Jennifer looked down at her notebook and shrugged, unable to take it the next step. "Unless you're suggesting I'm guilty of blackmail. How would that go? I know that Metalcote is negligent in its security arrangements because kids get in there and steal tulio. (Metalcote and half a dozen others along the river, but never mind.) I take that information to Metalcote and offer to go public with it unless they make a grant to my program. Is that it? First you're accusing me of sexual misconduct with my clients and now blackmail. What's next?"

Murder. Jennifer looked at Howell, hoping the word was legible in her gray eyes, because she didn't have the courage to say it.

Howell chuckled, a forced, constipated kind of chuckle. "You know I agreed to let you interview me because I thought some publicity might result in help for my clients. If I'd known you were going to get into all this tabloid stuff, I'd have steered clear."

"There's been another death. Three. Three in a row." When Jennifer said the word "death", Art stopped fussing with his equipment and leaned up against the wall in the back of Howell's office.

"I know. I thought that's what you were coming here to talk to me about. Not . . . not all this other stuff." Howell leaned back in his chair ready now with his prepared speech. "I told you the last time you were here that I didn't think tulio killed the first two boys. Now that there's been a third death I'm sure of it."

"Yes, how did you know?" There was a jarful of plastic toys on Howell's desk. Last time she had been in the office Jennifer had wondered about the toys, whether they were rewards for Howell's clients. This time she wondered about the jar.

"I told you tulio doesn't behave that way. There may be an occasional fatality but not three in a row. I'm convinced those kids died of something else."

Jennifer nodded. Howell had said that. Was it just in the interest of truth or was he laying groundwork for something else he knew about those boys and their deaths? The police had been perfectly willing to believe the boys died as a result of their glue-sniffing habits. Of course, they had failed to do the math: three deaths. Howell was ahead of them there. He had been adding all along. "Why didn't you go to the police?"

"I haven't had a lot of luck with the police in the past. They don't really want to be bothered with . . . my population. Glue-sniffers are largely harmless. Maybe because their drug of choice makes them kind of slow and dopey, but the most they do is a little shoplifting. They don't get into fights, they don't kill each other like other types of drug users do, and the police are happy not to be bothered with them. Besides, you called. I shared what I knew with you."

I am not the authorities, Jennifer reminded him silently, just a novice reporter, who is struggling with an oversized story. "You're right. They didn't die from glue-sniffing."

"No. Really? I thought so. What was it then?"

"Noth . . . Well, they don't know. It didn't show up in the autopsy."

"Nothing showed up in the autopsy?" Howell sat forward. "What did they die of then?"

"Nobody knows." Well, somebody knew. Maybe even Howell. There was something a little staged about his surprise and concern.

"Incredible. I wonder what it was. They must have gotten hold of something besides toluene, some other chemical from one of those plants down by the river. I can't imagine what would do that, disappear and not leave a trace, but there must be some substance that fits the bill."

"What if . . . it didn't come from one of those plants? What . . . if it came from here? This is a hospital. There are drugs here." As Jennifer spoke, she winced in anticipation of Howell's reaction. Here after all she was obliquely linking him to the murders.

But Howell either genuinely didn't know the boys were murdered or was determined not to reveal that he knew. "We have very tight controls on drugs here. There is virtually no way those boys could have stolen anything from here. No way. Maybe . . . possibly if they had some inside help, but that isn't likely."

Jennifer decided not to tell him that the three victims had definitely had help—somebody who offered them poison in a jar. Instead she took another tack. "When Jimmie died, I was out on the river in that new steamboat. I could have been passing Benton Park at the very moment he died." The self-admission came more easily to her than the accusations had. Perhaps it was a more innately female way to extract information.

"I was probably at home . . . what night was it?

"About three weeks ago. Thursday. October 15th." Jennifer pretended to consult her notes about this. She didn't want Howell to see the snare.

He flipped through his desktop calendar. "Yeah. No engagements that night. I must have been at home with my wife."

Wife? He had a wife? Jennifer had assumed he was single. There was something sort of uncared for in the wearing of polyester suits. A wife seemed unlikely to let her husband out of the house with one of those on. But that was her own prejudice showing, Jennifer reminded herself.

"Even if I'd been out on the streets there was probably nothing I could have done."

If Howell had been home with his wife, he hadn't been out snuffing Jimmie. If he had a wife in the first place, maybe he hadn't been sexually pursuing young boys in the park. Here for the first time Jennifer found testimony for Howell's defense. She had gotten something with her back-door approach, something that hadn't come out when she shoved that microphone in the poor guy's face.

"Nothing in the autopsy." Howell shook his head over it. "How strange. How really strange. Listen, I've got Pete Cobb, the guy you interviewed, waiting down the hall. I had thought you might want to talk to him and see what he has to say since he's out there in the middle of all this. And now with this new information, maybe he's heard about tainted chemical or something."

He got up from behind his desk to get Pete, an overweight man who cared (or professed to care) about a hopeless, unredeemable group of people more than he did about his own reputation. Jennifer sank her head in her hands, wanting him to be a good guy. He was so needed.

"Do you want me to shoot this?" Art asked from his position against the back wall.

"No. Let's see what he has to say first."

Pete Cobb was wearing what appeared to be the same open-necked blue shirt he had worn at their last interview. This time it was covered with a cheap tan jacket that couldn't possibly have kept him warm enough that early November morning.

Jennifer stood up and extended her hand. "How are you?"

"Fahn." From the grin on his face Jennifer judged he probably felt . . . fine. But she reminded herself that he didn't know enough to know when he wasn't.

Howell pushed through the door with another chair in his hands. He set it down beside Jennifer's in front of his desk. "Here you go, Pete." Pete sat down and stuck his chin in the air like a dog who was waiting for the wind to bring him a scent and wasn't sure which direction it would come from.

Jennifer waited, deferring to Howell. This was his show, the second time he had brought on Pete, and she wanted to see what performance he was going to elicit.

"Well, Pete. Ms. Burgess and I got you down here to ask you some questions."

Pete said something in his garbled way that Jennifer did not catch.

"No, this has nothing to do with your therapy. Now, Pete, I want ya to hang in there with me. Do you remember when your brother died in August and how we talked about it then? How we said that's what happens sometimes when you sniff glue?"

"Yeah'zz a good reason t'stayway frumt. Ss'badstuff." Pete was wary as if he knew this was leading somewhere and had his suspicions about it.

"Right. Well, since then two more boys have died. A boy named Hoyt Jenkins in September . . ." Howell turned to Jennifer. "As I told you, Hoyt was not a client of mine, but Pete knew him. Right Pete?" Pete nodded vigorously. "So okay, he died in September. Then in October Jimmie Smith died. Now Pete, that's three boys dying in three months. All about the same age. Eight, nine, ten years old."

Pete shook his head. "SS'badstuff."

"You're right. Okay, but let's forget that for just a minute." Howell's concentration on his client was complete. "We think there may be some connection, some . . . reason that these three boys died. Something other than the tulio."

"Zat tulio's bad ferya." Once again, the party line.

Jennifer suddenly remembered that the last time she interviewed Pete he had said it *wasn't* tulio that killed his brother. Something else, he had said. Bad stuff. She spoke up. "When I interviewed you in September you said Mike didn't die from tulio. That it was something else. Do you remember that?"

Pete cocked one eye in Jennifer's direction as if appraising her question and then the other in Howell's. Whatever he saw there seemed to inhibit his answer. "Ss'bad stuff tulio. Ll'kill ya."

"You're right. Tulio is very bad stuff. Very bad stuff. But, Pete, it wouldn't kill three boys in three months like that. Remember, we've talked about it. Sometimes tulio will kill you quickly, but only very, very rarely. It's more likely to kill you slowly over a long period of time. We want to know if you've heard anything in the neighborhood about some bad stuff." Howell let the question sink in before moving on to the next one. "Or, if you know about a new place where people are getting tulio. Or maybe from a new person? Maybe somebody's selling it or giving it away?"

Pete had listened carefully to each new hypothesis. At the last one he laughed. A little uneasily? Jennifer thought so. "S'no money. S'no money fer tulio. S'ain't nobody . . ." Whatever Pete said after that was lost in his slurred speech.

"What?"

"He says only a crazy person would give it away," Howell translated. "What about bad stuff, Pete?" Pete shook his head. His face took on a cunning expression. Combined with the vacancy in his eyes it was . . . Well, it gave Jennifer the chills. "Is there a new place where everybody's getting tulio?" Pete dropped his head and shook it again.

"What about that company, Metalcote?" Jennifer interjected.

That brought Pete's head up abruptly. The cunning expression deepened, making his face look like a plastic halloween mask. "Ss'tulio there . . . inna white barrels."

"What about other barrels at Metalcote? Or tanks . . . or . . . or other containers with chemicals in them?"

Once again Pete referred to his therapist, and whatever he saw there brought him back to square one. "Ss'tulio's badstuff. Badstuff."

"Washington University Science Department."

"Professor Gil Holt, please." Hecklepeck swooshed some paper off his desk so he could rest his feet there without slipping. Waiting for the operator to put him through, he explained to himself that he didn't have to feel guilty. He was just nosing around, not by any means taking over the investigation of Jennifer's story. Besides, he had the contact and his curiosity had gotten the better of him.

"Yup." Gil Holt had one of those midwestern accents with a bite to it.

Hecklepeck identified himself and asked how the professor was doing, picturing him as he did so in his clear plastic glasses, a man whose face had never been troubled with a smile.

"Fine." Gil Holt didn't seem to believe that conversations should be filled up with talk. There was a lag now as Hecklepeck waited vainly for him to return the ball.

"Uh, that's good. I'm calling to test your expertise. Specifically, I'm looking for a chemical that's capable of killing somebody by direct inhalation. But here's the difficult part: After that it's got to evaporate, leaving no trace either in the victim's body or in the container from which the substance was inhaled." Hecklepeck waited for an answer.

Gil Holt's voice, when he employed it, was slightly belligerent, as if he were challenging the listener to take issue with him. "I could do a computer check, but I'm not sure what would come up. The system's not really set up to handle that kind of inquiry." Another pause. "Better if you could give me some more information."

"How about this? What about chemicals used in the electroplating process? Is there anything there that would fit the bill?"

"Depends. What kind of electroplating?"

"Small stuff. Gold charms. Electronic components."

Silence fell on the other end of the line again, but at least, Hecklepeck told himself, he knew where Gil Holt was this time: reviewing the chemicals used in electroplating.

"Nope."

"Nope? You mean none of the chemicals used in electroplating fit the bill?"

"Yep. As far as I can tell from the information you've given me."

"Figures," Hecklepeck sighed. "We'd already figured out that hydrogen cyanide is too toxic to carry around in a jar for the purposes of murder, and the chlorofluorocarbons—"

"Chlorofluorocarbons?"

"Yeah, they can be carried around in a jar, but they wouldn't kill anybody."

"Chlorofluorocarbons aren't normally used in the electroplating process."

"Well, they are in this case, for degreasing. It doesn't matter anyway—"

"You didn't mention chlorofluorocarbons." Gil Holt sounded aggrieved. Because Hecklepeck hadn't given him all the information?

"Well, it doesn't matter. It's not important."

Whatever vexed Gil had cured him of his conversational lag syndrome. He was suddenly right on top of it. "Chlorofluorocarbons are inert."

"Oh? They are? What does that mean?"

"They don't react with other substances. They wouldn't, for instance, dissolve in a person's bloodstream. So, yes, they would be completely expelled from the body. Or they would just evaporate out of an open container. Their inertness is the trouble with them.

They migrate all the way to the stratosphere before reacting with sunlight to damage the ozone layer. Which one?"

"Which one? What?" Hecklepeck was still trying to absorb what he had just heard. It was his turn to lag.

"Which chlorofluorocarbon? There are lots of them, different combinations of chlorine and fluorine surrounding carbon atoms. They have numbers, eleven being probably the most common. It's in most of our air-conditioning systems."

"Oh, well which one is used for degreasing?"

Holt sighed audibly and put down the phone. In a few minutes he was back. "Refrigerant 113 most commonly."

"Okay. Is it lethal?"

Another pause, but at least this time Hecklepeck could hear the rustling of book pages in the background. "Underwriters' Laboratories says . . . it's less toxic than refrigerants in the Group 4 category but more toxic than Group 5." Hecklepeck rolled his eyes, the only expression of impatience he dared make. He needed Gil's help. "Group 4, according to the CRC Handbook of Chemistry and Physics, is 'gases or vapors which in concentrations of the order of 2 to 2½ percent for durations of exposure of the order of 2 hours are lethal or produce serious injury.' " Gil Holt's reading was monotonal. "Now you understand 113 is not nearly as bad as that."

Yeah, Hecklepeck understood that much. But did the gobbledygook that Gil just read tell how bad 113 was? Was it the killer he was looking for? Specifically, what would breathing 100 percent (or close to it) refrigerant 113 do in five or six seconds? He put the last question to Gil Holt.

"Don't know," said the chemist. "I doubt the conditions of use have dictated that kind of testing."

17

WIFE? WHAT DOES his having a wife have to do with anything?"
Hecklepeck and Jennifer were discussing her interview with Howell in Hecklepeck's office. Hecklepeck was resting the back of his
head against one cinder-block wall and had his feet propped up on
one edge of the doorway into the newsroom.

"If he has a wife then maybe he doesn't need to go around
picking up chickens." On the other side of the doorway with no
door Jennifer was in Hecklepeck's extra chair, and her feet, too,
minus their high heels, were resting on the cinder-block wall in
front of her.

"Jen. Honey. Where have you been? Married guys do that kind
of thing all the time. Believe me. As far as I'm concerned the
evidence is incontrovertible. You saw Ben Howell out in Tower
Grove Park waving money in front of a male hooker."

"He says it's outreach. That he goes out there to find his clients
and get them away from bad influences."

"And you believed him?"

"I'm not sure. He could be telling the truth. He seems quite
dedicated. He definitely has a good rapport with his clients." Jennifer hadn't believed him. Not exactly. But she didn't disbelieve
him either, and she very much wanted Howell to be innocent for
the good he did.

"Well, we don't have to act as judge and jury on this."

"What do you mean?"

"We just have to present the facts and let the public decide."

Jennifer stared at Hecklepeck. "But what if he really is innocent?

The minute you put something like that on the air, people are going to think he's guilty no matter what."

"The evidence is pretty overwhelming that he is. Notwithstanding that we, as journalists, should not be judging him. All we do is present the facts and let the public decide. Sometimes that results in a miscarriage of justice, but more often than not, if we have done our homework, we perform a great service. If the guy is sexually abusing his clients, he has no business counseling them. We have a duty to bring that information forward."

"But if he's innocent it'll still be the end of his career, and there won't be anyone else to care for those poor, hopeless people."

Hecklepeck smiled what was intended to be a sort of professorial benediction. "So young and so little faith in the system. Do you think it's easy to get someone like Howell charged, tried, and convicted no matter how many stories we do? It isn't. In this country the benefit of the doubt makes it easy to get away with breaking the law."

He was being patronizing! That supercilious smile. Jennifer sat up, bringing her stockinged feet down onto the carpeted floor. "But short of conviction in a court of law, our story could ruin Howell's career. It might not go on his record but everybody would know. People would talk. They'd hold it against him."

Hecklepeck smiled that smile again. "People's memories are shorter than you know. That story will be forgotten as soon we get to weather in the same newscast."

Jennifer was seeing red. "I don't care. It's my story and unless I get some more positive proof I'm not going to crucify somebody who is doing this community a lot of good. One of the only people." Jennifer was now determined that Howell was going to be innocent no matter what argument Hecklepeck brought forward.

"Come on, Jen. Nobody does outreach in Tower Grove Park in the middle of the night. His story is weak and you caught him in the act. Besides, there's more at stake here than just a little sexual misconduct. This is a question of murder. Mur-der. Three boys dead. And Howell is very much a suspect. We can't sit on it."

"I haven't got enough to go on with the murder stuff. Nothing but a jar with nothing in it and a boy who died of nothing. So, if I can't air that, how can I connect Howell to it?"

"You don't have to. Besides,—"

"Line three, Heck," a voice from the newsroom called out.

He picked up the phone, grateful for the interruption. It would give Jennifer a chance to cool down. "William Hecklepeck." The prolonged silence on the other end told him it was either a prank call or . . . it could be Gil.

"Gil Holt here."

"How are you?"

Once moving, Gil Holt was not to be diverted with pleasantries. "I called a former classmate of mine who works at one of the companies that manufactures refrigerant 113. Now this is not for publication." Gil Holt evidently got his media mixed up. His voice was stern. "He says a few years ago they ran a test on the stuff to see if it could be used in a new dry-cleaning process. One of the lab workers collapsed. His heart went into fibrillation—arrythmia— and he died before the medics could get to him. No history of heart trouble. No other explanation except that he had his face in 113."

"Wow. I don't believe it."

"Yep. But I want to impress on you again this isn't for publication. It's not common knowledge. The company evidently hushed the whole thing up to preserve the integrity of its product. So you could get my friend in serious trouble if you printed it."

Hecklepeck assured Gil Holt that he wouldn't and thanked him. As soon as he hung up the phone, he told Jennifer. "So it looks like it could well have been the chlorofluorocarbons that killed Jimmie and the other boys. They fill the bill perfectly. They're lethal and they evaporate," Hecklepeck wound up, triumphantly laying the booty at his lady's feet.

"What?" The expression on Jennifer's face was thunderous. "What were you doing making calls about my story?" Far from calming down while Hecklepeck was on the phone, she had grown more angry and his interference, never mind the new information, was another log on the fire.

Irritation came over the anchorman. This wasn't how mentoring went. Jennifer was supposed to listen and admire, not argue. "It was just a phone call. I was trying to help and look what I got. I would say my effort paid off."

"That's how it is with you, isn't it? The ends justify the means, no matter who gets trampled along the way. First Ben Howell and now me."

"It's hardly the same. You are my friend and colleague. I'm trying to help you put together a good story, and one phone call doesn't seem to be a particularly immoral act. Ben Howell is an entirely different story. He's a probable pederast and a murder suspect. In fact I would say we have a moral duty—"

Jennifer couldn't let go of it. "But you don't know that about him. What if he isn't? What if he really is a caring social worker who is willing to give up his paychecks to help people?"

Was that a dig at his own overlarge paycheck? Of course not. However, Hecklepeck glared right back at Jennifer. This woman, whom he had been thinking of in endearing terms, had turned on him, and now he was finding that he could be right there to meet her. He hadn't foreseen this. "Surely you can at least see that there's a small possibility your friend Howell is covering something up."

"Innocent until proven guilty. You haven't proven anything."

"What the hell is proof then? Let me restate it yet another time: You've got the guy offering a fistful of cash to a teenage male hooker. If that's not proof, what is it?"

"That is circumstantial. He explained that."

"You're not the judge, Jen. You're not a twelve-member jury panel. You're just a journalist, and it is your job to bring this stuff out in the daylight so judges and juries can get a whack at it."

They were going round in circles, and with each circumnavigation the argument was getting fiercer. Jennifer stood up. "Well, I don't want to. I don't want to take that responsibility."

"Oh, that's a good persuasive argument. Did you think being a journalist was going to be easy? Did you think it was all fan mail and viewer recognition? It's not. It's hard, tough choices that affect people's lives, choices that will also affect your life because you're going to have to live with them."

Jennifer was fishing around on the floor for her shoes. She grabbed them and started out the door without bothering to put them on. But before the exit was complete she turned back, her eyes flashing with anger. "Maybe I don't want to be a journalist. Did you ever think of that?"

Hecklepeck drew back into the vacuum left by her departure. No, he hadn't thought of that. He certainly hadn't.

The knocker fell with a dull thud on the big wooden door. It sounded even more muted than it had the first time Jennifer had been there. But perhaps she was reading circumstances into it.

This little pilgrimage was all her idea. She had been writing the second part of her series on glue-sniffing, now due to air in only a week, and she had suddenly felt an urgent need to make this visit. It didn't seem right to use Jimmie Smith's pictures and his words without the blessing of his parents.

Jennifer had been looking at the videotapes of the boy, and all the pathos of his predicament came back to her. His cowlick—that tuft of black hair that stuck up from the back of his head, his little swagger, and all the eagerness with which he had led her into the secrets of his world just made the reality of his death that much more pathetic. How could she violate his spirit by using him as a ratings grabber? The answer had been, Only with the approval of his parents after they had been fully informed.

Doubtless this was avoiding her own journalistic responsibility. But Jennifer just couldn't see that the bigger issues, the public's right to know, et cetera, outweighed the rights of one small, murdered boy. Mentally she told that to Hecklepeck, with whom she was still angry.

She hadn't spoken to him since their fight. Their work schedules barely overlapped, so it was easy to avoid him. Jennifer was seriously busy writing her series, which was turning out to be a general tutorial on glue-sniffing. The unanswered questions—Who killed three boys with a chlorofluorocarbon in a jar? and Which was Ben Howell, a dedicated drug counselor or a pervert?—nagged at her, but she did not have the time or the emotional fortitude to pursue them. There were just stories that never panned out, stories the public never saw.

Jennifer wanted to be finished with it. She was tired of aching for Jimmie, for Pete, even for Howell. What made her ache was the coupling of responsibility and impotence that came with being a reporter. She couldn't observe such sad, misguided lives without wanting to help, and she couldn't help without violating journalistic principles. It was a miserable place to be.

And it was lonely again. For a while Hecklepeck had been there to keep her company. In retrospect they spoke different languages, yet his presence had counted for something, and Jennifer missed it.

She pulled out the knocker again, but even as she released it she heard a shuffling on the other side of the door. Jimmie's mother looked exactly as she had the last time Jennifer saw her, even down to her dress. Was it the same faded cotton or one so similar as to be indistinguishable?

"Hello," said Jennifer. "I don't know if you remember me but I'm the reporter . . . with Channel Three . . . who came, oh, four weeks ago, to interview your son Jimmie. I'm so sorry about Jimmie. I just wanted to come and tell you . . . and talk to you."

The knot in Mrs. Smith's pale forehead deepened. She could have been reacting to the outdoor light, but Jennifer thought it was the pain of hearing Jimmie's name. She gestured weakly for Jennifer to come in.

The room also was unchanged, filled with the same unmade beds. The television was on, and Betty Smith once again had the room's one chair pulled up in front of it. The one difference was a plastic crucifix that had been nailed to the wall over the television. It was broken. Jesus was missing his right hand and the corresponding section of cross. Beneath the icon were two long-stemmed rosebuds, also plastic, in a glass jar, and as Jennifer walked by, she thought she saw a snapshot lying there too. Probably a picture of Jimmie, she thought, and felt a surge of pathos.

She seated herself very gingerly on the edge of one of the beds. "I wanted to tell you how sorry I am." The woman grunted. "He was so young, such a nice boy. You must feel awful." Jennifer had not taken her coat off, and she suddenly realized how hot the room was, hot enough for Betty Smith to be comfortable in her cotton dress.

Without taking her eyes off the television the woman lifted her rounded shoulders. "S'nuthin' I ken do bout it. E'hadn't oughta been sniffin nuthin.' "

"No. No, he shouldn't have." Jennifer had come to sympathize with the woman, but between the desire and its awful target rose the strong itch of curiosity. "Did you know what he was sniffing? Was it tulio? Or did he somehow get hold of something else?"

"S'tulio s'far s'I know."

"Well, I just want you to know how sorry I am. There was something special about Jimmie . . . He was . . . quite captivating." Once again from out of nowhere Jennifer's curiosity tickled her violently. "Have you heard . . . was there anything strange, anything unexpected about Jimmie's death?" This was the last question, Jennifer told herself. She was here to commiserate, not extract information from poor, grieving people.

146

"Doan know nuthin'. Nuthin'. Nuthin'. Jimmie, he m'youngest."
Mrs. Smith began to rock back and forth in her vinyl swivel chair.
Was she cradling her baby or her pain? Both. Clearly both.

Jennifer debated unbuttoning her coat for a little relief from the
heat but decided it was better not to look like she was settling in.
She didn't know what to say. In the face of grief like Betty Smith
must be feeling, her own experience was lacking.

A chair creaked in the next room, followed by the shuffle of
movement. "I'm really sorry . . . sorry about Jimmie." Jennifer's
sudden words fell on Betty Smith's back. The sentient woman had
once again been absorbed by her TV set.

Homer Smith appeared in the doorway, the look of anxiety in his
eyes more rending than ever. He shuffled a few feet further into the
room and stood, swaying on his feet in a white tee shirt and gray
pants.

"I . . . I'm very sorry about Jimmie," Jennifer repeated. But the
incantation was losing any ability it might have had to protect her
emotionally. There was, she could see him, a person behind crazy
Homer Smith's pale eyes. She hadn't expected that nor that that
person would suffer so over the death of his son. Smith's pain
moved her deeply.

"Ja-Jimmie gone true da'narragate. Gonna hevin."

"Yes, I'm sure Jimmie's in heaven." Jennifer willed the father to
take solace. "He was a good boy."

"F'he asks fer bread, d'ya give'm a stone?" Homer Smith shook
his head. However, it looked like somebody unseen was doing it for
him. He moved like a painful puppet on strings. "D'ya give'm a
stone?"

Betty Smith turned halfway around in her chair and looked at her
husband. But his disturbed gaze never seemed to rest on anything.
"Only a few is given to find the narragate. The rest'es oner wide
road." Homer Smith shot that last at the ceiling and then, with a
tormented smile, found Jennifer. "Them'es find the narragate,
them'es angels."

"Yes, I know Jimmie is an angel." Jennifer's eyes filled with
tears, for Jimmie, who was probably better off as an angel than
growing up here with a lunatic father. But the tears were also for
the father who had loved his son. "I came to tell you how sorry I
am and to talk with you about the television—"

"When you gone putuss on tee vee?" Betty Smith wanted to know.

"Well, that's what I wanted to talk to you about. My series is scheduled to start next Monday and I want to do a lot with Jimmie in it, but since he died, I wanted to ask . . . well, see if it is still all right with you."

"M'I gonna be in't?"

"Well, yes. I had planned on putting you in it. I need you to show what kind of background Jimmie comes from. I know it seems like I'm sort of using him, but it could do some good. I don't know how much I believe in it myself, but there are other children like Jimmie out there who sniff tulio and maybe one of them would see the program or maybe . . ." She was wasting her time. Betty Smith had turned back to her television program. Her husband was muttering to himself. Neither was listening.

It was one of those afternoons that would not lighten up. It lowered with the promise of snow or the threat of night, depending on the individual point of view. Jennifer felt the weight of both. For some reason she could not get back into her car and drive away from Jimmie's neighborhood. Instead she walked down the block in the direction of Benton Park.

Heck would have laughed at her for making such a visit. She was almost crying. Poor Jimmie. No one cared about his legacy, his recorded image and voice, except her, and she was no more sure of the right course than she had been before. But now she understood it was her decision whether or not to air it and her decision alone. That was what Heck had meant by journalistic responsibility.

Jennifer wished she felt better for knowing.

Benton Park was browner than it had been when she was last there in late September. The grass had died. She walked toward the swing set where the second boy, Hoyt Jenkins, had been found and sat on the end swing, the one furthest from his swing. She tucked her red coat in around her.

To Jennifer the cold was a relief after the thick heat of the Smiths' apartment. But it must have kept the children away. No one was playing. Jennifer wondered if children ever played at normal children's games in Benton Park, if they engaged in activities that were not perverted with drugs or stealing or the like. She doubted it.

In her mind she changed the park into a snowscape filled with children squealing downhill and the park lake into an ice-skating rink. Of course Jimmie and Hoyt, and Mike, the first boy to die, would not have had sleds or skates. No Flexible Flyers in the garage the way Jennifer had had, growing up.

Jimmie could have improvised, though, scavenged some cardboard or an old tray. That was what had so charmed Jennifer about him, his ability to use his environment in imaginative play. Unfortunately the game had been glue-sniffing. Because of it Jimmie had died.

Jennifer shivered and almost lost her balance. She grabbed the swing chain to steady herself, her hand protected in a white knitted glove. Jimmie's own game. But someone had pulled a switch on him. A deadly chemical, refrigerant 113 probably, instead of tulio. It could have been an accident on the part of somebody who, unlike Jimmie, didn't know enough to stay away from the yellow barrels. But wouldn't that person have died from sniffing the chlorofluorocarbon himself? Or, if that person were not a glue-sniffer, wouldn't he have made the connection when the first boy, Mike Cobb, died? Wouldn't he have stayed away from the yellow barrels after that?

Yes, yes, and yes. Which meant it had to be deliberate—the evidence of the missing jars borne out. Somebody had intentionally tapped the yellow barrels at Metalcote and delivered refrigerant 113 to Benton Park's glue-sniffers. Probably that person had not known the chlorofluorocarbons were lethal, but he would have found out and yet he didn't stop, eventually killing three boys on three Thursdays in three successive months.

Jennifer swallowed queasily. It was a sick variation on a sick game. Because that's what it was, had to be. Some unknown player took such glee in what his medicine did to one boy that he administered it to two others.

The horror of this conclusion dazed Jennifer. She couldn't see to take her deductions any further and instead let the gentle movement of the swing take over. Back and forth. Back and forth. After a while the swing seemed to be talking to her. Three boys. Dead. On Thursdays all. One each month. For three months. Three boys . . . dead. Thursdays all. August. September. October. Nov . . . November! Jennifer slammed both feet into the ground to stop the swing. Was it possible? No, it couldn't be. She counted on her fingers. There were three more Thursdays to go in the month. Could it be?

But the game was over wasn't it? Three boys had died. That was enough. No more. She lifted her feet. Three . . . boys dead, the swing said. Thursdays . . . always. Month after month. August-Sept . . . emberOct . . . oberNov . . .

18

WILLIAM HECKLEPECK PARKED the Porsche carelessly without regard for the long-term welfare of its tires. Bumper metal scraped against the curbstone, which, given his recent priorities, should have registered. He didn't hear it. Hecklepeck got out and slammed the car door. Then he walked off without putting a quarter in the parking meter.

The truth was he could have been driving a Chevrolet . . . a Yugo . . . a golf cart for all the notice he took. His mind was elsewhere, and it wasn't sunken in the muddy hollow of panicky depression. On the contrary, he was a man puffed up with purpose, bread dough rising to smother all opposition.

A master of the universe! Well, no. Not that. Not that at all. Specifically he was the man who took on those who dared to think they might be masters of the universe and brought them down to just under human size. So, what did that make him exactly? A master of masters of the universe? No! How could he think such a thing? He was just a journalist doing his job. But, oh, what a job it was sometimes. Hecklepeck was looking forward to confronting Gustavius Bussard VI about the gambling profits that hadn't been reported along with the ticket receipts from the drug benefit on his steamboat. He was going to sock it to Gus Bus.

He paused in front of the deco Bussard Tower and realized he had one important decision to make before he entered. He thought for a moment. Baked chicken. If he had to order something it would be the baked chicken. As he remembered the dining room menu, it was the simplest, most unadorned, most undersold of all the dishes listed. But safest. Hecklepeck figured anything on that menu that sounded remotely appetizing or, even worse, French was to be avoided. What Gus Bus's kitchen staff meant by sauce velouté was doused-in-canned-cream-of-mushroom-soup. What they meant by bouquet garnis was one tired old bay leaf and too much oregano. Definitely, the baked chicken, and he would insist on paying for it.

Blind fool that he had been he had accepted too much from Gus. He had let Gus buy away his objectivity with one tired, tasteless lunch, two tickets for a gambling party, and the promise of a steamboat trip to New Orleans. What a pathetic exchange for his journalistic integrity! Why hadn't he seen it happening?

Well, no matter now. It was time to reclaim his independence. Hecklepeck pushed through the revolving door into the front lobby.

Gus Bus kept him waiting at the white-draped table in the executive dining room. He could have had a drink but he waved it away and instead passed the time observing Bussard-Dusay executives eating their lunches. Almost invariably they were alone, most often perusing some report propped up against the condiments. Were they trying to appear conscientious or were they simply unable to find anyone willing to eat with them in the company dining room?

The result was an oppressive silence, the kind that made it difficult to swallow unobtrusively. Maybe that's why there were so many gold drapes, hung to deaden the sound of diners trying to swallow the inedible.

Gus Bus arrived like a sudden wind. Movement and rustling surrounded him. Some of the diners put aside their reports to be ready with a greeting; others dug in deeper, ostentatiously turning pages; waiters bowed; and even the crockery, heretofore oddly silent, clinked and clacked.

Gus stopped at one or two of the tables and murmured something to the executives there before taking the chair opposite Hecklepeck. No sooner had he done so than a drink was placed at his elbow by the same waiter who had waited on them the last time Hecklepeck had lunched with Gus Bus. They were sitting at the same table, toward the back and under what would have been a window were it not draped into oblivion. The table had a good view of the rest of the dining room.

"Ah, the winds of November." Gus raised his glass in greeting. He was once again wearing his coke-bottle glasses. They glinted out of the dark hollow of his chair.

Hecklepeck looked at them with irritation. This was what it was about Gus. The truth could now be told. He always made remarks like that. They were said in an affected, upper-nasal-passage manner that called attention, not to their meaning, but to the fact that they had meaning, *poetic* meaning. The trouble was they hadn't. Gus's utterances were fatuous nonsense, and they left Hecklepeck with no reply except the one he shouldn't make: Cut the crap, Gus.

"Ah, Henry." Gus wasn't waiting for an answer. "Is there a ghost of a chance Miz Jackson made vegetable soup today?"

"Yes suh. She sho' did."

"Hmmm-hmmm. Well, I'll have some of that. How about you Heck? It's mighty good."

Hecklepeck's mouth dropped open. It was the same vegetable soup conversation Gus had had the last time. If he had vegetable soup every day, why did he always inquire about its existence? Or was this some sort of nursery world game—flirting with the idea of no vegetable soup in order to be surprised when it turned out there was some? "Nothing," Hecklepeck was firm. Best to let Gus know from the start that he meant business.

"Nothing? Are you sure? There's some good cream of . . . cream of something soup if you'd prefer it." Gus twisted out of his chair to confirm this with Henry.

The waiter nodded. "Broccoli. Cream of broccoli."

"No! No. I'm not hungry. I'm here because I have to talk to you about something that I view as fairly serious."

"Oh. Well, bring Mr. Hecklepeck some bread sticks, Henry, and some ice tea. Oh, and the vegetable dip platter."

Gus was trying to buy him with cut-up carrot sticks! As if journalists could be bought off that cheaply. The anchorman leaned forward to meet the enemy. "I can't—"

"Rah Rah Ra." It was said in Gus's *meaning here* tone. "Just think, in a week or so we we will be basking in the southern sun. Although . . ."

In November? Basking? More likely rah rah rotting in the winter rains. Not that Hecklepeck would have minded that. It would have increased the challenge. "I'm not going." Did it hurt to say it? Only the slightest twinge.

"What? Well, actually I was going to put it off another week. I have this club. Are we a club? Not really. Just a group of old friends, we all went to Country Day together, that normally meets the third Thursday of every month at the Missouri Athletic Club. We just talk, you know, sort of solve the world's problems." Gus paused while Henry set his vegetable soup in front of him.

"I've invited several members of this informal group to make the trip to New Orleans, but they've indicated to me they don't want to miss the meeting next week. It's a special one, a dinner meeting. The topic of conversation is 'Meritocracy in a Global Marketplace.' I thought I'd wait and raise the Gus Boat's anchor the Saturday afterward. Which would make it a Thanksgiving trip; we could stop for turkey at some port along the way."

At least this time Gus had come up with something besides those souvenir tins stowed in the hold of his boat as an excuse to delay. Hecklepeck was tired of that business. "It doesn't matter to me. I can't go now and I can't go then. I'm not going at all."

"Oh?" Gus was holding his soupspoon in midair.

Hecklepeck resisted the urge to find out what the thick white glob was that passed as vegetable dip. "I can't. It's a question of journalistic integrity. You're too much in-the-news in St. Louis for me to socialize with you. It gives the appearance of tainting, if it doesn't actually taint, my point of view."

"Oh-oh." Hecklepeck could almost see Gus measuring and weighing this turn of events to see what its worth was.

"In fact"—Hecklepeck reached into the pocket inside his suit jacket and pulled out a check.—"I want to reimburse Public Advancement for the gambling cruise tickets and you for the lunch you bought me in September."

"That's not necessary." Gus waved it away. "What do you media people do for friends?"

Hecklepeck tucked the check under the pot full of sugar packets. "There are lots of people to be friends with who don't figure in the news."

"Really?" He could almost hear Gus thinking how odd it was to prefer friendships with nobodies to those with people like himself. "Most media people seem to move around constantly, but you've been here a long time."

But still not long enough to be one of us. Hecklepeck mentally supplied the unspoken thought. Whether it was the snobbery or the reference to his own stagnation, a wave of anger passed over him.

"I don't see why you have to cut yourself off from . . . just because you might do a story on one of us or something."

Hecklepeck leaned forward, taking Gus in with a severe gaze.

This was it. "If the story were inconsequential, maybe not. If it were a matter of a ribbon cutting or two, no problem. Unfortunately what we have here is a serious question about the revenues from the charitable fund-raiser you, as a member of Public Advancement, had a hand in organizing."

"Question? We raised and donated over 80,000 dollars to St. Louis Without Drugs. What can possibly be wrong with that?"

"Nothing, as far as it goes. That 80,000 came from ticket receipts, right? You raised 125,000 from sales of tickets, gave 80,000 to charity, and used 45,000 for expenses."

"Yes, of course." Impossible to see the expression, if there was one, in Gus's eyes, but his long fingers fiddled with his white damask napkin.

"What happened then to the gambling receipts? To the money you had to have taken in for all those gold and silver chips that all those people were betting on all those games? I figure you raised as much or almost as much on the gambling as you did at the door. Where did that money go?"

Gus let go of his napkin. "I wouldn't say we raised that much on the gambling."

"Gus, I was there. Those were very appealing prizes you offered. I saw what people were betting: hundreds of dollars. I did myself. But let's say it added up to only 50,000 dollars. I think that's low, but okay, I ask you again, where did the money go?"

Gus shrugged against the chair upholstery. "Expenses. We had a lot of expenses."

"Expenses? What you're telling me is that you spent more money on the fund-raiser than you gave to the cause you were raising money for?"

There was something pouty about the set of Gus's lips. "You enjoyed yourself, didn't you? I saw you having a good time."

"Yes, to my regret. But I would have had an equally good time without gambling for inscribed silver trays or munching on caviar or listening to half the symphony orchestra perform as well as numerous other musical entertainers. Is that what you spent the money on?"

Gus inclined his head. "And waiters. And costumes. And all the gambling equipment. And the steamboat rental. And . . ."

"Steamboat rental? You charged for that?"

"Well, yes, I had to. My board of directors wouldn't allow me to just lend it, even for a good cause. A matter of precedent and recouping our investment." Henry, the waiter, appeared at Gus's elbow to take the lunch order. Gus ignored him.

"Your board of directors!" Hecklepeck was full of contempt, and his face showed every bit of it. "Your board of directors is the same bunch that makes up Public Advancement, the same cozy little group that put on the fund-raiser. You could have saved that expense, held the fund-raiser at somebody's house. Instead, you voted to pay yourselves. Now tell me. Your board of directors and the one at Tom Honigger's company, Korporate Keepsakes, are one and the same. Am I right?"

"Well, no. Gordon isn't on at Korporate Keepsakes. Neither is Zip Forrest—"

"Yeah, but the similarity is unmistakable, let's face it. And the Korporate Keepsakes board said it had to be reimbursed for all those gold-plated key chains that were handed out at the fund-raiser. Right? Am I right?"

"Board members have to speak up for the best business interests of the corporation. When I sit on the Korporate Keepsakes board I think only in terms of that company's welfare."

"I see. You want me to believe that you handily forget about your own company and about Public Advancement, that quasi-public service organization that has more than once been accused of trying to sway public policy. No. You don't forget. It all works because the interests of all these entities are wrapped in and around each other like spaghetti. And this, this alleged fund-raiser illustrates perfectly the way it all works." Henry was still standing beside Gus's chair, looking into the middle distance to demonstrate that while he couldn't avoid hearing, he understood nothing.

Gus's coke-bottle lenses were directed unwaveringly at Hecklepeck. "We raised 80,000 dollars to combat drug abuse in this community. That's a lot of money. We didn't have to do it at all."

"No, but once you said you were going to do it you had an obligation to do it honestly and not as a profit maker for yourselves. What about all those people who bought tickets and bet money, thinking their money was going to charity. What about the people who donated goods and services to what they thought was a good cause?"

"It was a good party. Nobody complained."

"That's because nobody's figured it out yet."

156

"Your role, I suppose, is to let the world know?"

"Yes, indeed." Hecklepeck stood up.

"How are you going to explain that you were there gratis 500 dollars in complimentary tickets?"

"I'm just going to explain it." Hecklepeck rapped on the table with his knuckle as he spoke. "Everybody acts stupidly once in a while." He walked out of the dining room. As he crossed the middle distance, the corners of Henry's mouth twitched slightly as if a smile were trying to break out.

"Oh, the usual." Gus's voice was peevish.

Henry acknowledged the order and left. His boss reached across the table and picked up Hecklepeck's check. It was for 550 dollars, enough to more than cover the price of the gambling cruise tickets and one lunch. Gus started to tear the check up. Then he thought better of it and slipped it into his jacket pocket.

Outside Hecklepeck absentmindedly did the same with the parking ticket he plucked off his windshield. He got into the car, took hold of the wheel with both hands, and rested his head on it. Something was bothering him. Something amorphous at the back of his mind. Something that had happened during the interview with Gus.

It wasn't the story. Hecklepeck was pleased about that. He had fairly caught Gus and his cronies and, as soon as he shot some visuals, could air their transgressions. They would make a good story, but not a great one. Those guys had always operated that way and they had been caught before, here and there. But the occasional cornering didn't change them or the way they did business. Maybe, possibly, it kept them more honest than they otherwise would have been. Hecklepeck doubted even that. Gus and his friends really believed the rules didn't apply to them.

Hecklepeck also wasn't bothered by his own shortcomings in the affair. True, he had to explain to Turnbull that he wasn't taking a steamboat trip, that he was doing this story instead. But that was all. Turnbull could draw his own conclusions or he could try to dig further. It didn't matter. Self-recrimination being largely unknown to Hecklepeck, his conscience was as light and airy as gauze. He relished the prospect of telling the story to greater St. Louis. He'd do a little commentary at the end about journalistic integrity and being ever-vigilant because even the best, the most experienced, could find themselves on the wrong side of that ill-defined line that must separate the reporter from his subject.

He turned the key in the ignition and pulled out of the parking space, once again scraping the curb and again taking no notice. So what was that niggling at him back there?

Hunger? Was he wanting lunch after the one he had been glad to be unable to eat at Gus's? Yes, but he felt that in an entirely different part of his body. It was not nearly as bothersome as the tug in the back corner of his mind.

All right, he silently declared, anybody with any complaints back there, come forward now. Let's hear them. Driving the car automatically through downtown traffic, Hecklepeck settled back in his leather seat, cleared his mind, and waited for whatever would come up.

Jennifer, as he had last seen her with her eyes flashing and a strand loose from her ponytail. He did feel badly about the fight they had had. It had been his fault; he had gotten too caught up in his self-appointed role as teacher. But when the opportunity arose, he would make it up to her. They would agree that she should have been telling him more about her feelings all along and that he should have inquired more. Of course there it was again: The real problem was words. But if it was troublesome not to be able to get a simple news story across to a viewer, it was really frightening that he couldn't communicate with Jennifer. Another sign of his mid-life affliction, whatever it was all about? Hecklepeck refused to dwell on it.

Getting back on track, what did Jennifer have to do with his lunch with Gus? Her name hadn't come up. Neither had her story, really, only insofar as Gus's cheating on the alleged fund-raiser bore on the deaths of three poverty-stricken boys in Benton Park. There didn't seem to be much of a link there, just Metalcote. Tom Honigger and Metalcote, straddling the fence between one world and the other, supplying gold-plated key chains for the delectation of the very rich and chlorofluorocarbons for the eradication of the poor. Hecklepeck wished he had a more substantial reason to go after the arrogant Honigger but he didn't.

The truck in front of him double-parked, and he stopped behind it, waiting for the traffic to pass so that he could get around. What had Gus said? Rah Rah Ra. Hecklepeck grimaced again over that one. He'd said that it was his right to give a big party and write it off as a fund-raiser. Gus was so blinded by wealth and privilege that he just didn't see what was wrong with that. What was truly amazing was how little he gained by it. How much could he have charged anyway for the use of his steamboat? Twenty thousand dollars? Thirty? Small amounts for him. Bussard-Dussay could have done almost as well by donating the use of the boat and taking a tax deduction. Of course Gus was probably getting his deduction anyway. Having his cake and eating it too.

Just as he had when he asked Hecklepeck to make the steamboat ride with him, thus insuring he'd get publicity for his Gus Boat, and from all appearances at lunch he didn't think it much of a loss.

Well, Hecklepeck had known he was being used for something. He had no illusions about friendship with Gus. Gus's friends were born, not made, and Hecklepeck would have been surprised if there were any exception to the rule. Members of his discussion group had all gone to prep school together. So when they sat down to discuss their relative importance in the world, they could agree on exactly what that was. Just to be sure, they rehashed it once a month anyway: Every third Thursday Gus Bus and his friends met to talk about why they were better than everybody else. Every third Thursday? Every third . . .

The words repeated themselves in Hecklepeck's mind. Third Thursday. That was it! That's what was bothering him. He shoved the gearshift into neutral and hauled on the parking brake. From his breast pocket he took out his wallet, rifling through it so that pieces of paper flew all over the car. He stopped when he got to his pocket calendar.

19

T HEY RAN INTO each other in the station parking lot. "It's going to . . . it could . . . what if it happens again?" gasped Jennifer. "I mean I think there could be another murder."

"I agree. Next week to be exact. November 19th."

"How—"

Hecklepeck pulled out his pocket calendar. "We figured out that all the murders happened on Thursday, but what we didn't see was that each of them happened on the third Thursday of the month. So if there's going to be another murder, and I agree with you it's likely, then it's going to happen next week."

"The third Thursday of the month." Jennifer said the words reflectively as she turned the pages of the calendar. With her finger she located August 20th, September 17th, October 15th, and the upcoming November 19th—all of them Thursdays, each of them the third Thursday of the month. "Why?" She handed the calendar back to him.

"Your guess is as good as mine." For a moment they stared at each other wide-eyed in the glare of this new information.

Jennifer sat on top of the station's two front steps unmindful of the dank cold they had soaked up. "On the third Thursday of the month somebody steals a jarful of refrigerant 113 from Metalcote Inc. Then that person takes it to Benton Park and gives it to young boys with glue-sniffing habits." She shook her head. It sounded so unbelievable when she said it. "They inhale it and die."

"Right. Exactly." Hecklepeck leaned up against the bronze statue that stood in front of the station, that of a female reporter with her

160

microphone outstretched. "The real question is how to use that information."

"We could tell the police." Somehow Jennifer knew they were not going to tell the police.

"We could, but we really don't have anything substantial to go to them with. Besides, this is our . . . your story. Do you really want to give it away, hand it over to the men in blue without a denouement?" Jennifer shook her head. Strangely, she did feel proprietary about the story. What had the police done with it anyway? "Right, so let's see what we've got by way of unanswered questions. Then we can use what we do know to come up with solutions."

"I don't see how anybody could use refrigerant 113 to commit murder because nobody knew it was capable of killing." Jennifer blurted out something that had been troubling her. "Only the people at the company that makes it knew."

"And maybe some industry insiders. Word would have gotten around. But I think you raise a really good point. Maybe . . . may I make a suggestion?" Determined to be considerate, Hecklepeck waited for her nod. "Maybe if we . . . uh, you . . . review some of these guys who could have done it."

"Ben Howell. Pete Cobb. Tom Honigger . . ."

"Hold on. One at a time. Ben Howell. His motive." Hecklepeck propped himself up against the statue with his elbow.

"Assuming he is into sex with young boys, maybe he also likes to kill them. Or, maybe he has to so they won't tell."

"Opportunity?"

Jennifer rummaged through her purse until she found her notebook. "He told me he was home with his wife the night of the third murder, of Jimmie's death, in October. Well, he wasn't sure. There were no engagements for that night marked on his calendar."

"So he could have been wandering through the park."

"Yes, but how would he have known about refrigerant 113?"

"We-ell, he could have heard about it on the street. Didn't you tell me Jimmie knew that the contents of those yellow drums, the chlorofluorocarbons, was bad stuff? Howell could have heard about it from one of his clients. In fact he could have gotten one of his clients to steal the stuff from Metalcote for him. I have to tell you, I like him as a suspect."

"I don't," said Jennifer shortly.

"Who's next?" Hecklepeck was quick to avoid the argument.

"Pete Cobb. He's really weird. He's been sniffing glue for so long he doesn't seem to have much mind left. So I guess he could have gotten refrigerant 113 by mistake when he thought he was filling his jar with tulio."

"Then why didn't he inhale it? Why didn't it kill him?"

Jennifer shook her head. She didn't have a good answer. "He could have offered it to one of the boys first and seen what it did to him. Then after that he would have done it deliberately. Because . . . I don't know . . . because he enjoyed it."

"Or it gave him a sense of power?"

"Maybe. There's something really creepy about Pete."

"Would he know enough to wipe his fingerprints off the jar?"

Jennifer shrugged. "Who knows? Maybe. Everybody knows about fingerprints."

"Tom Honigger." There was a certain relish in Hecklepeck's voice. "He could have heard that refrigerant 113 was lethal through the company he bought it from. But it's hard to see him murdering three insignificant boys by getting them to sniff a jar of the stuff."

"What if he knew the boys were climbing his fence and stealing toluene and he was worried about his company's liability?"

"Yeah but I don't see him handling it that way. Arranging for his wife to dole out a 10,000 dollar grant to Howell is more his style. A payoff that doesn't look like a payoff and doesn't even come out of his own pocket. Howell works to keep the boys out of Metalcote, and there are no inconvenient bodies lying around. But give me an argument. He's far and away my sentimental favorite."

Jennifer sighed. "He couldn't have done it anyway."

"Why not?"

"He was on that steamboat with us the night Jimmie was killed."

"He was, wasn't he? So was his wife." For some reason the vision of Marion Honigger came to Hecklepeck's mind as she had been at the roulette table, focused and mean. "But the boat returned to home port just after nine o'clock. He could have left then and even come back, since the party continued on the waterfront until very late. I don't think I saw either of the Honiggers after we docked."

"Me neither." Another look of shared significance passed between them.

"Of course, if we're reaching for the stars, it would be nice to link Gus Bus up with this mess. Him and his mysterious souvenir coffee and spice tins."

"What?" Jennifer hadn't heard about the tins.

Hecklepeck waved it aside. "It doesn't matter. The closest I can get Gus Bus to Metalcote is passing by on his boat, and he seems to have an alibi for third Thursdays. I'd like there to be a connection, but there doesn't seem to be one. So who does that leave?"

"That's all. No! Frank Sempepos."

"Metalcote plant manager. What do you like about him?"

"I don't know. He was so jumpy when I asked him about chemicals. I had the feeling he was hiding something."

"Something like a chemical that might have been used to snuff out three neighborhood boys."

"Well, maybe. Yes." Jennifer tried the shoe out and it fit. "Like Honigger he could have known about refrigerant 113 from the company where it was purchased."

"What's the motivation?"

That was tougher. "I don't know. He's very proud of Metalcote's security. Maybe he doesn't like it being breached by young boys in search of chemicals to sniff."

"Nyah, weak. But what if Sempepos were supplying glue to the glue-sniffers and decided to retire from the business by killing off clients who could identify him."

Jennifer shook her head. "Those kids couldn't have paid him anything."

"No. No. But what if they performed some service for him, something illegal. Then he would have had to get them out of the way to prevent them from telling on him."

"Like what service?"

"I don't know. Theft ring? Prostitution?" But chronic glue-sniffers did not seem to have the stuff good business partners were made of, even partners in crime. "I know! What if the boys saw something they weren't supposed to see when they broke into Metalcote? Something that might have gotten Sempepos in trouble. So he had to get them out of the way."

"Ehhhh." Jennifer drew in her breath sharply, and her eyes grew big and round, as though inflated. "The flashing light! The flashing light! Oh, my God."

"What, what, what?"

"Don't you remember? When you were piloting the steamboat. There was a light flashing at Metalcote."

Hecklepeck didn't remember. He had been too caught up with steering the boat. "So what?"

"It wasn't just a regular flashing like a warning light. It was like a signal. Oh . . . and then I asked Sempepos about it and he got really defensive. He said it couldn't possibly be Metalcote's light because none of their lights had malfunctioned recently. But the way he said it! He was lying."

"Really." The look on Hecklepeck's face was appraising. Sempepos was the man who had failed to listen to his talk and then dared to ask him about it. A little man in some kind of silky synthetic shirt that had been open several notches at the neck, revealing a mat of black chest hair. Hecklepeck remembered the fur rather than anything about Sempepos's face. He had been standing in that crowd of Rotarians, all waiting to have their word with an anchorman. But that was just it, wasn't it? "Sempepos has an alibi. I met him at the Rotary Club meeting the night the second boy was killed. If he was at the meeting, he couldn't have been over at Metalcote whipping up lethal chemical potions."

"We-ell . . ." Jennifer was unwilling to let Sempepos off so easily. "What time did the meeting end?"

"Ten. After ten, closer to ten-thirty. If only we knew the exact time of death of that second boy."

"Hoyt Jenkins," said Jennifer automatically. "Sempepos came up to you at the end of the meeting, right?" Hecklepeck indicated that he had. "Did you see him—were you aware of him earlier, when the meeting was going on?"

Good question. All Hecklepeck could remember was seeing red because he had to sit through all that interminable Rotarian business before he could speak. Not true. He could recall a face or two in the crowd. The moony, vacuous one. Some guy with red hair and a clashing red face. The man with horse teeth whose clothes were too big for him. "No, I don't remember Sempepos, not until the question and answer period at the end of the meeting, which means—"

"He could have ducked out in the middle and done . . . anything."

"Not anything. But he could have easily gotten to Metalcote, which is only a few minutes away from where they hold the Rotary Club meetings on, I might add, *the third Thursday of the month*. He would have had plenty of time to fill a jar with that mysterious, disappearing chemical, take it to Benton Park, and wait for his victim. Or maybe he prearranged it, agreed to meet the guy there. That would give him time to burn, time for a burger and fries before he had to get back in order to give me his card."

"You think he did that only to prove he'd been at the meeting?" Jennifer hugged her knees. She liked this line of reasoning.

"It's certainly possible. Did you get the impression Metalcote was really out to get some publicity?"

"No. They were uptight when we were there. They wanted to control every shot we took."

"Exactly." It was a verbal flourish. After delivering it, Hecklepeck folded his arms and rested his head on the statue behind him.

Jennifer too was silent in contemplation of the house of cards they had just built. That was just what it was in her view, flimsy and insubstantial. It got them nowhere, not even a footing from which to pull themselves onto firm ground. She expressed her doubts to Hecklepeck.

"Not so, Bucko. We may not have the foggiest idea which of these characters is going around killing people, and it may be somebody who's not on the list we just drew up. But we do know where and when. All we have to do is be there."

"Be where? Metalcote?"

"Yes . . . or Benton Park, since that's where all three of the murders happened. Well, except the first. Mike Cobb was found on the corner, just outside the park."

"Are you suggesting a stakeout? Thursday night?" The idea sent a shiver up from the base of Jennifer's spine.

Hecklepeck *was* suggesting a stakeout. And as he contemplated the logistics of such a thing, an unholy glint, tiny, almost imperceptible, appeared in his eyes. "The trouble is there are two locations that ought to be watched: Metalcote and Benton Park."

That made sense. Refrigerant 113 was stolen from Metalcote and put to its deadly use at Benton Park. "Maybe you could take one and I'll take the other."

Hecklepeck congratulated himself on his diplomacy. He had just been invited to participate. Now for the tough part. He cleared his throat a little in order to deepen the credibility of his voice. "There is something to be said for approaching Metalcote by river, since the flashing light would indicate something is happening on the water-front."

Jennifer looked at her friend with instant suspicion. "Oh, come on."

"I'm serious." The light in Hecklepeck's eyes was glowing more intensely now. He avoided looking directly at Jennifer lest she see it. "How else are we going to get inside? You know better than I do what kind of security they have. Small boys may be able to slip by the guards but not television news crews. On the other hand they probably don't have any guard posts along the waterfront. It's one way to get in and find out what's going on."

"I suppose you have some ideas about how to make this amphibi-ous assault?" Jennifer's tone was as dry as toast.

"Well, yes, a few."

She zeroed in on him with all her woman's intuition. "It's got something to do with that steamboat, doesn't it? Doesn't it? Oh God, you're not going to steal it, are you?"

On William Hecklepeck's face, a blanket of new-fallen snow. "No! Of course not. I was just going to . . . hitch a ride. You know, 'Proud Mary'." He sang the chorus of the John Fogerty song until he caught the expression in Jennifer's eye and stopped singing abruptly. "So, what'll it be, land or sea?"

"I will patrol the park," said Jennifer, a little stuffily.

"With Art. You should take Art with you. And listen to me, Jennifer." Hecklepeck was suddenly very serious. "You maintain a low profile. You are only going to be there to observe, not to get involved. If something starts to go down, you get on the two-way and have someone at the station call the police. We're dealing with a triple murderer here."

"I know." Did she ever! The very thought sent charges that were at once electric and chilling through her. "What about you?"

"I'm going to leave a car by the street entrance to Metalcote so I can come through and join you as quickly as possible, hopefully with the news that somebody was caught in the act stealing refriger-ant 113 with intent to kill. But if not, I'll be able to help you patrol."

Words evaporated into one more long, direct look between them. It expressed excitement. But it also said a lot about worry and the concern that their best-laid plans and joint effort could somehow miss, letting a three-time murderer slip between two sets of fingers.

Suddenly they were both aware of how chilly it was.

"Oh," said Jennifer, "what about Turnbull? He's expecting me to air my series next week. They're about to start promoting it."

"Leave him to me." Hecklepeck stepped away from the statue against which he'd been reclining. "I think I can offer him something that will keep him happy."

20

HECKLEPECK BEGAN BY informing Jim Turnbull he was not going down to New Orleans in the company of Gus Bus. This, he rightly thought, would soften the news director up.

But Turnbull was not one to hand off the advantage. "Oh, why not?" he asked with a complete absence of inflection.

"I . . . ," Hecklepeck cleared his face of anything that wasn't altruistic, "felt I had to step aside in favor of some new information that has come my way."

"O-oh?" On the other side of the glass wall, newsroom employees were getting ready to go home. The six o'clock news had just ended. Not for the first time Turnbull found himself wishing he had the kind of relationship with his employees that would allow him to go out and have a beer with a group of them after work. It would be preferable to going home. Turnbull wondered if he should call up front and see if anyone on his level in sales or promotion wanted to have drinks before going home. The truth was he would have enjoyed newsroom company more.

Hecklepeck was explaining about Gus Bus's fund-raiser and the gambling money that hadn't been reported. At first, lost in his own thoughts, Turnbull didn't take it in. Then it dawned on him that Hecklepeck was talking about doing a story, a real story, not some sort of self-promoting puff piece. He leaned way back in his chair and eyed the anchorman.

To Hecklepeck it felt as if his boss had a pair of high-powered binoculars attached to his retinas. He squirmed a little. "So, I, uh, could have it ready to go for you at the beginning of next week."

"The beginning of next week." Turnbull said it with wonder.

After a year of acting like he was too good to go out and dirty his feet in the reportorial trenches, William Hecklepeck was volunteering to do a story. "The beginning of next week."

What was the matter with the man? This was a simple scheduling matter. "Yeah, next week. I thought it might make a good swap for Jennifer's—"

"So your friend, Gus Bus, is a crook?"

"We-ll, friend . . ." With a gesture Hecklepeck dismissed the word as too strong. Then without a breath he quickly explained why Jennifer's piece had to be postponed, why she needed more time.

This time Turnbull's eyes got wider in spite of himself. "You're telling me that Jennifer thinks these boys were murdered and that she can track down who did it?" Hecklepeck nodded. "That's a . . . good story." Turnbull gazed out into the newsroom as he pondered it. "She can have the extra time, but what is she doing to back herself up next Thursday night? I don't want her to get hurt."

"Oh . . ." Hecklepeck couldn't possibly explain to Turnbull that he was hitching a ride on the boat belonging to the crook he was about to expose. Turnbull just wouldn't have given it his whole-hearted approval. He wouldn't have understood what a favor Hecklepeck was doing for Captain McNiff and his crew, who spent their evenings traveling up and down the same boring stretch of river just to keep themselves in practice. "If I were relieved of my anchor duties, I'm familiar with the story and I could be there to back Jennifer up."

Normally Turnbull would have picked up on the airy vagueness of this. But he was too dumbfounded by what appeared to be Hecklepeck's involvement in not just one but two good news stories. "Yes, well, could be arranged. That's good."

Walking out of the news director's office, Hecklepeck realized he hadn't asked for a photographer. He would need one to record whatever went down at Metalcote next Thursday. Photographers were union employees, who must be paid for overtime work; therefore, they had to be approved by the man in charge of the newsroom budget, Turnbull.

Hecklepeck swung around, intending to go back into the news director's office. But the sight of the man, deep in contemplation of his television monitor on which was rolling an audition tape sent by an anchorman in Tulsa, stopped him dead in his tracks. How was he going to explain to Turnbull that he needed a photographer when he was officially just riding back-up on Jennifer, just trailing around after her in case she needed him?

Turnbull was tight with newsroom money, but he would probably buy the argument that this story merited two photographers. The trouble was Hecklepeck had . . . well, not lied, just omitted the part about the steamboat, and to request a photographer was to get in deeper. Turnbull would be a lot more interested in his movements if he were accompanied by someone with a price tag attached.

Better to make his own arrangements. Hecklepeck scanned the newsroom until he found who he was looking for, Richard Markowitz.

"Little Richard."

Richard barely looked up from his slug sheet, which listed summaries of the day's stories. He was deciding which ones he would like rewritten for the ten o'clock news.

"Richard, I have to come clean with you about the story, Jennifer's story. It's really big."

That got the producer. He looked up, ready to listen. Hecklepeck told him about refrigerant 113 and its possible bearing on the deaths of the three boys. He explained about the third Thursday and the stakeout that he and Jennifer were planning. As he did, the producer's eyes grew wide. "So I was wondering if you could possibly scrounge up some photographic equipment and come along with me to shoot." Richard had started out in the news business as a photographer and had made the switch to producing because it was on the management track. But in doing so he had sacrificed income. Producers were not union employees and they were never reimbursed for extra hours. Hecklepeck knew Turnbull wouldn't care how much work Richard did on his time off.

The producer thought it over. There was a running argument among KYYY's photographers about whether nonunion personnel were even allowed to touch photographic equipment. Some of the shooters said yes, that nonunion members should be allowed to handle it for the purpose of helping them carry it around. But others argued that that kind of behavior was bound to lead to nonunioners actually taking pictures.

Richard knew what the photographers would think of Hecklepeck's proposal, and he knew about the grievance they would surely file. Having once been one of the brotherhood, he sympathized with them. But when Hecklepeck went gonzo, nothing, not union rules or anything, could stop him. Hecklepeck was a powerful drug, a chemical coursing through Richard's bloodstream. He promised altered consciousness and high adventure.

Richard knew one of the photographers was on vacation; it was just a matter of quietly, temporarily appropriating his gear. He could do that and . . . "I'll see if I can't switch schedules with Marta that day. Wow, Heck, do you have any idea who could be pushing this refrigerant 113?"

The anchorman promised to brief him about all of it. All of it except the steamboat. He didn't want to set Richard off on that subject again, and he wasn't altogether sure the producer would keep it quiet.

"I was right; I knew this was a good story," Richard enthused. "It's instinct. The kind of instinct that comes with experience. All this time you've been looking into it. And that steamboat stuff, that was just a cover-up, wasn't it? Hey, man, I've really got to apologize, I really feel bad about saying that you're going through male menopause."

Hecklepeck accepted the apology. What else could he do?

The evening of Thursday, November 19, William Hecklepeck walked up the *Gustavius Bussard*'s gangplank with a load of photographic equipment that clearly lacked organization. Among other things he hugged some stand lights that were dragging their plugs. In one hand he held a jumble of mike cords and other cables. Under one armpit was a tripod.

At the top of the gangplank Captain McNiff saluted. "Welcome aboard."

Hecklepeck dropped the pile of stuff and returned the captain's salute. "Thank you. It's good to be here."

"Aye. A sense of mission. Men engaged in a worthy endeavor. Let me tell you it's a relief after so much aimless wandering." McNiff threw his arms out wide. "There is nothing that does a man's heart more good than some righteous ass-kicking." He brought his fists back to his chest and held them there for a moment before dropping them.

From the bottom of the gangplank came a groan, and both men turned to watch another heavily laden figure struggle up the incline.

This guy had battery belts hanging from both shoulders, as well as a videotape deck. He was clutching a camera. It seemed to obscure his vision in some way, because he felt each step before he took it with the toe of a running shoe.

The *Gustavius* rolled with another kick of the wind, and he almost lost his balance, letting out a low, animal moan. Hecklepeck regarded him with a mixture of fondness and disgust. McNiff looked at him sternly.

Reaching the top of the gangplank at last, he let everything he was holding slide on top of the pile that Hecklepeck had dropped and grabbed the rail.

"Richard Markowitz, Captain James McNiff. He's acting as my photographer tonight."

Richard looked straight at McNiff and announced balefully, "I get seasick."

The captain chuckled. "Well, you be sure and stick to the leeward deck. We weigh anchor promptly at eighteen hundred hours, five minutes." He turned and began giving orders to pull up the gangplank.

"You didn't tell me we were going to be rolling around on some boat," Richard snarled at Hecklepeck.

"If I had, you wouldn't have come."

"Damn straight. Damn straight I wouldn't have come. I don't want any part of these manifestations of your mid-life crisis and, oh yes, you are in the middle of one. You're so sick, so hormone starved, that you bend everything—even a serious story like this one—to fit your fantasy. So, fine! But why did you have to drag me along? It's like being forced to share someone's hallucination. Why couldn't you just tell Turnbull what you were up to and get him to assign you a real photographer? He would have paid the overtime."

"How could I explain to Turnbull that I'm taking a ride on the *Gustavius Bussard* after I just finished exposing its owner for a crook on the five, six, and ten o'clock news shows?"

As it often did at that time of night, the *Gustavius Bussard* pulled away from the waterfront, blowing a sporty blast from its whistle. Richard shuddered a little.

"You'd better get that stuff snapped together," said Hecklepeck. "It won't be too long before you're called on to use it." In reply Richard threw him a look that would have stopped an invasion of masticating army ants.

Hecklepeck walked toward the bow, out of its range, and gazed out over the black expanse of water. This had to be the dream of the boy inside every man. He was riding through the black night to guaranteed adventure. Under his feet the hearty steam engines chugged, fueled with the sweat of the boat's engineer. A cold, damp wind slicked back his hair, and the Mississippi's pong reverberated in his nose. It should have been glorious!

However, Hecklepeck's spirits were not soaring. He was worried. It was easy to blow down other people's concerns with breezy confidence, but for some reason this time he could not quell his own. Somebody who had murdered three children was on the loose out there, probably looking to kill a fourth. Instead of calling in the authorities, prevailing upon Lieutenant Berger to arrange a stakeout of Benton Park (and Berger would have done it for him; Hecklepeck knew that), he had sent one lone novice reporter and an experienced but not overly bright photographer into the breach. These two innocents were circling Benton Park in an unmarked news unit, comfortable in the knowledge that help in the form of William Hecklepeck was just around the corner.

Well, just around a bend in the river. Hecklepeck felt the portable two-way radio in the pocket of his down jacket. And if they called, sent out an SOS, what was he going to do? Swim to their aid? Hecklepeck mentally kicked himself for not having taken a more responsible attitude. Maybe Richard was right about the mid-life crisis business. Maybe it was clouding his judgment, causing him to make decisions that had more to do with his desire to play than with common sense. He should have been circling Benton Park in another unmarked news unit. At least that way if Jennifer needed him, he'd be able to help her.

Hecklepeck shoved his hands deep into his pockets and headed up to the pilothouse. It couldn't be helped now; the best he could do was try to hurry things along.

"We're just below the Poplar Street Bridge." McNiff pointed to his chart. "Just passed mile 179 and headed down to just below 177. Now which of these companies along here are we going to?"

Hecklepeck bent over the chart until he located the triangular symbol that represented Metalcote's dock. "Here. A company called Metalcote."

"Metalcote? Metalcote you say?" In spite of his muttonchop

whiskers and florid complexion, McNiff was a man to be reckoned with. "Well, now that's a coincidence. I've been there before."

"You have?"

"Oh, yes. Oui, oui. That's where we took on those bloody tins."

"Whaaat? Those souvenir tins of Gus's? You picked them up from Metalcote?" Hecklepeck didn't know why he hadn't thought of it before. Of course, Gus Bus would have had his souvenirs made by his good friend Tom Honigger's company, Korporate Keepsakes. But why had he lied about it, insisting that he was picking the tins up in New Orleans instead of in St. Louis at Metalcote? Here it was, another mysterious link with Metalcote. Hard to come up with a motive, but Hecklepeck mentally added Gus Bus to the list of murder suspects he and Jennifer had drawn up. At the very least Gus was someone to watch.

McNiff was looking at him like he too was making the same connections. But of course he couldn't be. Hecklepeck had given him only the most general outline of his investigation. If something went wrong, better McNiff shouldn't know what he was a part of. "Almost didn't get out tonight. Gus Bus was over in the afternoon with some of his corporates, asking questions. Liability. Tax stuff. Didn't think he was going to let me go." McNiff delivered this as if it had significance. Then he abruptly turned back to the chart. "This makes it easy. I know that water now, can get up close enough to kiss a girl standing on the bank."

"I don't want to get that close." Hecklepeck was slightly alarmed.

"Don't worry. Calmez vous. We'll set down several hundred yards out. You and that, uh, photographer of yours can go the rest of the distance in one of the lifeboats. I'll have some of the crew ferry you over."

"Thank you. I really appreciate this." The new worry-burdened, chastened Hecklepeck did not ask to pilot the boat. Tonight he was the investigative reporter, and McNiff, the steamboat captain.

"Oh, ree-anh, ree-anh. Pas de too. Pas de too." McNiff was full of relish.

The lights in the KYYY newsroom always seemed brighter at night even though there were no windows. Darkness seeped through the concrete walls as if the big, messy room could feel the hour. Turnbull could, anyway, as he wandered among the desks.

He was driving the nighttime assignment editor crazy. Not that she wasn't used to having Turnbull around. The news director often spent his evenings in his office doing something or other. But at those times he was "under glass" and she didn't feel bothered by him.

Tonight he was right there, treading heavily among the desks and touching things. He wasn't saying much. The nighttime assignment editor had tried several times to engage him in conversation in the hopes that he would be impressed and get the idea to move her onto days. But his answers were so noncommittal that she got the idea he didn't find her worthy of notice, and her discomfort grew.

The nighttime assignment editor's worthiness had not even entered into Turnbull's calculations. What occupied him was solely a matter of responsibility, his own for his employees. He had met Jennifer's father when he had come to visit her once. Allan Burgess was a protective, even a doting parent.

He would never allow a daughter of his to hang out in a dangerous slum area after dark. He would never understand why Turnbull had allowed it. But Turnbull had hired Jennifer to be a reporter. True, he had had the morning news in mind, that and some feature reporting, cute stuff that would keep her well out of trouble. However, if Jennifer showed the desire and, more importantly, the ability to tackle harder news, wasn't he obligated to let her go? Sure, not only for her sake, not even primarily for her sake, but in the interest of emergent truth.

The trouble was Turnbull kept imagining having to explain to Jennifer's doting father if something were to happen. For that reason he was going to stay as close to the two-way radio as he could. If the cry went out for help, he wanted to be there and be sure it was handled right.

Turnbull rounded the corner of a desk and shuffled some papers that were sitting on top of it. He did have one consolation, and that was the knowledge that William Hecklepeck, experienced investigative reporter, was out there with Jennifer. Hecklepeck could get to her quickly if the need arose.

It was Art who pressed the automatic door lock. Jennifer hadn't thought of it but she was glad he had. She felt safe inside the car. The white noise of the fan and the cozy warmth that emanated from the car heater seemed to place her in a protective metal cocoon.

They were circling Benton Park, driving along Jefferson Avenue. The park was dark in contrast to the well-lit street and it looked vast. Jennifer suddenly realized how hopeless her task was. She somehow had to be in the right place at the right time to see somebody sneaking over the grass with a jar full of chlorofluorocarbon. The odds against that were formidable

Given the traffic and the traffic lights she couldn't get around the park's periphery fast enough to catch anyone who slipped into the park. And once there, obscured by the gloom, that person could kill half a dozen little boys while Jennifer continued circling uselessly.

She bit her lip. That didn't cut it. Somehow she had to find a way to ensure that Jimmie's murderer was caught. It was the least she could do for the boy who had been so seduced by her TV camera. She absolutely owed him that much.

"Hey, look at that guy," Art hissed as he pulled up to the traffic light. A man in a tan raincoat was coming toward them, out of the park. "He looks like Ben Howell."

Jennifer squinted at the square figure in the raincoat. It did look like Howell. But they were too far away to be sure of anything. "He's going in the wrong direction. Anyway, he doesn't have a jar."

"Maybe he's done it already and tossed the jar. Do you want me to follow him?"

Jennifer shook her head. "I think we'd better stick with the park. It's too early. There are still a lot of people walking around on their way home from work." But she wasn't sure of the timing either. She and Hecklepeck had discussed it. They didn't know at what hour the three boys had been killed. They assumed it wasn't too late in the evening because even these boys would not have been wandering the streets in the early morning hours. But that still left a long stretch of time—Jennifer looked at her watch—between the current 6:25 and midnight. Five and a half hours to be vigilant in.

"How do you know that guy . . . Howell . . . didn't already find a dark, quiet corner of the park and murder somebody? How do you know that woman over there didn't do it?" Art put his camera finger down on what was wrong with their assignment.

Jennifer sighed. He was right, right, right. What she was praying for was that something would catch her eye. But there was no guarantee of that, and if another boy was killed because they were circling the wrong part of the block or because the murderer slipped by them, she would never be able to live with herself again.

Art made the turn onto Arsenal Street while Jennifer scanned the park from the new angle. "Do you want me to go around again?" Art was showing a photographer's unwillingness to waste time on a project that wouldn't sit with his common sense.

"No, stay straight on this and let's take a run past Metalcote." Hugging herself anxiously, Jennifer did not take her eyes away from the panorama outside her window. Nor did she stop searching when they left the park behind them. She scrutinized all pedestrians, peered into dark doorways and down dark alleys, looked down along the base of the great brewery wall. All the time she willed Jimmie's murderer to appear so she could identify him and cut a long, tense vigil short.

As they rounded the corner onto Second Street, where Metalcote was, she saw Hecklepeck's car parked by the curb. "Jesus, he left his Porsche down here." Art was astounded. "And he thinks it's going to be here in one piece when he comes to get it? He's crazy."

Jennifer was not interested in the fate of Hecklepeck's car. She was glad to see its familiar metallic gleam because it meant she wasn't alone in her responsibility for the safety of one unknown little boy, a boy who was even now on the path that would take him to a rendezvous with a murderer. Jennifer shuddered and hugged herself tighter.

Where was Hecklepeck anyway? Out on the river somewhere, playing steamboat captain. Why hadn't she insisted he keep his feet on the ground?

Art pulled the car up in front of the factory's gates. "That's funny." He pointed. "That small gate, the people gate, it's open." It was. In the light of several big security spotlights that lit up the entrance to Metalcote Jennifer could see it was wide open. On the other hand, the big chain-link gate, the one that swung open to admit vehicular traffic, was closed. It was kept that way by a heavy, padlocked chain. "I don't get it. They're so paranoid about security here."

Jennifer looked up at the guard shack. The light inside was on. She waited awhile to see the figure of the guard pass by the window. None did. She turned to Art and, although there was nobody to hear, whispered, "Where are the guards?"

He shook his head. "I don't see any."

Y E GODS! SACREY blooo . . ." McNiff peered out the window of his pilothouse.

"Yes," breathed Hecklepeck beside him, "yes, yes, yes."

In the corner Richard groaned. He had come inside to get out of the wind, but being in an enclosed space was not having a salutary effect on his stomach.

On the right-hand shoreline, where the Army Corps of Engineers chart placed Metalcote, a blinking light had appeared. McNiff squinted at it. "A. . . . X. . . . B. . . . T. . . . M . . . Whatever that's all about, it's not Morse. If it's anything, it's some private code."

"Maybe the light is just malfunctioning." But Hecklepeck knew better.

"Nope. A malfunctioning light would flicker or, you know, falter. That baby's sending a message to someone."

The two men peered into the darkness. They had been on the verge of excitement since the boat ride started, and now the adrenaline began to pump in earnest. To Hecklepeck it felt as if the steady throb of the steam engines had moved inside his body. Jennifer had been right! There was a light. She had seen it flashing on one third Thursday, and here it was again on another third Thursday. Could that be coincidence? No! sang out Hecklepeck's soul. But simultaneously his mind questioned the relationship between the light and three murdered boys. Was this some kind of diversion or were the two connected?

"Lookee that. Message received." McNiff pointed downriver, where running lights foretold the approach of another boat. "Looks like a tug with a barge. Hmmmph, only one." Hecklepeck was impressed at the captain's acumen. All he could discern was lights on the water. "What we'll do," McNiff swung toward him, "is continue downriver aways. Then we'll swing around and head up, but closer to shore. At that point we will see what we will see and make a decision about how you're going to board 'em. Sacrey bloo, my old shoe. This smells a lot like a contraband situation." McNiff's eyes all but glowed in the dark. The old DEA agent, a catlike creature, was coming out in him.

"Contraband? Like what? Drugs?"

"Could be drugs. Could be objects of some kind that Mr. Metalcote doesn't want to pay customs duty on."

"Like stuff for the company to electroplate?"

"Ay-ah or les objets for resale."

From Richard's corner came another groan. Something in the tone rang a warning bell with McNiff. "Boy! Get yourself outside. That side, out of the wind, and pull yourself together. We've got a night's work in front of us." The captain's voice was sharp, and even in extremity Richard recognized that it had to be obeyed. He stumbled out the door.

He would never know how much time he spent kneeling at the rail feeling horribly sick but also betrayed and kicked by his erstwhile friend, Hecklepeck. It was enough time to plot every conceivable nasty kind of revenge. At some point the boat changed course and the wind came around into his face. A short time after that Richard felt better.

He got unsteadily to his feet, a little surprised to find that his knees held, and stumbled back into the pilothouse, out of the wet air.

McNiff and Hecklepeck were behind the wheel just as they had been when he had left them. But now McNiff was holding a big pair of binoculars in front of his eyes. "Activity on the dock. But you know, that barge is empty. They're not unloading anything."

"Let me see. Let me see." Hecklepeck applied the binoculars to his own eyes. "No. They're loading. They're putting those barrels on the barge."

"Barrels?"

"Like 55-gallon drums." Hecklepeck swung around while handing the binoculars back to McNiff. "Richard! Did you bring the telephoto?"

Richard pulled his down jacket around so that the zipper was in the front. "Ye-es."

"Why don't you get hooked up and see if you can get some pictures of that activity there on the dock." Hecklepeck pointed off to the left front of the boat.

"It's pretty far away." But Richard was feeling better without the contents of his stomach, and he began to contemplate the possibilities of shooting the dock. "I could get something probably. It would be indistinct but something . . ."

"Try." Hecklepeck turned back to the captain. "Well? What are they doing?"

"I'd say it wasn't drugs. They'd be smuggling those in, not out."

"Then what?"

"Contraband of some sort." McNiff was guessing. "Something they want to ship out through New Orleans without paying taxes or duty."

"Like what? Gold-plated bullets?"

"No, mon a-me. There's no army in the world that can afford them."

"Okay, how about electronic circuitry?" Hecklepeck was serious this time. "Protected technology, maybe, that's not supposed to leave the country."

"Touchez." The two men looked at each other like wide-eyed children just offered a lollipop.

"There's only one way to find out."

"Board them as they lie!"

"Yeah. How do we go about that?"

"I'll bring the boat around. We'll head down below this Metalcote and then come up again, a leg nearer to shore. In the meantime we'll prepare to launch a lifeboat or two. When we get back, just above the plant, we'll throw her into neutral, weigh anchor, and some of the crew can take you ashore." McNiff began issuing orders over a telephone.

Hecklepeck returned to contemplation of the dock scene at Metalcote, which was now almost behind them, and tried to come up with a plan. Previous speculation had taken him to the area where the barrels were stored and a single murderer could be tapping out a jarful of refrigerant 113. He would be so cowed at the sight of Hecklepeck and a TV camera—Richard being the camera's legs—that he would fall down and confess.

Instead there was all this activity at Metalcote's dock, at least three people engaged in the loading of barrels and maybe a tugboat captain. The murderer might be part of that crew or he might be a solitary operator skulking in the shadows. No way to tell. But either way the opposition was formidable: a minimum of four people and all of them criminals to some degree or other, which meant they probably packed guns. Far from being intimidated, they were likely to consign Hecklepeck, his camera, and its legs to the bottom of the river.

The better part of valor, Hecklepeck decided, was to call in the police.

What Richard saw through the viewfinder was upside down and an indistinct gray. Images were always upside down in the viewfinder, but he had no idea what kind of picture he was getting, he shot so infrequently. It was going to be shaky for sure. Given his own trembling and the motion of the boat, he couldn't possibly keep the camera steady.

All of a sudden the picture in the viewfinder slid out of view and the eyepiece filled with black. Richard knew he was seeing the dark expanse that was the river. He cursed. The damn boat was coming around again. They'd just done that ten minutes ago. Now he had to pick up everything and schlepp around to the other side again.

He picked up the camera and lurched around the stern of the boat. Richard had come down to the lowest deck to get a head-on shot of the activity at Metalcote, and as he walked forward he noticed activity up ahead along the rail. Two lifeboats were suspended from the side of the boat and from all appearances were in the process of being launched.

For one awful moment Richard knew the steamboat was going down and the order had been given to abandon ship. But then as he heard the steam engines assertively power down, the truth came to him in an even more horrible flash. The crew wasn't abandoning anything except him and Hecklepeck. They alone were going to be set adrift in one of the open boats, and if they survived as far the shoreline they . . . Well, it didn't matter, they wouldn't survive. This was Hecklepeck's idea, Richard knew it, his idea of adventure, of testing his aging abilities against the elements. Richard could have killed him for it.

As these dark thoughts ran through his mind, Hecklepeck and

Captain McNiff came around the stern end of the boat. "As soon as we're launched, you call the cops," Hecklepeck was saying before he got within the range of Richard's hearing. "You can tell them—"

"Don't worry. I know how to pique their interest." The gleam in McNiff's eyes once again revealed his DEA agent soul. "Those boys will be there in force. I just wish I could be in on the kill too."

"You've got to stay with the ship?"

"Aye-ah. But you take good pictures for me."

"Yep," said Hecklepeck, reaching Richard's side. "This is the man who will do it." He clapped Richard on the back. McNiff looked at him dubiously. A crewmember approached carrying two life jackets.

"Do you . . . do you . . ." Richard sputtered, "expect me to go in one of those . . . of those boats?"

"You'll be okay. There's less chance of getting seasick there than here on the big boat." Hecklepeck took one of the two life jackets and put it on.

"I'd rather be seasick than swamped in the Mississippi. I'm not going."

"Richard, you have to. I need you to shoot."

"Shoot it yourself."

"Son," McNiff's voice was quiet but it was deadly with authority, "this isn't a game we're playing here. It's serious work and each one of us has a role to play. We may not like our roles, but the success of the operation depends on our playing them out. Now you are under my orders to get into that lifeboat and shoot everything that moves."

There was something about the captain that could not be disobeyed. Richard found himself automatically getting into his life preserver. Nor did he protest when two crewmembers lowered him into the bow of the open boat. He hunched miserably over his camera as the boat descended to water level, trying to take some consolation in the fact that at least he and Hecklepeck were not setting off alone. Three crewmen were on board the lifeboat, and clearly it was going to be their job to propel the thing safely through the water with those long oars.

In addition, a second lifeboat had been lowered and seemed to be hovering in the distance behind them. It too should have made Richard feel better, safer, but instead it impressed upon him that their mission was really dangerous. Not some macho fantasy of

Hecklepeck's but something McNiff and his crew were taking seriously. Richard looked over at the lit area of the shoreline. He had been so preoccupied with shooting them that he had not stopped to wonder what those men there were doing.

Turnbull came around the outside edge of the desk and started down the newsroom again. He wished the nighttime assignment editor would get off the two-way radio. But she was trying to help her crew find the home of an economist who had agreed to do an interview about St. Louis's unemployment figures, which had come out that day. Turnbull appreciated the fact that she needed the story. It was a slow, quiet news night.

But he wished she would leave the radio free for Hecklepeck and Jennifer. So far there had been nothing. Not a crackle. Turnbull was worried. With each aching minute he got more worried. But he wouldn't pick up the radio receiver and call them. That would have violated the trust he tried to put in his employees. They had gone out to do a job, and they had to be left alone to do it.

Turnbull had never been a reporter; he had walked straight into management. But he respected reporters and what they did. Each one of them he sent out into the field took a piece of him. When they came back with a good story, Turnbull claimed a share of the glory for himself. He felt he deserved it for letting his people follow their instincts and not tying them down to consultant-approved news material.

So far, in all his years of news directing, no one had gotten hurt pursuing a story. But Turnbull knew how he'd feel if they did.

He came around the desk at the far end of the newsroom. The nighttime assignment editor had hung up the two-way. Now she folded both her hands on top of her desk as if to show him that she wasn't up to anything.

Turnbull looked at his watch for the hundredth time. It was almost eight o'clock.

22

T HERE WERE NO guards along the river, but Metalcote had continued the chain-link fence. It was not too dark an evening for Hecklepeck to see that. From the stern of the lifeboat about twenty feet out, he estimated the fence was nine to twelve feet tall, growing out of a concrete embankment.

Hecklepeck looked downstream in the direction of the light. He and Richard had to disembark on Metalcote property, but well out of sight of the men on the dock. Not that those guys, who were in any case busy loading the barge, could see much beyond the circle of illumination, but Hecklepeck did not want to take any chance of being caught. The other difficulty was to find a place where they could land.

"What do you think?" Hecklepeck asked the crewman in charge.

"I think you're going to have to go over the fence, sir. We can drift down a little further, but I wouldn't want to risk much more."

"Well, it wouldn't be any problem for me," he said, giving the impression that Richard would have trouble. What Hecklepeck was really worrying about was the camera. "Do you have any rope?" The crewman nodded. "Okay, let's tie up here." The crewman passed the word down to his fellow crewmembers, who nimbly and silently set about making the lifeboat fast to the fence at the bow and the stern. "Tell Richard to pass the camera and recorder down here."

Richard regarded the chain-link fence with some relief. They couldn't land here; they couldn't land at all. They'd have to pack it in and go back to the *Gustavius Bussard,* mission unaccomplished. It was too bad, of course. A good story, but good stories didn't always pan out. Richard looked at the chain-link fence and whistled "Whistle a Happy Tune" under his breath.

Then came the request to pass down the camera and recorder. "Why?" he asked, instantly suspicious. "What's he want them for?" Picking up the recorder and pulling on it, the crewman said he didn't know. "Wait, wait, wait, wait." Richard unhooked the recorder from the camera and let it be conveyed away. Similarly he yielded the camera, but he looked down the dark boat after them, his worry returning.

Hecklepeck took off his life jacket and wrapped it around the recorder, weaving the ties in and around before tying them in secure knots. Satisfied that the recorder was secure, he looked around. "Tell Richard I need his life jacket."

The crewman transmitted the message. "Nooo!" shrieked Richard sotto voce. "I need it to go back with. I can't go back in an open boat without a life jacket." He held on to the life jacket with both hands.

"You're not going back," whispered the crewman, who simply began to unfasten the life preserver.

"Yes I am. Yes I am. Where else is there to go?" Richard tried to brush his hands away.

The crewman nodded toward the fence. "There."

"Over the fence? No. No way." Richard stood up to voice his objections to Hecklepeck.

The crewman pulled him down again. "You don't stand up in a boat."

"Well, I need to get to . . . to talk to *him*."

"Stay low and as close to the center of the boat as possible." The crewman steered Richard toward Hecklepeck, glad to be able to deliver the life jacket, especially with Richard still in it.

Lurching with the motion of the boat, Richard fell onto the seat next to Hecklepeck. "Are you crazy? We can't go over that fence. What do you want to do? Set us up to be picked off the top like sitting ducks?"

"I haven't got time to argue with you, Richard. Give me your life jacket."

"No. I'm going back to the boat." Just because some deep-seated self-hatred had made him accede to all the anchorman's wishes in the past didn't mean he had to now. It was never too late to learn to love yourself.

"There's no danger here. Nobody can see us go over the fence. It's too dark. And once we get to the other side, the police will be there."

"The police?" Like many children of the sixties, Richard had no use for the police unless he needed them. Now he needed them. "Why didn't you tell me that?"

Hecklepeck finished bundling up the camera in Richard's life jacket. "Okay, go ahead."

"Go ahead?"

"Climb over the fence." Richard's face must have shown the dismay he felt. "You can do it. Give me the battery belt. That's heavy. We'll steady the boat so that you can get a good footing. Then all you have to do is climb. Just like when you were a kid."

Thinking that his self-hatred must be running very deep at the moment, Richard stood up, unbuckled the battery belt, and handed it to Hecklepeck. The crew directed him to the center of the boat. On either side of him they grabbed the chain-link fence and held on, thus providing a relatively steady platform from which Richard could take his first big step to the top of the concrete wall in which the fence was set. He grabbed the fence with both hands, counted to three, and hauled himself up.

From there it was just a matter of getting his toes securely into the holes in the fence and pulling himself up step by step. As he dug his toes in, Richard was thankful for his running shoes, not that anybody had told him to wear them. He hoisted himself up, keeping his eyes on the fence top and telling himself to forget there was anything underneath him.

He reached the top quicker than he had expected and for a moment dithered about the best way to go over without losing his balance. But the right order of hands and feet and rights and lefts seemed to come to him out of the mists of his past. He got over, climbing down the far side with ease.

On the ground again Richard raised his fists like a prizefighter in victory, and the crew responded in kind. Hecklepeck was already beginning his climb.

Richard was amazed how lithe he was for a tall man. And an older man. At forty-six, wasn't he supposed to have prostate problems or something? Hecklepeck had the added handicap of the battery belt around his waist. He also had a rope tied around his torso above the belt. It dangled into the boat behind him.

He climbed to the top of the fence with the same assurance with which he anchored the news and swung himself over the top. But instead of descending, he dug himself in there.

Richard quickly realized why. From the top of the fence Hecklepeck was carefully pulling up the life-preserver-encased recorder. It hit several times against the fence but, given the protection of the life jacket, could not have been hurt.

Hecklepeck balanced the equipment briefly on top of the fence while he shifted his position in order to lower it to Richard. Richard understood without being told that he was to unload the recorder and send the life preserver back to the boat.

The same method was used with the camera. After Hecklepeck returned the life preserver it was packaged in, he dropped the rope into the boat and climbed down on Richard's side of the fence.

Richard had gotten a lift from his successful negotiation of the fence. But now as the lifeboat cast off, the quiet fell like a lead blanket. He felt abandoned and foredoomed.

Hecklepeck looked around them. They were on some kind of blacktop, a roadway, he judged, that perhaps went around the outer perimeter of Metalcote along with the fence. On the other side of the blacktop was the dark wall of a building. Hecklepeck had no doubt that if they followed the road they would come to the dock.

But the activity at the dock, as intriguing as it was, wasn't his main objective. He had to first find the barrels of refrigerant 113 and position himself or perhaps Richard to keep an eye on them. After that he would be free to investigate the dock. "We'll follow this road until we get past the end of the building," he whispered cheerily. "Then we'll duck off and try to work ourselves around to where we can see what's going on."

Richard was looking at the taping equipment lying at his feet. He felt like crying. He was supposed to pick all that up and stumble through the dark with it into . . . what? Discovery and certain death.

Hecklepeck put a hand on his shoulder. "If you can manage the tape recorder"—It was the least awkward of the two pieces of equipment.—"I'll get the camera. Richard, you're doing great."

They each picked up their equipment, Richard feeling better for the sympathy. As they started down the road, Hecklepeck was thankful that the night was not that dark, since he hadn't thought to bring a flashlight.

In the distance the pink haze of civilization was visible—almost, it seemed, within reach. But Hecklepeck knew how far they were from stepping out onto the city streets. They could not go back the way they had come, and there was no way out of the Metalcote jungle until the police came to the rescue. Hecklepeck could only hope that whatever McNiff had told the police would be enough to get them moving.

If so, the police would take care of the four or however many men were on the dock. But what sent shivers up his spine was the possibility of unexpectedly stumbling into someone else, someone who had already murdered three young boys and was looking to do so again. While the movement of the group was confined to the circle of light around the dock, a free-agent murderer could be slipping silently among the shadows, mayonnaise jar in hand. He could be anywhere.

The sound of their footsteps on the blacktop suddenly seemed alarmingly loud. Hecklepeck had to resist the impulse to break into a sprint; he was better off taking it slow, measured, and quiet. Richard obviously had the same urge. He kept speeding up and then slowing down again to Hecklepeck's pace before racing again.

When they reached the end of the building, Richard, tape recorder slung over his shoulder, launched himself at it and hugged the painted cinder block, his arms spread wide while his right cheek rested on the cool surface.

Hecklepeck peered around the corner. He guessed the building whose shelter they were taking was the main Metalcote plant Jennifer had described. "We'll walk down here along the side of the building."

Richard inched his body to the building edge. "There's a light down that way."

"Yeah. A security light. But it's pretty dim, and if we stay in the shadow of the building, we'll be all right. My guess is that most, if not all, activity, is down around that dock." Richard was rubbing his cheek in little circles against the cinder block. He didn't ask what the activity was that wasn't at the dock.

Hecklepeck wished he still smoked cigarettes and had one to smoke. It would allow him to stay where he was until the cigarette was finished. Cigarettes had been useful that way. As it was, he had to use his intuition to discriminate between a rest period and reluctance to get on with it.

He stared down the way they were about to go. No activity there.

Unless . . . no, that was just the shadowy flicker of something in the breeze. If he waited long enough no telling what he'd see crawling around down there. "Come on." Hecklepeck picked up the TV camera and pulled Richard around the corner.

Finding himself suddenly exposed and vulnerable, Richard backed as far as possible into the wall of the building and proceeded sideways with his back against it as if he expected at any second to be rained on with automatic weapon fire. Not as dramatic, Hecklepeck too was careful to stay close to the building, well in its shadow. On the other side of the concrete walkway from the building was some sort of storage area for large equipment, a forklift, some trucks. Hecklepeck scrutinized them carefully. They made such good hiding places.

After about fifty yards, they came to a flight of steps leading to a doorway into the plant. Hecklepeck pushed Richard down behind the steps and surveyed the situation. The big equipment was silent. In an open, dimly lit area in front of them was a sea of 55-gallon drums.

"Bingo," Hecklepeck breathed. *This* was where somebody would come to fill up a mayonnaise jar with refrigerant 113. *This* was where they had to set up surveillance. He carefully scanned the yellow and white barrels for signs of activity and discerned none.

Looking to his right Hecklepeck saw a boxcar, probably on a spur line. Above it he could see the top of the omnipresent chain-link fence. At two o'clock was a building, presumably the office building Jennifer had described. If so, the guard tower was on the other side of it. Crucial questions: Where were the security guards?, Did they make rounds?, and How often? Hecklepeck watched for a few moments and saw no movement that could be attributed to the guards.

He turned his attention to ten o'clock beyond the barrels. There was movement there all right, largely obscured by some low buildings. But in the gap between them, Hecklepeck could see men passing. Whatever they were doing was quiet. He could hear nothing, not even the sound of voices, but maybe he was still too far away.

If . . . if they could get to the other side of the barrels and hunker down behind one of those low buildings, they could maybe kill two birds with one stone: watch the barrels and at the same time spy on the men at the dock.

Getting there was the trick. The odds were formidable. The guards had to be somewhere, there were men down on the dock, and someplace was the guy with the mayonnaise jar. Funny how menacing something as mundane as a mayonnaise jar could become. Hecklepeck had to remind himself that the jar's ability to kill depended on the willing cooperation of the victim. No way could anybody force him to take a whiff of refrigerant 113. Yet the image of the phantom with the jar did not lose its creepiness.

"We have to get over there," Hecklepeck whispered to Richard. "The trick is to stay down as low as possible and get as much shelter from the barrels as you can."

Richard threw him a look that said, *you're telling me?* But for once he didn't verbally object. He was past that. Instead Richard hugged the tape recorder with both arms. With only a moment's contemplation and no warning to Hecklepeck he suddenly sprinted out behind the barrels, bent well over at the waist.

Hecklepeck hung back. No point in them both taking the risk at once. Watching . . . watching to the right where the guards presumably were, to the left where the dockmen were, and all over among the barrels for the wild card with the jar. Was that . . . ? No, nothing. Nothing stirred, and Richard reached the shelter of the shed on the opposite side, the safety of the shadows.

Metalcote seemed almost too quiet, too deserted. Hecklepeck hadn't seen even a hint of a security guard. Shouldn't they be making some kind of rounds soon? he asked himself uneasily. No way to know; he just had to risk it. He let out some air, transferred the camera to his right hand, and ran with it, crouching low among the yellow and white barrels. Expecting at any second to hear a voice or feel a hand on his shoulder, he too met with no opposition.

He came into the shadow with a sigh of relief and for some reason squeezed Richard's shoulder. They had made it! It felt safe in the dark of the shed; they could now see what they needed to see without being detected. "Hook up the camera," he whispered. "I need you to stay here and keep an eye on the barrels. If you see anybody, shoot. I'm going to reconnoiter a little."

Richard quietly moved around some empty barrels that were standing on their ends. He hooked the camera to the tape recorder and took up a position with the barrels all around him. He was protected and had space for shooting.

Meanwhile Hecklepeck worked his way to the edge of the shed

and peered around it. The light was so bright compared to what he was used to that it made him blink. When his eyes cleared, he saw that the men still had a few barrels to load onto the barge, and they were doing it as carefully as if each one contained something either very fragile or very unstable. Hecklepeck supposed that electronic circuits were delicate. He liked his theory about selling protected technology to foreign governments. But the truth was the barrels looked more like chemical drums than packing barrels. Why would Metalcote be clandestinely shipping out chemicals?

The question was absorbing. So absorbing that Hecklepeck stopped looking back over his shoulder. He and Richard had come so far he failed to remember they were still in a Bermuda Triangle of risk.

"Don't move!" The voice at Hecklepeck's back was low but commanding. Hecklepeck froze. This was what he hadn't wanted to happen! He had hoped to lay low until the police were on the scene and his safety and Richard's could be assured. Oh, how he had hoped that. Now . . . well, it depended on who was behind him. If it was a security guard, maybe they would just be tossed off the premises. But if it was one of the men on the dock or the man with the jar or both working together, they were in serious jeopardy. They could simply disappear and the authorities would never know. Not until later, when they talked to McNiff, *if* they talked to McNiff.

"Spread your arms out wide." Hecklepeck did, wondering if the owner of the voice had discovered Richard too.

Behind him he could hear a whispered conversation. There were two of them, and one of them moved. More whispered conversation. "Turn around."

Hecklepeck delayed for assessment. Could he gain something by not complying? Some element of surprise maybe? No, he was more likely to be shot in the back. By inches and fractions of inches he turned around. At least he could show these people there was fight in him, that he would go down with his boots on.

On the other side Hecklepeck found himself face to face with two members of the St. Louis city police special operations branch, each with a gun pointed in his direction. They looked as surprised as he felt. One of them lowered his weapon in disgust. "What are you doing here?"

Hecklepeck shrugged. "Well, you know. News."

"Got a tip from someone, hey?" The policeman was young and trying to be uncompromisingly tough. Perhaps it was his blond hair that brought Hitler Youth to mind.

"You might say that." Hecklepeck did not feel it necessary to divulge that he was the source of the tip the police had received.

The second policeman, slower and more thoughtful, dropped his gun and leaned over to whisper in the ear of his companion, "This thing came down so fast he could only have gotten the word from one of the higher-ups."

"Yeah?"

"So we'd better not mess with him."

"Yeah. Oh, yeah." The first policeman suddenly and deliberately dropped the tension in his shoulders and, under his breath, cleared his throat. "Okay, but you stay behind us. We don't want you to get hurt."

"Thanks. I don't want to get hurt either."

Hecklepeck sidled up to the policemen with a now-that-I'm-in-on-the-secret swagger. "What's the plan?" This wasn't so bad. He'd been discovered by the good guys. And they hadn't found Richard, so he was still keeping watch over the barrels. Things could yet work out.

"We've got that dock area surrounded. When the signal is given, we close in."

Hecklepeck nodded sagely and tried to think of a way to frame another question. He was handicapped having no idea what McNiff had told the police to get them there and at the same time not wanting to divulge the real reason he himself was there. Adding to that his essential ignorance about what was really happening on the dock, there didn't seem to be any point of departure for discussion.

The young, tough policeman swung toward him, his red-rimmed eyes burning. "You got here first? You seen any of them?"

Any of them what? Men on the dock? "Sure, there are at least four."

The young policeman's hand tightened on his gun, and he pushed past Hecklepeck to the edge of the shed, where he took up a position, poised for attack. His companion followed.

23

T HIS IS THE police. You are surrounded. Cease all activity and do not move." Moments later the signal came over a public-address system.

The three men in the lit area were in the process of maneuvering the last barrel down a wheeled ramp to the barge. They did not drop it but stood there holding it, blinking into the shadows to see if there really was a police presence.

The megaphoned announcement was repeated, and this time policemen stepped out of the dark all around. From behind the barge being loaded came the sound of police boats.

One of the three men said something to the other two, and they ever-so-carefully rolled the barrel back down the ramp until they reached the concrete loading platform. Holding the barrel there, the three of them got into a discussion. Surrounded on all sides by weapon-packing policemen, they were clearly arguing about something. It was surprising behavior to say the least. Why didn't they raise their hands, Hecklepeck wondered, fall flat on their faces, do something a normal human being, whether guilty or innocent, would do?

The police were a little baffled too. "Er, um," the megaphone stumbled, "put your hands on your heads and do not move. Repeat, do not move."

One of the men, who had been waving his hands excitedly in the air, dropped them to his sides. But the debate continued until one man, darting glances all around, left the group and walked toward the edge of the loading platform. He moved his hands back and forth in the air as if to say, "I'm okay. Don't shoot." At the edge of the platform he stopped, looked all around again, and hopped off. The policemen in front of Hecklepeck hunkered down a little further, minds and weapons trained on the man who was now walking up a little rise toward a small office building that obviously oversaw dock operations. What would the police do if he tried to duck inside?

The man with the megaphone was asking himself the same question. "Stay right where you are. Do not move! If you do we cannot answer for your safety."

The man bent over suddenly and picked something up, sending a ripple of tension around the circle of policemen. He straightened up and held up both hands to show that in each one was a piece of wood. The policemen relaxed slightly as the man returned to his companions and wedged both pieces of wood underneath the barrel. The three men tested the barrel and, when they were apparently satisfied that it wouldn't roll, they stood up, put their hands on their heads, and froze.

"Whoa," breathed Hecklepeck. What was so frightening about that barrel that those three men were more afraid of it than fifteen to twenty policemen with guns? Did the contents of the barrel have something to do with the deaths of three young boys?

The police were moving in. Some of them surrounded the three men at the barrel. Others pounded on the door of the little office building and pushed the door open.

Coming out from behind their little shed on the heels of the two policemen, Hecklepeck saw two men emerge from the office building. The one in the pea jacket was a complete stranger, captain of the tugboat, Hecklepeck guessed. But the man in the leather coat was familiar. Somewhere under the belted leather, Hecklepeck knew, was a carpet of black chest hair, the same hair he had seen at the Rotary Club meeting, belonging to Frank Sempepos.

Sempepos! He and Jennifer had been on the right track when they theorized about him. He was clearly in charge of a clandestine smuggling . . . well, shipping . . . something operation. Whatever, it was definitely clandestine. Sending out secretly coded signals to barge operators in the dark of the night on prearranged days smelled covert as hell. The flashing light signal was obviously to let the tugboat captain know the coast was clear. He could then dock and load up with . . . whatever it was he was loading up with.

If Sempepos went to all that trouble to communicate rather than pick up a phone or a radio handle, what would he do to keep his operation from being discovered? Even if the discoverers were only young boys who happened to climb over the fence in search of a cheap high? Their murders would have been a cinch for Sempepos to arrange, like putting out bait for rats, poison for boy snoopers.

Hecklepeck imagined a boy, a dirty street boy, climbing over the Metalcote fence, smaller and more nimble than Richard had been. He would dart among the 55-gallon drums until he found the one with the toluene in it. From the other side of the barrel he would be invisible as he filled his jar with chemical. Then he would spring back the way he came. All Sempepos had to do was replace the toluene with the "bad stuff".

Hecklepeck devoutly hoped no boy was climbing the fence tonight. But Richard or the police would see him if he did.

The police captain in charge of the operation was approaching the Sempepos group with one of his lieutenants. He happened to glance in Hecklepeck's direction and did a double take. Then he scowled deeply and said something to his lieutenant.

Hecklepeck guessed the captain had just issued the order to evict the press since he, after all, had not authorized its presence. As soon as the lieutenant hurried off to pass the word down to the next in command, he ducked back behind the shed. He couldn't let them throw him out until he'd talked to Sempepos.

Safe in the sheltered dark, Hecklepeck grinned at the absurdity of it. The police wouldn't have been at Metalcote if he hadn't had them called in, and now *they* wanted to evict *him* because their presence here had somehow been leaked to him. No point in setting them straight, he knew that. The police bureaucracy's sense of humor didn't stretch to irony.

The question was how to get to Sempepos, who along with the police captain and various others had gone back into the office, and get him to confess to three murders without being tossed out. Hecklepeck was stumped.

"Hey." The young blond cop who had first come up behind him came into the shadows where he was lurking. "You told me you saw them. Four of them."

"Actually there were five." Hecklepeck was once again referring to the number of men involved in the barge-loading operation.

"Well, where are they?"

"Out there." Hecklepeck gestured toward the big, lit area. He wanted to be left alone. He didn't want this young police officer attracting any attention to him.

"I been all over out there. I didn't see no womin."

"Women?" What had McNiff said to get the police authorities to Metalcote? "Oh yes, those women." He couldn't afford to let his ignorance show. If he did, this policeman, like any normal policeman, would clam up. Hecklepeck had to demonstrate that he knew all to get him to talk.

"Yeah, those women. The ones in the white slave ring. You said you saw them. Where are they?"

"They're . . . These women came in from where?" That was the ticket. Swap information with information.

"Guatemala. Costa Rica. One of them Latin American countries." The policeman straightened up and put his hand on his gun belt. "Selling them into prostitution here in St. Louis. Can you beat that?"

"No." Hecklepeck couldn't. He was in utter awe of Captain McNiff's imagination. The captain had straight-out appealed to the police force's collective manliness. They were all coming to the rescue of young girls. It was a whacking bill of goods. But how had the captain gotten them to spring for it?

"Yep. This is going to go down as a big one. It's got everything. Sex and drugs."

"Yes. Is that where the drugs are? In the barrels?"

"I reckon. Now you tell me, where are the womin?"

"Oh . . . well, they're in the office building over there with your captain."

"Yeah . . ." The young officer goggled in that direction, and Hecklepeck realized with distaste that this particular cop was not so much interested in being part of the solution as he was in getting a piece of the action.

"Leo!" His partner came into the shadows. "What are you doing with him?" He cocked his head in Hecklepeck's direction. "The captain wants to see him. To bawl him out for trespassing on an official operation."

Marching toward the office between the two officers, Hecklepeck reflected that things might just work out all by themselves. They were taking him to where Sempepos was.

The three of them stepped inside the door of the little office building. It was one big, dusty room full of files, some of them in cabinets, some stacked on the floor. The room was also full of people, all of them men. When he realized there were no women, the young policeman gave Hecklepeck a brass knuckle look. Hecklepeck started to shrug.

"Chemical dumping!" The police captain strode down the center of the room. "I brought in every man I had to come down here on a case of chemical dumping! What a crock of shit!"

Hecklepeck drew in his breath sharply. That's what Sempepos was doing! He was shipping out Metalcote's production waste and illegally dumping it somewhere. Those barrels were probably full of chemical sludge left over after the electroplating process, sludge that was largely deadly hydrogen cyanide. No wonder the three men had been so careful in their handling of it! The merest whiff of that stuff could have killed one of them outright. Horrible to think that a ruptured barrel would have taken out half the city police force and a renegade television news crew.

Why would Metalcote want to take that kind of risk? The answer, of course, was money. It was probably cheaper to pack the stuff into barrels, although it would have to be done mechanically, than it was to install all the Environmental Protection Agency-mandated equipment to dilute it or neutralize it or whatever was required by way of disposal. But the cost to the environment was incalculable. Obviously the hydrogen cyanide was packed in barrels that were specially lined to keep the acid from eating through them, but surely those linings wouldn't last forever. Then when they deteriorated the deadly stuff would leak out, seep into the subsoil, and eventually leach into someone's well water. But that wasn't the absolute worst of it.

Hecklepeck's anger, mounting as he reviewed Metalcote's crimes, suddenly erupted and washed over him, red-hot. For God's sake, what about the river? They were transporting barrels and barrels of lethal acid on the open water. What if there had been an accident? In fact, who was to say there hadn't been one, and that hundreds upon hundreds of gallons of the stuff hadn't spilled into the Mississippi River, killing plant life, massacring fish, and finding its way to the intake for the city water supply?

Muttering under his breath, the police captain took up a stance in front of his lieutenant, who was standing near Hecklepeck. "This chemical dumping"—Hecklepeck put aside his anger to listen.—"is not even our jurisdiction. It belongs to the feds, to the boys at

EeePeeAy." The captain's tone said that he thought chemical dumping was not much of a crime and the Environmental Protection Agency even less of a crime fighter. "Chemicals: that's environmental. Transporting chemicals across state lines: definitely a federal matter, not local. What the fuck was Bob Dial thinking of when he called us out on this one?"

So that was how McNiff had pulled it off! He had gotten his old colleague, Bob Dial, the head of the local Drug Enforcement Agency office, to tip off the St. Louis police to the alleged sex and drugs ring. Dial had probably given some reason why he couldn't handle the bust himself, since it was as much in his bailiwick as that of the police. Whatever he had said they obviously jumped at it. Hecklepeck made a mental note to take McNiff out for an expensive dinner.

The tough young policemen took a sharp hold on Hecklepeck's elbow and cleared his throat. "Hhrrum. Sir? Hhhhhrummm. Sir?" The police captain looked over at him. "Here's Mr. Herkleperk, sir. You wanted to see him."

"Ho. Yes. Channel Three. Well, you have no business here. This is a police matter, not a public press circus. I'm going to have to ask you to leave . . . No! Come to think of it this is an EeeePeeeAy matter. Do what you want. But stay away from those barrels. They're dangerous."

Hecklepeck nodded at the captain's back and pulled his elbow out of the policeman's grasp. He had no intention of getting anywhere near the barrels. His quarry was Sempepos. He started to make his way down the room toward the end, where Sempepos sat in a metal chair, his head in his hands.

About ten feet from Sempepos, Hecklepeck took a deep breath and briefed the reporter in himself. Objective: to find out about the murders. Method of execution: extend sympathy until Sempepos is lulled into self-betrayal. Pitfall to be avoided: grabbing the polluting son-of-a-bitch and slamming him into the wall.

Hecklepeck approached the leather-wrapped man in the chair and spoke his name. Sempepos looked up, plainly a wretched man whose career had just come to a disastrous halt. But he did not grasp for whatever straw Hecklepeck might have offered. Instead his eyes hardened into BB pellets. "No comments for the press."

"I understand. I want to ask you about something else." Hecklepeck just knew the set of his face had not achieved sympathetic, that the anger was showing through. But, damn it, Sempepos wasn't giving him anything to work with.

"No comments about anything."

"This is off-the-record. For my own information. I have to know about the boys."

"See my lawyer."

The room was still full of police, but as far as William Hecklepeck was concerned there were only two people in it, himself and Frank Sempepos. He felt himself falling headfirst into the trap he had told himself to avoid. Grabbing Sempepos's collar with both hands, he lifted the little man bodily out of his chair and shoved him against the wall. "Tell me about the boys."

"Huh?" Sempepos had already sustained one shock that evening; this one didn't seem to be getting through to him.

Hecklepeck tightened his grip. "The three boys who died from glue-sniffing. But it wasn't glue, was it? It was one of your chemicals. Tell me."

"Glue?"

As angry as Hecklepeck was, he got the impression that Sempepos was genuinely bewildered. Out of the corner of his eye he saw policemen approaching. "Not glue but some chemical. They were murdered with it. Tellll me."

Sempepos shook his head, his gunmetal eyes threatening to become an unlikely source of water. "I don't know anything about murder. I swear it."

Hecklepeck scoured the man's face, then abruptly dropped him and, skirting the policemen, headed for the door of the office.

Sempepos was telling the truth, he was sure of it. He hadn't murdered the three boys, knew nothing about it. But then who had? Someone else connected with Metalcote's illegal chemical dumping? Someone unconnected?

Hecklepeck headed around the shed and over to the cluster of barrels where he knew Richard was hiding. He crouched down behind them.

"Wha-aa? Oh, it's you." Richard peered out through the space between two barrels. "I've been looking at all these barrels for so long they're beginning to move on me. But have I seen a person, a human being? Not a fucking one. What's going on over there? I heard a megaphone."

Hecklepeck sat down on the ground. Maybe the murderer had

been frightened off by all the evidence of police around the entrance to Metalcote. Maybe he had decided this was not the time to collect refrigerant 113 and use it to commit murder. Understandably.

If only he, Hecklepeck, hadn't called in the police . . . But then Sempepos would never have been apprehended, and he and Richard might be on their way to the bottom of the river with weights tied around their ankles. Calling the police had seemed to be the best course at the time and it still had its selling points.

Shit! He had wanted to wrap it up tonight.

"Are you going to let me out of here now? I want to go home. Nobody's going to come in here and steal chemicals with the police all over the place. They're either staying away or they've already been here but either way . . ."

Hecklepeck looked at the barrel that separated him and Richard as if it had just said something brilliant. Already been here. Why hadn't he thought of that?

If so . . . the phantom with the mayonnaise jar was even now haunting Benton Park, looking for a victim. Or had already found one. Hecklepeck sprang to his feet.

"Where are you going? What about me?" Richard's voice sounded hollow in his circle of 55-gallon drums.

He received no answer. Hecklepeck was sprinting through the darkness toward the front entrance of Metalcote.

24

Both of Metalcote's gates were wide open when Hecklepeck burst through. The Porsche was where he left it, parked on the street along with a string of police cars. He slid into the driver's seat.

It wasn't just that a murderer was wandering through Benton Park with a jarful of lethal chemical looking to shove someone's nose into it, although that was bad enough. There was also Jennifer, roaming the park too. Hecklepeck became almost physically sick when he thought that the two might come together and Jennifer . . . What kind of jeopardy was Jennifer in? Oh God, he didn't want to think.

Hecklepeck sped along the south side of Benton Park, scanning the curb for Art's unmarked white car. The car was supposed to be anonymous but it wasn't. Any pedestrian could have picked it out for some kind of news or law enforcement vehicle. For one thing it had a tall radio antenna set squarely in the middle of the roof. Easy to spot and Hecklepeck didn't see it.

He shook the steering wheel of his Porsche as if it were the car's fault. However, the blame was his. His, his, his! How could he let Jennifer, a young novice reporter, wander around where a murderer was supposed to be with only a photographer for back-up?

He should have been riding shotgun. Instead he had been steamboating into a net of red herrings—attending a fish fry when he should have been hauling in the big one.

Wyoming Street dead-ended, and Hecklepeck had to take a jog that took him away from the park, away from where he had any chance of seeing anything. He stopped behind several cars at the

Jefferson Avenue light and leaned on his horn. No time to wait for a traffic light.

Hecklepeck forced the Porsche up on the curb and passed each of the cars that was blocking his progress before bouncing back onto the roadway and swinging into the righthand lane on Jefferson Avenue.

All his attention, all his worry he trained on Benton Park. The Park's edges were illuminated by streetlights, but its depths were darker. Anything could be lurking in those shadowy places. Hecklepeck searched them for the slightest sign of movement, the merest flicker.

There! The reflection off a piece of glass. Hecklepeck's heart came up into his mouth. But it was a bottle, not a jar, and some man was drinking from it. Hecklepeck took a long, slow breath to calm himself.

The man with the bottle was about the only person not hurrying through the park. Maybe the liquor kept him from feeling the cold. What if Jennifer weren't at the park? Should he look elsewhere in the neighborhood or widen the search by notifying the police?

It was worrisome, a choice Hecklepeck didn't want to make, and as it happened he didn't have to. He saw the white car with its telltale antenna. It was parked the wrong way along the curb in a no-parking zone as if its occupants had been in too big a hurry to turn around and park properly.

Afraid to delve into the meaning of that, Hecklepeck pulled over to the curb so the two vehicles faced each other, front end to front end. Jennifer and Art must have gone into the park.

He didn't hesitate. Heart pounding with fear, he once again forced the Porsche onto the sidewalk. This time, however, he drove into the park, compelling an oncoming pedestrian to leap onto the grass and out of his way.

Slow-going as he surveyed the park. Now every shadow flickered, each piece of broken glass glittered malignantly at him, and branches swung as if with intent. Each movement yanked on him with a heart-stopping tug, pulling him off balance, off the course of urgency he felt.

Finally over the top of a small rise roughly mid-park he spotted a light. It was of an intensity that Hecklepeck associated with television production. Art's camera light.

He decided to abandon the car. His approach would be less

202

obtrusive on foot and give him the benefit of surprise if he needed it. Hecklepeck took the first part of the distance at a run.

The grass, by now stiff with frost, crunched beneath his feet. It sounded loud, too loud, to him. But, he reassured himself, there was nobody to hear. The only people who counted were still up ahead in the circle of light. Everything he had was concentrated on getting there fast.

About twenty-five feet away, however, he gave in to caution and slowed to a walk, keeping each step as silent as possible. They were between some trees. The light that Hecklepeck had seen was the light on Art's camera. Jennifer stood to one side, safe, watching with her back to Hecklepeck. Art was shooting.

"Narragate! Send'm through the narragate to hevin." There was some mumbling and then, "If yer son asks fer bread, willee give'm a stone? Nah, frewts of the tree. Know'm by ther frewts."

Hecklepeck tensed again. He had relaxed a little when he saw that Jennifer was all right, but what was going on here? Art moved slightly, revealing an intense little man in a dirty beige jacket and gray work pants. The man was now chanting or appeared to be. In any case he kept up a steady stream of unintelligible talk, all of which Art's camera eagerly recorded.

What riveted Hecklepeck was the glass jar the man held out in front of him. The contents were invisible because the jar was swathed in a soiled cotton print fabric, but the man held it as reverently as if it were a silver chalice being prepared for the Holy Eucharist. This man, whoever he was, was a murderer. But who was he?

Hecklepeck stepped forward and touched Jennifer on the elbow. She turned, startled, until she recognized Hecklepeck. Then her face broke into relief. "I'm so glad you're here . . . finally," she whispered. "We've been waiting for you—to get the police. We have to stay with him. He's all right as long as we're here, but if we go, he'll wander off somewhere and maybe kill somebody."

"I've never seen him before. Who the hell is he?"

"Homer Smith. He's Jimmie's father."

"It all started when Homer found the narrow gate." Jennifer and Hecklepeck were sitting at a table at Sebastion's well after the late news had ended. Richard and Turnbull were there too, Turnbull having broken down in his excitement over the story and asked his employees if they wanted to stop for a drink before going home. "It came out of a Bible passage he was made to learn in his childhood and still remembered."

" 'Strait is the gate, and narrow is the way, which leadeth unto life.' " Growing up, Turnbull had spent many less-than-eager hours in Bible class. " 'And few there be that find it.' Matthew, describing the Sermon on the Mount."

Jennifer nodded. "Homer Smith was walking along that street by the river one day and he found it, right there at the front entrance to Metalcote. The company has two gates, one wide one to let cars and trucks in, and a narrow one for foot traffic."

"Come on." Richard, as usual, was skeptical. "This guy sees a gate in a chain-link fence surrounding an industrial plant and thinks he's found the door to salvation?"

"Homer Smith's whole world was roughly the ten-block square of his neighborhood. You should have seen him when they took him down to the police station for booking. It too was a revelation. If all there are are ten square blocks, then it's not illogical to find the gate to salvation there." Hecklepeck caught himself. He was telling Jennifer's story. "At least that's my theory, the way I see it."

Jennifer was more concerned with making her point than any infraction of Hecklepeck's. "It's too easy to label him crazy. He was overwhelmed by life. He saw what was happening: no work, not enough food, children who were picking up nasty city ways like glue-sniffing. But he was helpless to do anything about it . . . until God showed him the way, the narrow gate. Everything he did made sense to him."

There was a slight pause before Jennifer picked up the story again. "Homer kept an eye on the narrow gate, which is usually kept tightly locked and is watched over by Metalcote's many security guards. Then one night he found it sitting wide open." Jennifer looked at Hecklepeck as if she'd just tossed the ball to him.

Hecklepeck carried it. "It would have been a Thursday night, the third Thursday of whatever month, because the Rotary Club of South St. Louis meets on third Thursdays."

"Oh, of course. I see it all now. Third Thursdays . . . Rotary Club . . . narrow gates." Richard put two fingers to the bridge of his nose as if all those things were coming together in some spiritual medium.

"The Rotary Club business is important because Metalcote's

manager, Frank Sempepos, was using it to create an alibi for himself. He'd show up for the first part of the meeting, cocktails, and let people know he was there. Then he'd duck out and go to Metalcote, where the security guards would be sent home, their shift over. That way no one was left at the plant except Sempepos to witness the loading of Metalcote's waste onto barges for illegal dumping."

"Do you mean to tell me that those Rotarians didn't notice this Sempepos guy ducking in and out?" Richard again.

"Some of them may have, but there was enough coming and going by other Rotarians that nobody would have been sure one way or the other. And Sempepos took pains to let me at least know he was there." Outrage crept into Hecklepeck's tone. "He came up and tried to get me to do a story on chlorofluorocarbons at Metalcote. But he didn't really want a story; he dragged his feet all over the place when Jennifer took him up on it. What he was actually doing was registering his presence with me. Ironically," Hecklepeck gave an evil smile, "what he did was register his absence. I had already talked about ozone in my speech and it was clear from what he said he hadn't been there to hear it."

"He was at Metalcote." Jennifer bounced a little in her chair, happy to take up the story again. "Loading barges with dangerous chemicals for illegal dumping in Illinois. And while all that was going on, the gate was left unlocked and unguarded."

"Enter Homer," declared Richard.

"Right, carrying a jar."

"Carrying a jar? How did he know to carry a jar?"

"Well, maybe he wasn't carrying a jar the first time." Jennifer wrinkled her brow. She wasn't entirely sure how the next part went. "He probably walked in and saw all the barrels full of chemicals. He must have known that's where Jimmie and the other kids went to get the glue they sniffed. So he either went back and got a jar or the next time he came with a jar. Either way, he filled it up with the chemical in the yellow barrels."

"And thus did fate change the course of human events," Hecklepeck intoned.

Turnbull leaned forward in his chair. "How so?"

"Because if Homer had filled his jar from one of the white barrels, he would have gotten toluene and not refrigerant 113. He might not have killed anybody."

"It's so sad." There were tears in Jennifer's eyes. "Homer didn't set out to murder anyone. He was using the glue-sniffing to relate to his son."

"And God led him into all this by revealing a gate in a chain-link fence to him?" Richard still hadn't gotten past the gate.

Jennifer nodded. "God showed him the way. And when the first boy died, that was God too. Homer realized then he had mistaken God's purpose."

Turnbull thoughtfully stroked the side of his face, which felt rough in the early morning hours. " 'If ye then, being evil, know how to give good gifts unto your children, how much more shall your Father, which is in heaven give good things to them?" he intoned. "Matthew again."

"Uh, yes." Jennifer had a hard time taking in King James' English. "Homer decided he was supposed to save other boys by helping them through the narrow gate to salvation. So whenever he found the gate open he went in and filled up his jar. He wrapped the jar in cloth like it was holy, a communion cup more or less. Because of that there weren't any fingerprints."

"Then he went around giving it to children, including his own son." Richard actually shuddered.

"Well, things were pretty bad. He thought they'd be better for Jimmie in heaven."

"Perhaps he was right." Hecklepeck spoke up. "Maybe death was the best gift he could give Jimmie." The rest of the group squirmed, uncomfortable with that notion. "Maybe in a chaotic world, chaos is the only answer."

After a few moments of silence Turnbull leaned back in his seat and took a last sip of scotch. " 'Ye shall know them by the fruits they bear.' " Whether it was the quotation or the bitterness of the drink or his own thoughts, Turnbull grimaced slightly. Setting down the glass, he said, "We'll meet in my office tomorrow morning at . . . ten o'clock to map out a strategy for getting this thing on the air. I think a series of hard news pieces tomorrow night and then an hour-long special next week sometime. Jennifer, I called Joe Handy earlier this evening. He'll do the morning news tomorrow and all next week while you're putting all this together."

Jennifer sighed the sigh of a tired person at the prospect of a long nap.

Turnbull stood up and reached for the bill. He would rather have stayed, but he sensed that if he didn't start the exodus they'd probably all be up most of the night. He wanted them fresh for the work ahead.

Turnbull pulled on his worn, whitish raincoat and reflected that this was as good as it got. You hired competent people and then did the hard thing, which was to leave them alone. When it all worked out, when they were inspired and the stars were right, this was what you got, a story of murder and of criminal activity that swept from the highest ranks of St. Louis society to the lowest. This was Emmy award material, maybe even a Peabody.

Turnbull scribbled his name and ripped out his credit card receipt. "Pretty good," he said. "Pretty good work."

"Pretty good?" Richard muttered after Turnbull left. "I risk my life and it's pretty good?" Richard was getting into his own jacket to go home because he knew who was going to be producing the hour-long special. Turnbull wouldn't dare give it to anybody else!

"How do you feel?" asked Hecklepeck when he and Jennifer were alone and had agreed not to have another drink.

Jennifer sighed. "Okay, but I can't help wishing the murderer had been somebody else. Like Tom Honigger, somebody who deserved it."

"Deserved to be a murderer?" Hecklepeck handed her her jacket. "No, I know what you mean. Deserved to suffer the consequences. Our idea of a villain and not just a puppet of fate. I would have liked for it to have been Honigger too, but I am amply consoled by the fact that he is up to his eyebrows in illegal chemical dumping as the owner of Metalcote and will suffer big for that. There's also the moral question involving the glue-sniffers."

"What moral question?" Jennifer followed him out of Sebastion's, and they walked down the block together in the direction of Hecklepeck's hotel.

"The fact that Honigger got that big grant for Ben Howell and his substance abuse clinic indicates that he knew or suspected toluene was being stolen from his company. Maybe he read about the glue-sniffing deaths in the newspaper and came to the conclusion that his chemicals were responsible. If so, he had the moral duty to do something about it. Instead, he paid out guilt money or had it paid out through his wife and St. Louis Against Drugs."

"So big deal. I doubt that whatever public defender Homer Smith gets is going to bring that out in court."

"No, but I know at least one local television station that's going to report it loud and clear."

Jennifer sighed again. "I still wish it hadn't been Homer Smith. He was so pathetic, as much a victim of our society as Jimmie was."

"At times like this, when there doesn't seem to be any redemption, I fall back on the story itself and the telling of it and the hope that it reaches one . . . no more . . . just one person." Hecklepeck did believe that, didn't he? At bottom, there it still was, a good, solid platform, built with seasoned hardwood: his philosophy.

It didn't impress Jennifer.

TAG

THE MONDAY AFTER the hour-long special aired, Jennifer turned in her two-week notice. "I'm going back to school to get a master's in social work," she explained to Hecklepeck. "I want to do something that really helps people. Like Jimmie Smith."

"Journalism helps people." Hecklepeck felt both hurt and sad. "You're a hell of a reporter." He didn't have to be her mentor. They could be equal partners, work together.

Jennifer shrugged off the compliment. "Maybe journalism helps in some overall sense, but it doesn't make people's lives better. Not day to day. Not on an individual basis."

"It can." But Jennifer looked like she had made up her mind. "You won't earn as much mon . . ." Hecklepeck stopped himself just in time. Money wasn't the issue. He knew that. He could remember when he left college before graduating because he got a job as a television reporter that paid a $110 a week. That was before there was any money in television, and it had been better that way.

He had taken that job with the same emotion, the same clean, shiny expression in his eyes that Jennifer's had now. Why? Because he wanted to help people, and he believed that journalism, by playing up injustice and riding herd on the powerful, was the way to do the most for the maximum number of people. No one had been able to dissuade him, although his parents had tried. What had happened to all that conviction? It had disappeared with his youthful energy. Now the mere prospect of trying to dissuade Jennifer made him weary. "I hope you let me take you out to dinner before you go."

"Of course. I'm going to be here for two more weeks."

But Hecklepeck had been through enough two-week moves to know how quickly that time went. Through his office doorway he watched Jennifer leave the newsroom in her bright red coat and felt the sensation of panic rise up through his body.

"So! Now that you're back in the reporting mode, as it were, what are you going to do for a follow-up?" Richard flung himself into the empty chair in Hecklepeck's office, the one Jennifer had perched on with the news of her resignation. "I say let's go after that discussion group of Gus Bus's, the one devoted to exploring various permutations of the thesis that being rich is being better. For instance why," Richard rolled his eyes madly, "do these guys always meet on third Thursdays?"

"Cocaine probably." Richard pulled back from the unexpected answer. "They probably do cocaine. That's why Gus is going down to New Orleans this week. To pick up a large shipment of it. He's planning to smuggle it back in tins of coffee and spices in the hold of his steamboat."

"What? How do you know that?"

"McNiff. He's an agent with the Drug Enforcement Agency. Undercover. He's going to come down on Gus." Hecklepeck was unable to drum up any enthusiasm.

"Hey—Gus Bust! And we get the story, I presume. That is far out."

Hecklepeck sighed. "What difference does it make? He'll get off. He'll hire the best lawyer in the country."

"So what? It's still a great story. Another great story, I might add. I'd like to see you come up with a better one."

With an effort Hecklepeck shoved the panic back and threw open the door to any thought that could supplant it. What came in was the flow of black water as he had last seen in against the side of a small, white boat, the funky smell of nearby river water, and the sweet dark of emotional oblivion.

He swung around to face his friend, knee to knee in the confined space. "We start at Lake Itasca in the spring and go the whole way—down to New Orleans. You can do the shooting. Well, a little practice wouldn't hurt. I'll want plenty of beauty shots."

Richard drew back from the onslaught. "Is this another steamboat scam? I can't believe it. I thought you got that out of your system."

"Steamboat?" Hecklepeck looked at his friend as if he hadn't been listening. "Steamboat? I'm talking about real frontline adventure, about braving the elemental blitz bare-assed. I'm talking about a canoe!"